Far Eastern

William Somerset Maugham was born in 1874 and
lived in Paris until he was ten. He was educated
at King's School, Canterbury, and at Heidelberg
University. He spent some time at St. Thomas's
Hospital with the idea of practising medicine, but
the success of his first novel, *Liza of Lambeth*,
published in 1897, won him over to letters. *Of
Human Bondage*, the first of his masterpieces,
came out in 1915, and with the publication in
1919 of *The Moon and Sixpence* his reputation
as a novelist was established. His position as a
successful playwright was being consolidated at
the same time. His first play, *A Man of Honour*,
was followed by a series of successes just before
and after World War I, and his career in the
theatre did not end until 1933 with *Sheppey*.

His fame as a short-story writer began with *The
Trembling of a Leaf*, sub-titled *Little Stories of
the South Sea Islands*, in 1921, after which he
published seven more collections. His other
works include travel books such as *On a Chinese
Screen* and *Don Fernando*, essays, criticism, and
the autobiographical *The Summing Up* and *A
Writer's Notebook*.

In 1927 Somerset Maugham settled in the South
of France and lived there until his death in 1965.

Also by W. Somerset Maugham and available from Mandarin Paperbacks

W. Somerset Maugham
Far Eastern Tales

Mandarin

This edition first published in the United Kingdom in 1993 by
Mandarin Paperbacks

9 10

Copyright © Royal Literary Fund

The stories in this collection have been selected by John Whitehead
from *Cosmopolitan*, *The Gentleman in the Parlour*, *The Casuarina Tree*,
Ah King and *A Traveller in Romance*

Mandarin Books
Random House UK Limited
20 Vauxhall Bridge Road, London SW1V 2SA

Random House Australia (Pty) Limited
20 Alfred Street, Milsons Point, Sydney
New South Wales 2061, Australia

Random House New Zealand Limited
18 Poland Road, Glenfield
Auckland 10, New Zealand

Random House South Africa (Pty) Limited
Endulini, 5a Jubilee Road, Parktown 2193, South Africa

Random House UK Limited Reg. No. 954009

A CIP catalogue record for this book
is available from the British Library

Papers used by Random House UK Limited
are natural, recyclable products made from wood grown in
sustainable forests. The manufacturing processes conform to
the environmental regulations of the country of origin.

Printed and bound in Great Britain by
Cox & Wyman Ltd, Reading, Berkshire

ISBN 0 7493 1602 0

Contents

Footprints in the Jungle

There is no place in Malaya that has more charm than Tanah Merah. It lies on the sea and the sandy shore is fringed with casuarinas. The government offices are still in the old Raad Huis that the Dutch built when they owned the land, and on the hill stand the grey ruins of the fort by aid of which the Portuguese maintained their hold over the unruly natives. Tanah Merah has a history and in the vast labyrinthine houses of the Chinese merchants, backing on the sea so that in the cool of the evening they may sit in their loggias and enjoy the salt breeze, families dwell that have been settled in the country for three centuries. Many have forgotten their native language and hold intercourse with one another in Malay and pidgin English. The imagination lingers here gratefully, for in the Federated Malay States the only past is within the memory for the most part of the fathers of living men.

Tanah Merah was for long the busiest mart of the Middle East and its harbour was crowded with shipping when the clipper and the junk still sailed the China Seas. But now it is dead. It has the sad and romantic air of all places that have once been of importance and live now on the recollection of a vanished grandeur. It is a sleepy little town and strangers that come to it, losing their native energy, insensibly drop into its easy and lethargic ways. Successive rubber booms bring it no prosperity and the ensuing slumps hasten its decay.

The European quarter is very silent. It is trim and

neat and clean. The houses of the white men—Government servants and agents of companies—stand round an immense padang, agreeable and roomy bungalows shaded by great cassias, and the padang is vast and green and well cared for, like the lawn of a cathedral close, and indeed there is in the aspect of this corner of Tanah Merah something quiet and delicately secluded that reminds you of the precincts of Canterbury.

The club faces the sea; it is a spacious but shabby building; it has an air of neglect and when you enter you feel that you intrude. It gives you the impression that it is closed really, for alterations and repairs, and that you have taken indiscreet advantage of an open door to go where you are not wanted. In the morning you may find there a couple of planters who have come in from their estates on business and are drinking a gin-sling before starting back again; and latish in the afternoon a lady or two may perhaps be seen looking with a furtive air through old numbers of the 'Illustrated London News'. At nightfall a few men saunter in and sit about the billiard-room watching the play and drinking sukus. But on Wednesdays there is a little more animation. On that day the gramophone is set going in the large room upstairs and people come in from the surrounding country to dance. There are sometimes no less than a dozen couples and it is even possible to make up two tables of bridge.

It was on one of these occasions that I met the Cartwrights. I was staying with a man called Gaze who was head of the police and he came into the billiard-room, where I was sitting, and asked me if I would make up a four. The Cartwrights were planters and they came in to Tanah Merah on Wednesdays because it gave their girl a chance of a little fun. They were very nice people, said Gaze, quiet and unobtrusive, and played a very pleasant game of bridge. I followed Gaze into the card-room and was introduced to them. They were already seated at a table and Mrs. Cartwright was shuffling the cards. It inspired me with confidence to see the competent way in which she did it. She took half the pack in each hand, and her hands were large and strong, deftly inserted the corners of one half under the corners of the other, and with a click and a neat bold gesture cascaded the cards together.

It had all the effect of a conjuring trick. The card-player knows that it can be done perfectly only after incessant practice. He can be fairly sure that anyone who can so shuffle a pack of cards loves cards for their own sake.

'Do you mind if my husband and I play together?' asked Mrs. Cartwright. 'It's no fun for us to win one another's money.'

'Of course not.'

We cut for deal and Gaze and I sat down.

Mrs. Cartwright drew an ace and while she dealt, quickly and neatly, chatted with Gaze of local affairs. But I was aware that she took stock of me. She looked shrewd, but good-natured.

She was a woman somewhere in the fifties (though in the East, where people age quickly, it is difficult to tell their ages), with white hair very untidily arranged, and a constant gesture with her was an impatient movement of the hand to push back a long wisp of hair that kept falling over her forehead. You wondered why she did not, by the use of a hairpin or two, save herself so much trouble. Her blue eyes were large, but pale and a little tired; her face was lined and sallow; I think it was her mouth that gave it the expression which I felt was characteristic of caustic but tolerant irony. You saw that here was a woman who knew her mind and was never afraid to speak it. She was a chatty player (which some people object to strongly, but which does not disconcert me, for I do not see why you should behave at the card-table as though you were at a memorial service) and it was soon apparent that she had an effective knack of badinage. It was pleasantly acid, but it was amusing enough to be offensive only to a fool. If now and then she uttered a remark so sarcastic that you wanted all your sense of humour to see the fun in it, you could not but quickly see that she was willing to take as much as she gave. Her large, thin mouth broke into a dry smile and her eyes shone brightly when by a lucky chance you brought off a repartee that turned the laugh against her.

I thought her a very agreeable person. I liked her frankness. I liked her quick wit. I liked her plain face. I never met a woman who obviously cared so little how she looked. It was not only her head that was untidy, everything about her was slovenly; she wore a high-necked silk blouse, but for coolness had unbuttoned the top buttons and showed a gaunt and withered neck; the blouse was crumpled and none too clean, for she smoked innumerable cigarettes and covered herself with ash. When she got up for a moment to speak to somebody I saw that her blue skirt was rather ragged at the hem and badly needed a brush, and she wore heavy, low-heeled boots. But none of this mattered. Everything she wore was perfectly in character.

And it was a pleasure to play bridge with her. She played very quickly, without hesitation, and she had not only knowledge but flair. Of course she knew Gaze's game, but I was a stranger and she soon took my measure. The team-work between her husband and herself was admirable; he was sound and cautious, but knowing him, she was able to be bold with assurance and brilliant with safety. Gaze was a player who founded a foolish optimism on the hope that his opponents would not have the sense to take advantage of his errors, and the pair of us were no match for the Cartwrights. We lost one rubber after another, and there was nothing to do but smile and look as if we liked it.

'I don't know what's the matter with the cards,' said Gaze at last, plaintively. 'Even when we have every card in the pack we go down.'

'It can't be anything to do with your play,' answered Mrs. Cartwright, looking him full in the face with those pale blue eyes of hers, 'it must be bad luck pure and simple. Now if you hadn't had your hearts mixed up with your diamonds in that last hand you'd have saved the game.'

Gaze began to explain at length how the misfortune, which had cost us dear, occurred, but Mrs. Cartwright, with a deft flick of the hand, spread out the cards in a great circle so that we should cut for deal. Cartwright looked at the time.

'This will have to be the last, my dear,' he said.

'Oh, will it?' She glanced at her watch and then called to a young man who was passing through the room. 'Oh, Mr. Bullen, if you're going upstairs tell Olive that we shall be going in a few minutes.' She turned to me. 'It takes us the best part of an hour to get back to the estate and poor Theo has to be up at the crack of dawn.'

'Oh, well, we only come in once a week,' said Cartwright, 'and it's the one chance Olive gets of being gay and abandoned.'

I thought Cartwright looked tired and old. He was a man of middle height, with a bald, shiny head, a stubbly grey moustache, and gold-rimmed spectacles. He wore white ducks and a black-and-white tie. He was rather neat and you could see he took much more pains with his clothes than his untidy wife. He talked little, but it was plain that he enjoyed his wife's caustic humour and sometimes he made quite a neat retort. They were evidently very good friends. It was pleasing to see so solid and tolerant an affection between two people who were almost elderly and must have lived together for so many years.

It took but two hands to finish the rubber and we had just ordered a final gin and bitters when Olive came down.

'Do you really want to go already, Mumsey?' she asked.

Mrs. Cartwright looked at her daughter with fond eyes.

'Yes, darling. It's nearly half-past eight. It'll be ten before we get our dinner.'

'Damn our dinner,' said Olive, gaily.

'Let her have one more dance before we go,' suggested Cartwright.

'Not one. You must have a good night's rest.'

Cartwright looked at Olive with a smile.

'If your mother has made up her mind, my dear, we may just as well give in without any fuss.'

'She's a determined woman,' said Olive, lovingly stroking her mother's wrinkled cheek.

Mrs. Cartwright patted her daughter's hand, and kissed it.

Olive was not very pretty, but she looked extremely nice. She was nineteen or twenty, I suppose, and she had still the plumpness of her age; she would be more attractive when she had fined down a little. She had none of the determination that gave her mother's face so much character, but resembled her father; she had his dark eyes and slightly aquiline nose, and his look of rather weak good nature. It was plain that she was strong and healthy. Her cheeks were red and her eyes bright. She had a vitality that he had long since lost. She seemed to be the perfectly normal English girl, with high spirits, a great desire to enjoy herself, and an excellent temper.

When we separated, Gaze and I set out to walk to his house.

'What did you think of the Cartwrights?" he asked me.

'I liked them. They must be a great asset in a place like this.'

'I wish they came oftener. They live a very quiet life.'

'It must be dull for the girl. The father and mother seem very well satisfied with one another's company.'

'Yes, it's been a great success.'

'Olive is the image of her father, isn't she?'

Gaze gave me a sidelong glance.

'Cartwright isn't her father. Mrs. Cartwright was a widow when he married her. Olive was born four months after her father's death.'

'Oh!'

I drew out the sound in order to put in it all I could of surprise, interest and curiosity. But Gaze said nothing and we walked the rest of the way in silence. The boy was waiting at the door as we entered the house and after a last gin pahit we sat down to dinner.

At first Gaze was inclined to be talkative. Owing to the restriction of the output of rubber there had sprung up a considerable activity among the smugglers and it was part of his duty to circumvent their knavishness. Two junks had been captured that day and he was rubbing his hands over his success. The go-downs were full of confiscated rubber and in a little while it was going to be solemnly burnt. But presently he fell into silence and we finished without a word. The boys brought in coffee and brandy and we lit our cheroots. Gaze leaned back in his chair. He looked at me reflectively and then looked at his brandy. The boys had left the room and we were alone.

'I've known Mrs. Cartwright for over twenty years,' he said slowly. 'She wasn't a bad-looking woman in those days. Always untidy, but when she was young it didn't seem to matter so much. It was rather attractive. She was married to a man called Bronson. Reggie Bronson. He was

7

a planter. He was manager of an estate up in Selantan and I was stationed at Alor Lipis. It was a much smaller place than it is now; I don't suppose there were more than twenty people in the whole community, but they had a jolly little club, and we used to have a very good time. I remember the first time I met Mrs. Bronson as though it was yesterday. There were no cars in those days and she and Bronson had ridden in on their bicycles. Of course then she didn't look so determined as she looks now. She was much thinner, she had a nice colour, and her eyes were very pretty—blue, you know—and she had a lot of dark hair. If she'd only taken more trouble with herself she'd have been rather stunning. As it was she was the best-looking woman there.'

I tried to construct in my mind a picture of what Mrs. Cartwright—Mrs. Bronson as she was then—looked like from what she was now and from Gaze's not very graphic description. In the solid woman, with her well-covered bones, who sat rather heavily at the bridge-table, I tried to see a slight young thing with buoyant movements and graceful, easy gestures. Her chin now was square and her nose decided, but the roundness of youth must have masked this: she must have been charming with a pink-and-white skin and her hair, carelessly dressed, brown and abundant. At that period she wore a long skirt, a tight waist and a picture hat. Or did women in Malaya still wear the topis that you see in old numbers of the illustrated papers?

'I hadn't seen her for—oh, nearly twenty years,' Gaze went on. 'I knew she was living somewhere in the F.M.S., but it was a surprise when I took this job and came here to run across her in the club just as I had up in Selantan so many years before. Of course she's an elderly woman now and she's changed out of all recognition. It was rather a shock to see her with a grown-up daughter, it made me realise how the time had passed; I was a young fellow when I met her last and now, by Jingo, I'm due to retire on the age limit in two or three years. Bit thick, isn't it?'

Gaze, a rueful grin on his ugly face, looked at me with faint indignation, as though I could help the hurrying march of the years as they trod upon one another's heels.

'I'm no chicken myself,' I replied.

'You haven't lived out East all your life. It ages one before one's time. One's an elderly man at fifty and at fifty-five one's good for nothing but the scrap-heap.'

But I did not want Gaze to wander off into a disquisition on old age.

'Did you recognise Mrs. Cartwright when you saw her again?' I asked.

'Well, I did and I didn't. At the first glance I thought I knew her, but couldn't quite place her. I thought perhaps she was someone I'd met on board ship when I was going on leave and had known only by sight. But the moment she spoke I remembered at once. I remembered the dry twinkle in her eyes and the crisp sound of her voice. There was something in her voice that seemed to mean: you're a bit of a damned fool, my lad, but you're not a bad sort and upon my soul I rather like you.'

'That's a good deal to read into the sound of a voice,' I smiled.

'She came up to me in the club and shook hands with me. "How do you do, Major Gaze? Do you remember me?" she said.

'"Of course I do."

'"A lot of water has passed under the bridge since we met last. We're none of us as young as we were. Have you seen Theo?"

'For a moment I couldn't think whom she meant. I suppose I looked rather stupid, because she gave a little smile, that chaffing smile that I knew so well, and explained.

'"I married Theo, you know. It seemed the best thing to do. I was lonely and he wanted it."

'"I heard you married him," I said. "I hope you've been very happy."

'"Oh, very. Theo's a perfect duck. He'll be here in a minute. He'll be so glad to see you."

'I wondered. I should have thought I was the last man Theo would wish to see. I shouldn't have thought she would wish it very much either. But women are funny.'

'Why shouldn't she wish to see you?' I asked.

'I'm coming to that later,' said Gaze. 'Then Theo turned up. I don't know why I call him Theo; I never called him anything but Cartwright, I never thought of him as anything but Cartwright. Theo was a shock. You know what he looks like now; I remembered him as a curly-headed youngster, very fresh and clean-looking; he was always neat and dapper, he had a good figure and he held himself well, like a man who's used to taking a lot of exercise. Now I come to think of it he wasn't bad-looking, not in a big, massive way, but graceful, you know, and lithe. When I saw this bowed, cadaverous, bald-headed old buffer with spectacles I could hardly believe my eyes. I shouldn't have known him from Adam. He seemed pleased to see me, at least, interested; he wasn't effusive, but he'd always been on the quiet side and I didn't expect him to be.

'"Are you surprised to find us here?" he asked me.

'"Well, I hadn't the faintest notion where you were."

'"We've kept track of your movements more or less. We've seen your name in the paper every now and then. You must come out one day and have a look at our place. We've been settled there a good many years, and I suppose we shall stay there till we go home for good. Have you ever been back to Alor Lipis?"

'"No, I haven't," I said.

'"It was a nice little place. I'm told it's grown. I've never been back."

'"It hasn't got the pleasantest recollections for us," said Mrs. Cartwright.

'I asked them if they'd have a drink and we called the boy. I daresay you noticed that Mrs. Cartwright likes her liquor; I don't mean that she gets tight or anything like that, but she drinks her stengah like a man. I couldn't help looking at them with a certain amount of curiosity. They seemed perfectly happy; I gathered that they hadn't done at all badly, and I found out later that they were quite well off. They had a very nice car, and when they went on leave they denied themselves nothing. They were on the best of terms with one another. You know how jolly it is to see two people who've been married a great many years obviously better pleased with their own company than anyone else's. Their marriage had evidently been a great success. And they were both of them devoted to Olive and very proud of her, Theo especially.'

'Although she was only his step-daughter?' I said.

'Although she was only his step-daughter,' answered Gaze. 'You'd think that she would have taken his name. But she hadn't. She called him Daddy, of course, he was the only father she'd ever known, but she signed her letters, Olive Bronson.'

'What was Bronson like, by the way?'

'Bronson? He was a great big fellow, very hearty, with a loud voice and a bellowing laugh, beefy, you know, and a fine athlete. There was not very much to him, but he was as straight as a die. He had a red face and red hair. Now I come to think of it I remember that I never saw a man sweat as much as he did. Water just poured off him, and when he played tennis he always used to bring a towel on the court with him.'

'It doesn't sound very attractive.'

'He was a handsome chap. He was always fit. He was keen on that. He hadn't much to talk about but rubber and games, tennis, you know, and golf and shooting; and I don't suppose he read a book from year's end to year's end. He was the typical public-school boy. He was about thirty-five when I first knew him, but he had the mind of a boy of eighteen. You know how many fellows when they come out East seem to stop growing.'

I did indeed. One of the most disconcerting things to the traveller is to see stout, middle-aged gentlemen, with bald heads, speaking and acting like schoolboys. You might almost think that no idea has entered their heads since they first passed through the Suez Canal. Though married and the fathers of children, and perhaps in control of a large business, they continue to look upon life from the standpoint of the sixth form.

'But he was no fool,' Gaze went on. 'He knew his work from A to Z. His estate was one of the best managed in the country and he knew how to handle his labour. He was a damned good sort, and if he did get on your nerves a little you couldn't help liking him. He was generous with his money, and always ready to do anybody a good turn. That's how Cartwright happened to turn up in the first instance.'

'Did the Bronsons get on well together?'

'Oh, yes, I think so. I'm sure they did. He was good-natured and she was very jolly and gay. She was very outspoken, you know. She can be damned amusing when she likes even now, but there's generally a sting lurking in the joke; when she was a young woman and married to Bronson it was just pure fun. She had high spirits and liked having a good time. She never cared a hang what she said, but it went with her type, if you understand what I mean; there was something so open and frank and careless about her that you didn't care what she said to you. They seemed very happy.

'Their estate was about five miles from Alor Lipis. They had a trap and they used to drive in most evenings about five. Of course it was a very small community and men were in the majority. There were only about six women. The Bronsons were a god-send. They bucked things up the moment they arrived. We used to have very jolly times in that little club. I've often thought of them since and I don't know that on the whole I've ever enjoyed myself more than I did when I was stationed there. Between six and eight-thirty the club at Alor Lipis twenty years ago was about as lively a place as you could find between Aden and Yokohama.

'One day Mrs. Bronson told us that they were expecting a friend to stay with them and a few days later they brought Cartwright along. It appeared that he was an old friend of Bronson's, they'd been at school together, Marlborough, or some place like that, and they'd first come out East on the same ship. Rubber had taken a toss and a lot of fellows had lost their jobs. Cartwright was one of them. He'd been out of work for the greater part of a year and he hadn't anything to fall back on. In those days planters were even worse paid than they are now and a man had to be very lucky to put by something for a rainy day. Cartwright had gone to Singapore. They all go there when there's a slump, you know. It's awful then, I've seen it; I've known of planters sleeping in the street because they hadn't the price of a night's lodging. I've known them stop strangers outside the 'Europe' and ask for a dollar to get a meal, and I think Cartwright had had a pretty rotten time.

'At last he wrote to Bronson and asked him if he couldn't do something for him. Bronson asked him to come and stay till things got better, at least it would be free board and lodging, and Cartwright jumped at the chance, but Bronson had to send him the money to pay his railway fare. When Cartwright arrived at Alor Lipis he hadn't ten cents in his pocket. Bronson had a little money of his own, two or three hundred a year, I think, and though his salary had been cut, he'd kept his job, so that he was better off than most planters. When Cartwright came Mrs. Bronson told him that he was to look upon the place as his home and stay as long he as liked.'

'It was very nice of her, wasn't it?' I remarked.

'Very.'

Gaze lit himself another cheroot and filled his glass. It was very still and but for the occasional croak of the chik-chak the silence was intense. We seemed to be alone in the tropical night and heaven only knows how far from the habitations of men. Gaze did not speak for so long that at last I was forced to say something.

'What sort of a man was Cartwright at that time?' I asked. 'Younger, of course, and you told me rather nice-looking; but in himself?'

'Well, to tell you the truth, I never paid much attention to him. He was pleasant and unassuming. He's very quiet now, as I daresay you noticed; well, he wasn't exactly lively then. But he was perfectly inoffensive. He was fond of reading and he played the piano rather nicely. You never minded having him about, he was never in the way, but you never bothered very much about him. He danced well and the women rather liked that, but he also played billiards quite decently and he wasn't bad at tennis. He fell into our little groove very naturally. I wouldn't say that he ever became wildly popular, but everybody liked him. Of course we were sorry for him, as one is for a man who's down and out, but there was nothing we could do, and, well, we just accepted him and then forgot that he hadn't always been there. He used to come in with the Bronsons every evening and pay for his drinks like everyone else, I suppose Bronson had lent a bit of money for current expenses, and he was always very civil. I'm rather vague about him, because really he didn't make any particular impression on me; in the East one meets such a lot of people, and he seemed very much like anybody else. He did everything he could to get something to do, but he had no luck; the fact is, there were no jobs going, and sometimes he seemed rather depressed about it. He was with the Bronsons for over a year. I remember his saying to me once:

'"After all I can't live with them for ever. They've been most awfully good to me, but there are limits."

'"I should think the Bronsons would be very glad to have you," I said. "It's not particularly gay on a rubber estate, and as far as your food and drink go, it must make precious little difference if you're there or not."'

Gaze stopped once more and looked at me with a sort of hesitation.

'What's the matter?' I asked.

'I'm afraid I'm telling you this story very badly,' he said. 'I seem to be just rambling on. I'm not a damned novelist, I'm a policeman, and I'm just telling you the facts as I saw them at the time; and from my point of view all the circumstances are important; it's important, I mean, to realise what sort of people they were.'

'Of course. Fire away.'

'I remember someone, a woman, I think it was, the doctor's wife, asking Mrs. Bronson if she didn't get tired sometimes of having a stranger in the house. You know, in places like Alor Lipis there isn't very much to talk about, and if you didn't talk about your neighbours there'd be nothing to talk about at all.

'"Oh, no," she said, "Theo's no trouble." She turned to her husband who was sitting there mopping his face. "We like having him, don't we?"

'"He's all right," said Bronson.

'"What does he do with himself all day long?"

'"Oh, I don't know," said Mrs. Bronson. "He walks round the estate with Reggie sometimes, and he shoots a bit. He talks to me."

'"He's always glad to make himself useful," said Bronson. "The other day when I had a go of fever, he took over my work and I just lay in bed and had a good time."'

'Hadn't the Bronsons any children?' I asked.

'No,' Gaze answered. 'I don't know why, they could well have afforded it.'

Gaze leant back in his chair. He took off his glasses and wiped them. They were very strong and hideously distorted his eyes. Without them he wasn't so homely. The chik-chak on the ceiling gave its strangely human cry. It was like the cackle of an idiot child.

'Bronson was killed,' said Gaze suddenly.

'Killed?'

'Yes, murdered. I shall never forget that night. We'd been playing tennis, Mrs. Bronson and the doctor's wife, Theo Cartwright and I; and then we played bridge. Cartwright had been off his game and when we sat down at the bridge-table Mrs. Bronson said to him: 'Well, Theo, if you play bridge as rottenly as you played tennis we shall lose our shirts.'

'We'd just had a drink, but she called the boy and ordered another round.

'"Put that down your throat," she said to him, "and don't call without top honours and an outside trick."

'Bronson hadn't turned up, he'd cycled in to Kabulong to get the money to pay his coolies their wages and was to come along to the club when he got back. The Bronsons' estate was nearer Alor Lipis than it was to Kabulong, but Kabulong was a more important place commercially, and Bronson banked there.

'"Reggie can cut in when he turns up," said Mrs. Bronson.

'"He's late, isn't he?" said the doctor's wife.

'"Very. He said he wouldn't get back in time for tennis, but would be here for a rubber. I have a suspicion that he went to the club at Kabulong instead of coming straight home and is having drinks, the ruffian."

'"Oh, well, he can put away a good many without their having much effect on him," I laughed.

'"He's getting fat, you know. He'll have to be careful."

'We sat by ourselves in the card-room and we could hear the crowd in the billiard-room talking and laughing. They were all on the merry side. It was getting on to Christmas Day and we were all letting ourselves go a little. There was going to be a dance on Christmas Eve.

'I remembered afterwards that when we sat down the doctor's wife asked Mrs. Bronson if she wasn't tired.

'"Not a bit," she said. "Why should I be?"

'I didn't know why she flushed.

'"I was afraid the tennis might have been too much for you," said the doctor's wife.

'"Oh, no," answered Mrs. Bronson, a trifle abruptly, I thought, as though she didn't want to discuss the matter.

'I didn't know what they meant, and indeed it wasn't till later that I remembered the incident.

'We played three or four rubbers and still Bronson didn't turn up.

'"I wonder what's happened to him," said his wife. "I can't think why he should be so late."

'Cartwright was always silent, but this evening he had hardly opened his mouth. I thought he was tired and asked him what he'd been doing.

'"Nothing very much," he said. "I went out after tiffin to shoot pigeon."

'"Did you have any luck?" I asked.

'"Oh, I got half a dozen. They were very shy."

17

'But now he said: "If Reggie got back late, I daresay he thought it wasn't worth while to come here. I expect he's had a bath and when we get in we shall find him asleep in his chair.'

'"It's a good long ride from Kabulong," said the doctor's wife.

'"He doesn't take the road, you know," Mrs. Bronson explained. "He takes the short cut through the jungle."

'"Can he get along on his bicycle?" I asked.

'"Oh, yes, it's a very good track. It saves about a couple of miles."

'We had just started another rubber when the barboy came in and said there was a police-sergeant outside who wanted to speak to me.

'"What does he want?" I asked.

'The boy said he didn't know, but he had two coolies with him.

'"Curse him," I said. "I'll give him hell if I find he's disturbed me for nothing."

'I told the boy I'd come and I finished playing the hand. Then I got up.

'"I won't be a minute," I said. "Deal for me, will you?" I added to Cartwright.

'I went out and found the sergeant with two Malays waiting for me on the steps. I asked him what the devil he wanted. You can imagine my consternation when he told me that the Malays had come to the police-station and said there was a white man lying dead on the path that led through the jungle to Kabulong. I immediately thought of Bronson.

'"Dead?" I cried.

'"Yes, shot. Shot through the head. A white man with red hair."

'Then I knew it was Reggie Bronson, and indeed, one of them naming his estate said he'd recognised him as the man. It was an awful shock. And there was Mrs. Bronson in the card-room waiting impatiently for me to sort my cards and make a bid. For a moment I really didn't know what to do. I was frightfully upset. It was dreadful to give her such a terrible and unexpected blow without a word of preparation, but I found myself quite unable to think of any way to soften it. I told the sergeant and the coolies to wait and went back into the club. I tried to pull myself together. As I entered the card-room Mrs. Bronson said: 'You've been an awful long time.' Then she caught sight of my face. 'Is anything the matter?' I saw her clench her fists and go white. You'd have thought she had a presentiment of evil.

'"Something dreadful has happened," I said, and my throat was all closed up so that my voice sounded even to myself hoarse and uncanny. "There's been an accident. Your husband's been wounded."

'She gave a long gasp, it was not exactly a scream, it reminded me oddly of a piece of silk torn in two.

'"Wounded?"

'She leapt to her feet and with her eyes starting from her head stared at Cartwright. The effect on him was ghastly, he fell back in his chair and went as white as death.

'"Very, very badly, I'm afraid," I added.

'I knew that I must tell her the truth, and tell it then, but I couldn't bring myself to tell it all at once.

'"Is he,' her lips trembled so that she could hardly form the words, 'is he—conscious?'

'I looked at her for a moment without answering. I'd have given a thousand pounds not to have to.

'"No, I'm afraid he isn't.'

'Mrs. Bronson stared at me as though she were trying to see right into my brain.

'"Is he dead?'

'I thought the only thing was to get it out and have done with it.

'"Yes, he was dead when they found him.'

'Mrs. Bronson collapsed into her chair and burst into tears.

'"Oh, my God," she muttered. "Oh, my God."

'The doctor's wife went to her and put her arms round her. Mrs. Bronson with her face in her hands swayed to and fro weeping hysterically. Cartwright, with that livid face, sat quite still, his mouth open, and stared at her. You might have thought he was turned to stone.

'"Oh, my dear, my dear," said the doctor's wife, "you must try and pull yourself together." Then, turning to me. "Get her a glass of water and fetch Harry."

'Harry was her husband and he was playing billiards. I went in and told him what had happened.

'"A glass of water be damned," he said. "What she wants is a good long peg of brandy."

'We took it in to her and forced her to drink it and gradually the violence of her emotion exhausted itself. In a few minutes the doctor's wife was able to take her into the ladies' lavatory to wash her face. I'd made up my mind now what had better be done. I could see that Cartwright wasn't good for much; he was all to pieces. I could understand that it was a fearful shock to him, for after all Bronson was his greatest friend and had done everything in the world for him.

'"You look as though you'd be all the better for a drop of brandy yourself, old man," I said to him.

'He made an effort.

'"It's shaken me, you know," he said. "I . . . I didn't . . ." He stopped as though his mind was wandering; he was still fearfully pale; he took out a packet of cigarettes and struck a match, but his hand was shaking so that he could hardly manage it.

'"Yes, I'll have a brandy."

'"Boy," I shouted, and then to Cartwright: "Now, are you fit to take Mrs. Bronson home?"

'"Oh, yes," he answered.

'"That's good. The doctor and I will go along with the coolies and some police to where the body is."

'"Will you bring him back to the bungalow?" asked Cartwright.

'"I think he'd better be taken straight to the mortuary," said the doctor before I could answer. "I shall have to do a P.M."

'When Mrs. Bronson, now so much calmer that I was amazed, came back, I told her what I suggested. The doctor's wife, kind woman, offered to go with her and spend the night at the bungalow, but Mrs. Bronson wouldn't hear of it. She said she would be perfectly all right, and when the doctor's wife insisted—you know how bent some people are on forcing their kindness on those in trouble—she turned on her almost fiercely.

'"No, no, I must be alone," she said. "I really must. And Theo will be there."

'They got into the trap. Theo took the reins and they drove off. We started after them, the doctor and I, while the sergeant and the coolies followed. I had sent my seis to the police station with instructions to send two men to the place where the body was lying. We soon passed Mrs. Bronson and Cartwright.

'"All right?" I called.

'"Yes," he answered.

'For some time the doctor and I drove without saying a word; we were both of us deeply shocked. I was worried as well. Somehow or other I'd got to find the murderers and I foresaw that it would be no easy matter.

'"Do you suppose it was gang robbery?" said the doctor at last.

'He might have been reading my thoughts.

'"I don't think there's a doubt of it," I answered. "They knew he'd gone into Kabulong to get the wages and lay in wait for him on the way back. Of course he should never have come alone through the jungle when everyone knew he had a packet of money with him."

'"He'd done it for years," said the doctor. "And he's not the only one."

'"I know. The question is, how we're going to get hold of the fellows that did it."

'"You don't think the two coolies who say they found him could have had anything to do with it?"

'"No. They wouldn't have the nerve. I think a pair of Chinks might think out a trick like that, but I don't believe Malays would. They'd be much too frightened. Of course we'll keep an eye on them. We shall soon see if they seem to have any money to fling about."

'"It's awful for Mrs. Bronson," said the doctor. "It would have been bad enough at any time, but now she's going to have a baby . . ."

'"I didn't know that," I said, interrupting him.

'"No, for some reason she wanted to keep it dark. She was rather funny about it, I thought."

'I recollected then that little passage between Mrs. Bronson and the doctor's wife. I understood why that good woman had been so anxious that Mrs. Bronson should not overtire herself.

'"It's strange her having a baby after being married so many years."

'"It happens, you know. But it was a surprise to her. When first she came to see me and I told her what was the matter she fainted, and then she began to cry. I should have thought she'd be as pleased as Punch. She told me that Bronson didn't like children and he'd be awfully bored at the idea, and she made me promise to say nothing about it till she had had a chance of breaking it to him gradually."

'I reflected for a moment.

'"He was the kind of breezy, hearty cove whom you'd expect to be as keen as mustard on having kids."

'"You never can tell. Some people are very selfish and just don't want the bother."

'"Well, how did he take it when she did tell him? Wasn't he rather bucked?"

'"I don't know that she ever told him. Though she couldn't have waited much longer; unless I'm very much mistaken she ought to be confined in about five months."

'"Poor devil," I said. "You know, I've got a notion that he'd have been most awfully pleased to know."

'We drove in silence for the rest of the way and at last came to the point at which the short cut to Kabulong branched off from the road. Here we stopped and in a minute or two my trap, in which were the police-sergeant and the two Malays, came up. We took the head-lamps to light us on our way. I left the doctor's seis to look after the ponies and told him that when the policemen came they were to follow the path till they found us. The two coolies, carrying the lamps, walked ahead and we followed them. It was a fairly broad track, wide enough for a small cart to pass, and before the road was built it had been the highway between Kabulong and Alor Lipis. It was firm to the foot and good walking. The surface here and there was sandy and in places you could see quite plainly the mark of a bicycle wheel. It was the track Bronson had left on his way to Kabulong.

'We walked twenty minutes, I should think, in single file, and on a sudden the coolies, with a cry, stopped sharply. The sight had come upon them so abruptly that notwithstanding they were expecting it they were startled. There, in the middle of the pathway lit dimly by the lamps the coolies carried, lay Bronson; he'd fallen over his bicycle and lay across it in an ungainly heap. I was too shocked to speak, and I think the doctor was, too. But in our silence the din of the jungle was deafening; those damned cicadas and the bull-frogs were making

23

enough row to wake the dead. Even under ordinary circumstances the noise of the jungle at night is uncanny; because you feel that at that hour there should be utter silence it has an odd effect on you, that ceaseless and invisible uproar that beats upon your nerves. It surrounds you and hems you in. But just then, believe me, it was terrifying. That poor fellow lay dead and all round him the restless life of the jungle pursued its indifferent and ferocious course.

'He was lying face downwards. The sergeant and the coolies looked at me as though awaiting an order. I was a young fellow then and I'm afraid I felt a little frightened. Though I couldn't see the face I had no doubt that it was Bronson, but I felt that I ought to turn the body over to make sure. I suppose we all have our little squeamishnesses; you know, I've always had a horrible distaste for touching dead bodies. I've had to do it fairly often now, but it still makes me feel slightly sick.

'"It's Bronson, all right," I said.

'The doctor—by George, it was lucky for me he was there—the doctor bent down and turned the head. The sergeant directed the lamp on the dead face.

'"My God, half his head's been shot away," I cried.

'"Yes."

'The doctor stood up straight and wiped his hands on the leaves of a tree that grew beside the path.

'"Is he quite dead?" I asked.

'"Oh, yes. Death must have been instantaneous. Whoever shot him must have fired at pretty close range."

'"How long has he been dead, d'you think?"

'"Oh, I don't know, several hours."

'"He would have passed here about five o'clock, I suppose, if he was expecting to get to the club for a rubber at six."

'"There's no sign of any struggle," said the doctor.

'"No, there wouldn't be. He was shot as he was riding along."

'I looked at the body for a little while. I couldn't help thinking how short a time ago it was since Bronson, noisy and loud-voiced, had been so full of hearty life.

'"You haven't forgotten that he had the coolies' wages on him," said the doctor.

'"No, we'd better search him."

'"Shall we turn him over?"

'"Wait a minute. Let us just have a look at the ground first."

'I took the lamp and as carefully as I could looked all about me. Just where he had fallen the sandy pathway was trodden and confused; there were our footprints and the footprints of the coolies who had found him. I walked two or three paces and then saw quite clearly the mark of his bicycle wheels; he had been riding straight and steadily. I followed it to the spot where he had fallen, to just before that rather, and there saw very distinctly the prints on each side of the wheels of his heavy boots. He had evidently stopped there and put his feet to the ground, then he'd started off again, there was a great wobble of the wheel, and he'd crashed.

'"Now let's search him," I said.

'The doctor and the sergeant turned the body over and one of the coolies dragged the bicycle away. They laid Bronson on his back. I supposed he would have had the money partly in notes and partly in silver. The silver would have been in a bag attached to the bicycle and a glance told me that it was not there. The notes he would have put in a wallet. It would have been a good thick bundle. I felt him all over, but there was nothing; then I turned out the pockets, they were all empty except the right trouser pocket, in which there was a little small change.

'"Didn't he always wear a watch?" asked the doctor.

'"Yes, of course he did."

'I remembered that he wore the chain through the buttonhole in the lapel of his coat and the watch and some seals and things in his handkerchief pocket. But watch and chain were gone.

'"Well, there's not much doubt now, is there?" I said.

'It was clear that he had been attacked by gang robbers who knew he had money on him. After killing him they had stripped him of everything. I suddenly remembered the footprints that proved that for a moment he had stood still. I saw exactly how it had been done. One of them had stopped him on some pretext and then, just as he started off again, another, slipping out of the jungle behind him, had emptied the two barrels of a gun into his head.

'"Well," I said to the doctor, "it's up to me to catch them, and I'll tell you what, it'll be a real pleasure to me to see them hanged."

'Of course there was an inquest. Mrs. Bronson gave evidence, but she had nothing to say that we didn't know already. Bronson had left the bungalow about eleven, he was to have tiffin at Kabulong and was to be back between five and six. He asked her not to wait for him, he said he would just put the money in the safe and come straight to the club. Cartwright confirmed this. He had lunched alone with Mrs. Bronson and after a smoke had gone out with a gun to shoot pigeon. He had got in about five, a little before perhaps, had a bath and changed to play tennis. He was shooting not far from the place where Bronson was killed, but never heard a shot. That, of course, meant nothing; what with the cicadas and the frogs, and the other sounds of the jungle he would have had to be very near to hear anything; and besides, Cartwright was probably back in the bungalow before Bronson was killed. We traced Bronson's movements. He had lunched at the club, he had got money at the bank just before it closed, had gone back to the club and had one more drink, and then started off on his bicycle. He had crossed the river by the ferry, the ferryman remembered distinctly seeing him, but was positive that no one else with a bicycle had crossed. That looked as though the murderers were not following, but lying in wait for him. He rode along the main road for a couple of miles and then took the path which was a short cut to his bungalow.

'It looked as though he had been killed by men who knew his habits, and suspicion, of course, fell immediately on the coolies of his estate. We examined them all—pretty carefully—but there was not a scrap of evidence to connect any of them with the crime. In fact, most of them were able satisfactorily to account for their actions and those who couldn't seemed to me for one reason and another out of the running. There were a few bad characters among the Chinese at Alor Lipis and I had them looked up. But somehow I didn't think it was the work of the Chinese; I had a feeling that Chinese would have used revolvers and not a shot-gun. Anyhow, I could find out nothing there. So then we offered a reward of a thousand dollars to anyone who could put us in the way of discovering the murderers. I thought there were a good many people to whom it would appeal to do a public service and at the same time earn a tidy sum. But I knew that an informer would take no risks, he wouldn't want to tell what he knew till he knew he could tell it safely, and I armed myself with patience. The reward had brightened the interest of my police and I knew they would use every means they had to bring the criminals to trial. In a case like this they could do more than I.

'But it was strange, nothing happened; the reward seemed to tempt no one. I cast my net a little wider. There were two or three kampongs along the road and I wondered if the murderers were there; I saw the headmen, but got no help from them. It was not that they would tell me nothing, I was sure they had nothing to tell. I talked to the bad hats, but there was absolutely nothing to connect them with the murder. There was not the shadow of a clue.

'"Very well, my lads," I said to myself, as I drove back to Alor Lipis, "there's no hurry; the rope won't spoil by keeping."

'The scoundrels had got away with a considerable sum, but money is no good unless you spend it. I felt I knew the native temperament enough to be sure that the possession of it was a constant temptation. The Malays are an extravagant race, and a race of gamblers, and the Chinese are gamblers, too; sooner or later someone would start flinging his money about, and then I should want to know where it came from. With a few well-directed questions I thought I could put the fear of God into the fellow and then, if I knew my business, it shouldn't be hard to get a full confession.

'The only thing now was to sit down and wait till the hue and cry had died down and the murderers thought the affair was forgotten. The itch to spend those ill-gotten dollars would grow more and more intolerable till at last it could be resisted no longer. I would go about my business, but I meant never to relax my watch, and one day, sooner or later, my time must come.

'Cartwright took Mrs. Bronson down to Singapore. The company Bronson had worked for asked him if he would care to take Bronson's place, but he said, very naturally, that he didn't like the idea of it; so they put another man in and told Cartwright that he could have the job that Bronson's successor had vacated. It was the management of the estate that Cartwright lives on now. He moved in at once. Four months after this Olive was born at Singapore, and a few months later, when Bronson had been dead just over a year, Cartwright and Mrs. Bronson were married. I was surprised; but on thinking it over I couldn't help confessing that it was very natural. After the trouble Mrs. Bronson had leant much on Cartwright and he had arranged everything for her; she must have been lonely, and rather lost, and I daresay she was grateful for his kindness, he did behave like a brick; and so far as he was concerned I imagined he was sorry for her, it was a dreadful position for a woman, she had nowhere to go, and all they'd gone through must have been a tie between them. There was every reason for them to marry and it was probably the best thing for them both.

'It looked as though Bronson's murderers would never be caught, for that plan of mine didn't work; there was no one in the district who spent more money than he could account for, and if anyone had that hoard buried away under his floor he was showing a self-control that was super-human. A year had passed and to all intents and purposes the thing was forgotten. Could anyone be so prudent as after so long not to let a little money dribble out? It was incredible. I began to think that Bronson had been killed by a couple of wandering Chinese who had got away, to Singapore perhaps, where there would be small chance of catching them. At last I gave it up. If you come to think of it, as a rule, it's just those crimes, crimes of robbery, in which there is least chance of getting the culprit; for there's nothing to attach suspicion to him, and if he's caught it can only be by his own carelessness. It's different with crimes of passion or vengeance, then you can find out who had a motive to put the victim out of the way.

'It's no use grizzling over one's failures, and bringing my common sense to bear I did my best to put the matter out of my mind. No one likes to be beaten, but beaten I was and I had to put as good a face on it as I could. And then a Chinaman was caught trying to pawn poor Bronson's watch.

'I told you that Bronson's watch and chain had been taken, and of course Mrs. Bronson was able to give us a fairly accurate description of it. It was a half-hunter, by Benson, there was a gold chain, three or four seals and a sovereign purse. The pawnbroker was a smart fellow and when the Chinaman brought the watch he recognised it at once. On some pretext he kept the man waiting and sent for a policeman. The man was arrested and immediately brought to me. I greeted him like a long-lost brother. I was never so pleased to see anyone in my life. I have no feeling about criminals, you know; I'm rather sorry for them, because they're playing a game in which their opponents hold all the aces and kings; but when I catch one it gives me a little thrill of satisfaction, like bringing off a neat finesse at bridge. At last the mystery was going to be cleared up, for if the Chinaman hadn't done the thing himself we were pretty sure through him to trace the murderers. I beamed on him.

'I asked him to account for his possession of the watch. He said he had bought it from a man he didn't know. That was very thin. I explained the circumstances briefly and told him he would be charged with murder. I meant to frighten him and I did. He said then that he'd found the watch.

'"Found it?" I said. "Fancy that. Where?"

'His answer staggered me; he said he'd found it in the jungle; I laughed at him; I asked him if he thought watches were likely to be left lying about in the jungle; then he said he'd been coming along the pathway that led from Kabulong to Alor Lipis, and had gone into the jungle and caught sight of something gleaming and there was the watch. That was odd. Why should he have said he found the watch just there? It was either true or excessively astute. I asked him where the chain and the seals were, and he produced them immediately. I'd got him scared, and he was pale and shaking; he was a knock-kneed little fellow and I should have been a fool not to see that I hadn't got hold of the murderer there. But his terror suggested that he knew something.

'I asked him when he'd found the watch.

'"Yesterday," he said.

'I asked him what he was doing on the short-cut from Kabulong to Alor Lipis. He said he'd been working in Singapore and had gone to Kabulong because his father was ill, and that he himself had come to Alor Lipis to work. A friend of his father, a carpenter by trade, had given him a job. He gave me the name of the man with whom he had worked in Singapore and the name of the man who had engaged him at Alor Lipis. All he said seemed plausible and could so easily be verified that it was hardly likely to be false. Of course it occurred to me that if he had found the watch as he said it must have been lying in the jungle for more than a year. It could hardly be in very good condition; I tried to open it, but couldn't. The pawnbroker had come to the police-station and was waiting in the next room. Luckily he was also something of a watch-maker. I sent for him and asked him to look at the watch; when he opened it he gave a little whistle, the works were thick with rust.

'"This watch no good," he said, shaking his head. "Him never go now."

'I asked him what had put it in such a state, and without a word from me he said that it had been long exposed to wet. For the moral effect I had the prisoner put in a cell and I sent for his employer. I sent a wire to Kabulong and another to Singapore. While I waited I did my best to put two and two together. I was inclined to believe the man's story true; his fear might be ascribed to no more guilt than consisted in his having found something and tried to sell it. Even quite innocent persons are apt to be nervous when they're in the hands of the police; I don't know what there is about a policeman, people are never very much at their ease in his company. But if he really had found the watch where he said, someone had thrown it there. Now that was funny. Even if the murderers had thought the watch a dangerous thing to possess, one would have expected them to melt down the gold case; that would be a very simple thing for any native to do; and the chain was of so ordinary a pattern they could hardly have thought it possible to trace that. There were chains like it in every jeweller's shop in the country. Of course there was the possibility that they had plunged into the jungle and having dropped the watch in their hurry had been afraid to go back and look for it. I didn't think that very likely: the Malays are used to keeping things tucked away in their sarongs, and the Chinese have pockets in their coats. Besides, the moment they got into the jungle they knew there was no hurry; they probably waited and divided the swag then and there.

'In a few minutes the man I had sent for came to the police-station and confirmed what the prisoner had said, and in an hour I got an answer from Kabulong. The police had seen his father who told them that the boy had gone to Alor Lipis to get a job with a carpenter. So far everything he had said seemed true. I had him brought in again, and told him I was going to take him to the place where he said he had found the watch and he must show me the exact spot. I handcuffed him to a policeman, though it was hardly necessary, for the poor devil was shaking with fright, and took a couple of men besides. We drove out to where the track joined the road and walked along it; within five yards of the place where Bronson was killed the Chinaman stopped.

'"Here," he said.

'He pointed to the jungle and we followed him in. We went in about ten yards and he pointed to a chink between two large boulders and said that he found the watch there. It could only have been by the merest chance that he noticed it, and if he really had found it there it looked very much as though someone had put it there to hide it.'

Gaze stopped and gave me a reflective look.

'What would you have thought then?' he asked.

'I don't know,' I answered.

'Well, I'll tell you what I thought. I thought that if the watch was there the money might be there, too. It seemed worth while having a look. Of course, to look for something in the jungle makes looking for a needle in a bundle of hay a drawing-room pastime. I couldn't help that. I released the Chinaman, I wanted all the help I could get, and set him to work. I set my three men to work, and I started in myself. We made a line—there were five of us—and we searched from the road; for fifty yards on each side of the place at which Bronson was murdered and for a hundred yards in we went over the ground foot by foot. We routed among dead leaves and peered in bushes, we looked under boulders and in the hollows of trees. I knew it was a foolish thing to do, for the chances against us were a thousand to one; my only hope was that anyone who had just committed a murder would be rattled and if he wanted to hide anything would hide it quickly; he would choose the first obvious hiding-place that offered itself. That is what he had done when he hid the watch. My only reason for looking in so circumscribed an area was that as the watch had been found so near the road, the person who wanted to get rid of the things must have wanted to get rid of them quickly.

'We worked on. I began to grow tired and cross. We were sweating like pigs. I had a maddening thirst and nothing in the world to drink. At last I came to the conclusion that we must give it up as a bad job, for that day at least, when suddenly the Chinaman—he must have had sharp eyes, that young man—uttered a guttural cry. He stooped down and from under the winding root of a tree drew out a messy, mouldering, stinking thing. It was a pocket-book that had been out in the rain for a year, that had been eaten by ants and beetles and God knows what, that was sodden and foul, but it was a pocket-book all right, Bronson's, and inside were the shapeless, mushed-up, fetid remains of the Singapore notes he had got from the bank at Kabulong. There was still the silver and I was convinced that it was hidden somewhere about, but I wasn't going to bother about that. I had found out something very important; whoever had murdered Bronson had made no money out of it.

'Do you remember my telling you that I'd noticed the print of Bronson's feet on each side of the broad line of the pneumatic tyre, where he had stopped, and presumably spoken to someone? He was a heavy man and the prints were well marked. He hadn't just put his feet on the soft sand and taken them off, but must have stopped at least for a minute or two. My explanation was that he had stopped to chat with a Malay or a Chinaman, but the more I thought of it the less I liked it. Why the devil should he? Bronson wanted to get home, and though a jovial chap, he certainly was not hail-fellow-well-met with the natives. His relations towards them were those of master and servants. Those footprints had always puzzled me. And now the truth flashed across me. Whoever had murdered Bronson hadn't murdered him to rob and if he'd stopped to talk with someone it could only be with a friend. I knew at last who the murderer was.'

I have always thought the detective story a most diverting and ingenious variety of fiction, and have regretted that I never had the skill to write one, but I have read a good many, and I flatter myself it is rarely that I have not solved the mystery before it was disclosed to me; and now for some time I had foreseen what Gaze was going to say, but when at last he said it I confess that it gave me, notwithstanding, somewhat of a shock.

'The man he met was Cartwright. Cartwright was pigeon-shooting. He stopped and asked him what sport he had had, and as he rode on Cartwright raised his gun and discharged both barrels into his head. Cartwright took the money and the watch in order to make it look like the work of gang robbers and hurriedly hid them in the jungle, then made his way along the edge till he got to the road, went back to the bungalow, changed into his tennis things and drove with Mrs. Bronson to the club.

'I remembered how badly he'd played tennis, and how he'd collapsed when, in order to break the news more gently to Mrs. Bronson, I said Bronson was wounded and not dead. If he was only wounded he might have been able to speak. By George, I bet that was a bad moment. The child was Cartwright's. Look at Olive: why, you saw the likeness yourself. The doctor had said that Mrs. Bronson was upset when he told her she was going to have a baby and made him promise not to tell Bronson. Why? Because Bronson knew that he couldn't be the father of the child.'

'Do you think that Mrs. Bronson knew what Cartwright had done?' I asked.

'I'm sure of it. When I look back on her behaviour that evening at the club I am convinced of it. She was upset, but not because Bronson was killed; she was upset because I said he was wounded; on my telling her that he was dead when they found him she burst out crying, but from relief. I know that woman. Look at that square chin of hers and tell me that she hasn't got the courage of the devil. She has a will of iron. She made Cartwright do it. She planned every detail and every move. He was completely under her influence; he is now.'

'But do you mean to tell me that neither you nor

anyone else ever suspected that there was anything between them?'

'Never. Never.'

'If they were in love with one another and knew that she was going to have a baby, why didn't they just bolt?'

'How could they? It was Bronson who had the money; she hadn't a bean and neither had Cartwright. He was out of a job. Do you think he would have got another with that story round his neck? Bronson had taken him in when he was starving and he'd stolen his wife from him. They wouldn't have had a dog's chance. They couldn't afford to let the truth come out, their only chance was to get Bronson out of the way, and they got him out of the way.'

'They might have thrown themselves on his mercy.'

'Yes, but I think they were ashamed. He'd been so good to them, he was such a decent chap, I don't think they had the heart to tell him the truth. They preferred to kill him.'

There was a moment's silence while I reflected over what Gaze said.

'Well, what did you do about it?' I asked.

'Nothing. What was there to do? What was the evidence? That the watch and notes had been found? They might easily have been hidden by someone who was afterwards afraid to come and get them. The murderer might have been quite content to get away with the silver. The footprints? Bronson might have stopped to light a cigarette or there might have been a tree-trunk across the path and he waited while the coolies he met there by chance moved it away. Who could prove that the child that a perfectly decent, respectable woman had had four months after her husband's death was not his child? No jury would have convicted Cartwright. I held my tongue and the Bronson murder was forgotten.'

'I don't suppose the Cartwrights have forgotten,' I suggested.

'I shouldn't be surprised. Human memory is astonishingly short and if you want my professional opinion I don't mind telling you that I don't believe remorse for a crime ever sits very heavily on a man when he's absolutely sure he'll never be found out.'

I thought once more of the pair I had met that afternoon, the thin, elderly, bald man with gold-rimmed spectacles, and that white-haired untidy woman with her frank speech and kindly, caustic smile. It was almost impossible to imagine that in the distant past they had been swayed by so turbulent a passion, for that alone made their behaviour explicable, that it had brought them in the end to such a pass that they could see no other issue than a cruel and cold-blooded murder.

'Doesn't it make you feel a little uncomfortable to be with them?" I asked Gaze. 'For, without wishing to be censorious, I'm bound to say that I don't think they can be very nice people.'

'That's where you're wrong. They are very nice people; they're about the pleasantest people here. Mrs. Cartwright is a thoroughly good sort and a very amusing woman. It's my business to prevent crime and to catch the culprit when crime is committed, but I've known far too many criminals to think that on the whole they're worse than anybody else. A perfectly decent fellow may be driven by circumstances to commit a crime and if he's found out he's punished; but he may very well remain a perfectly decent fellow. Of course society punishes him if he breaks its laws, and it's quite right, but it's not always his actions that indicate the essential man. If you'd been a policeman as long as I have, you'd know it's not what people do that really matters, it's what they are. Luckily a policeman has nothing to do with their thoughts, only with their deeds; if he had, it would be a very different, a much more difficult matter.'

Gaze flicked the ash from his cheroot and gave me his wry, sardonic, but agreeable smile.

'I'll tell you what, there's one job I *shouldn't* like,' he said.

'What is that?' I asked.

'God's, at the Judgment Day,' said Gaze. 'No, sir.'

Mabel

I was at Pagan, in Burma, and from there I took the steamer to Mandalay, but a couple of days before I got there, when the boat tied up for the night at a riverside village, I made up my mind to go ashore. The skipper told me that there was there a pleasant little club in which I had only to make myself at home; they were quite used to having strangers drop off like that from the steamer, and the secretary was a very decent chap; I might even get a game of bridge. I had nothing in the world to do, so I got into one of the bullock-carts that were waiting at the landing-stage and was driven to the club. There was a man sitting on the verandah and as I walked up he nodded to me and asked whether I would have a whisky and soda or a gin and bitters. The possibility that I would have nothing at all did not even occur to him. I chose the longer drink and sat down. He was a tall, thin, bronzed man, with a big moustache, and he wore khaki shorts and a khaki shirt. I never knew his name, but when we had been chatting a little while another man came in who told me he was the secretary, and he addressed my friend as George.

'Have you heard from your wife yet?' he asked him.

The other's eyes brightened.

'Yes, I had letters by this mail. She's having no end of a time.'

'Did she tell you not to fret?'

George gave a little chuckle, but was I mistaken in thinking that there was in it the shadow of a sob?

'In point of fact she did. But that's easier said than

done. Of course I know she wants a holiday, and I'm glad she should have it, but it's devilish hard on a chap.' He turned to me. 'You see, this is the first time I've ever been separated from my missus, and I'm like a lost dog without her.'

'How long have you been married?'

'Five minutes.'

The secretary of the club laughed.

'Don't be a fool, George. You've been married eight years.'

After we had talked for a little George, looking at his watch, said he must go and change his clothes for dinner and left us. The secretary watched him disappear into the night with a smile of not unkindly irony.

'We all ask him as much as we can now that he's alone,' he told me. 'He mopes so terribly since his wife went home.'

'It must be very pleasant for her to know that her husband is as devoted to her as all that.'

'Mabel is a remarkable woman.'

He called the boy and ordered more drinks. In this hospitable place they did not ask you if you would have anything; they took it for granted. Then he settled himself in his long chair and lit a cheroot. He told me the story of George and Mabel.

They became engaged when he was home on leave, and when he returned to Burma it was arranged that she should join him in six months. But one difficulty cropped up after another; Mabel's father died, the war came, George was sent to a district unsuitable for a white woman; so that in the end it was seven years before she was able to start. He made all arrangements for the marriage, which was to take place on the day of her arrival, and went down to Rangoon to meet her. On the morning on which the ship was due he borrowed a motor-car and drove along to the dock. He paced the quay.

Then, suddenly, without warning, his nerve failed him. He had not seen Mabel for seven years. He had forgotten what she was like. She was a total stranger. He felt a terrible sinking in the pit of his stomach and his knees began to wobble. He couldn't go through with it. He must tell Mabel that he was very sorry, but he couldn't, he really couldn't marry her. But how could a man tell a girl a thing like that when she had been engaged to him for seven years and had come six thousand miles to marry him? He hadn't the nerve for that either. George was seized with the courage of despair. There was a boat at the quay on the very point of starting for Singapore; he wrote a hurried letter to Mabel, and without a stick of luggage, just in the clothes he stood up in, leaped on board.

The letter Mabel received ran somewhat as follows:

Dearest Mabel, I have been suddenly called away on business and do not know when I shall be back. I think it would be much wiser if you returned to England. My plans are very uncertain. Your loving George.

But when he arrived at Singapore he found a cable waiting for him.

Quite understand. Don't worry. Love. Mabel.

Terror made him quick-witted.

'By Jove, I believe she's following me,' he said.

He telegraphed to the shipping-office at Rangoon and sure enough her name was on the passenger list of the ship that was now on its way to Singapore. There was not a moment to lose. He jumped on the train to Bangkok. But he was uneasy; she would have no difficulty in finding out that he had gone to Bangkok and it was just as simple for her to take the train as it had been for him. Fortunately there was a French tramp sailing next day for Saigon. He took it. At Saigon he would be safe; it would never occur to her that he had gone there; and if it did, surely by now she would have taken the hint. It is five days journey from Bangkok to Saigon and the boat is dirty, cramped and uncomfortable. He was glad to arrive and took a rickshaw to the hotel. He signed his name in the visitors' book and a telegram was immediately handed to him. It contained but two words: *Love. Mabel.* They were enough to make him break into a cold sweat.

'When is the next boat for Hong-Kong?' he asked.

Now his flight grew serious. He sailed to Hong-Kong, but dared not stay there; he went to Manila; Manila was ominous; he went on to Shanghai: Shanghai was nerve-racking; every time he went out of the hotel he expected to run straight into Mabel's arms; no, Shanghai would never do. The only thing was to go to Yokohama. At the Grand Hotel at Yokohama a cable awaited him.

'*So sorry to have missed you at Manila. Love. Mabel.*'

He scanned the shipping intelligence with a fevered brow. Where was she now? He doubled back to Shanghai. This time he went straight to the club and asked for a telegram. It was handed to him.

'*Arriving shortly. Love. Mabel.*'

No, no, he was not so easy to catch as all that. He had already made his plans. The Yangtze is a long river and the Yangtze was falling. He could just about catch the last steamer that could get up to Chungking and then no one could travel till the following spring except by junk. Such a journey was out of the question for a woman alone. He went to Hankow and from Hankow to Ichang, he changed boats here and from Ichang through the rapids went to Chungking. But he was desperate now, he was not going to take any risks: there was a place called Cheng-tu, the capital of Szechuan, and it was four hundred miles away. It could only be reached by road, and the road was infested with brigands. A man would be safe there.

George collected chair-bearers and coolies and set out.

It was with a sigh of relief that he saw at last the crenellated walls of the lonely Chinese city. From those walls at sunset you could see the snowy mountains of Tibet.

He could rest at last: Mabel would never find him there. The consul happened to be a friend of his and he stayed with him. He enjoyed the comfort of a luxurious house, he enjoyed his idleness after that strenuous escape across Asia, and above all he enjoyed his divine security. The weeks passed lazily one after the other.

One morning George and the consul were in the courtyard looking at some curios that a Chinese had brought for their inspection when there was a loud knocking at the great door of the Consulate. The doorman flung it open. A chair borne by four coolies entered, advanced, and was set down. Mabel stepped out. She was neat and cool and fresh. There was nothing in her appearance to suggest that she had just come in after a fortnight on the road. George was petrified. He was as pale as death. She went up to him.

'Hulloa, George, I was so afraid I'd missed you again.'

'Hulloa, Mabel,' he faltered.

He did not know what to say. He looked this way and that: she stood between him and the doorway. She looked at him with a smile in her blue eyes.

'You haven't altered at all,' she said. 'Men can go off so dreadfully in seven years and I was afraid you'd got fat and bald. I've been so nervous. It would have been terrible if after all these years I simply hadn't been able to bring myself to marry you after all.'

She turned to George's host.

'Are you the consul?' she asked.

'I am.'

'That's all right. I'm ready to marry him as soon as I've had a bath.'

And she did.

P. & O.

Mrs. Hamlyn lay on her long chair and lazily watched the passengers come along the gangway. The ship had reached Singapore in the night, and since dawn had been taking on cargo; the winches had been grinding away all day, but by now her ears were accustomed to their insistent clamour. She had lunched at the Europe, and for lack of anything better to do had driven in a rickshaw through the gay, multitudinous streets of the city. Singapore is the meeting place of many races. The Malays, though natives of the soil, dwell uneasily in towns, and are few; and it is the Chinese, supple, alert and industrious, who throng the streets; the dark-skinned Tamils walk on their silent, naked feet, as though they were but brief sojourners in a strange land, but the Bengalis, sleek and prosperous, are easy in their surroundings, and self-assured; the sly and obsequious Japanese seem busy with pressing and secret affairs; and the English in their topees and white ducks, speeding past in motor-cars or at leisure in their rickshaws, wear a nonchalant and careless air. The rulers of these teeming peoples take their authority with a smiling unconcern. And now, tired and hot, Mrs. Hamlyn waited for the ship to set out again on her long journey across the Indian Ocean.

She waved a rather large hand, for she was a big woman, to the doctor and Mrs. Linsell as they came on board. She had been on the ship since she left Yokohama, and had watched with acid amusement the intimacy which had sprung up between the two. Linsell

44

was a naval officer who had been attached to the British Embassy at Tokio, and she had wondered at the indifference with which he took the attentions that the doctor paid his wife. Two men came along the gangway, new passengers, and she amused herself by trying to discover from their demeanour whether they were single or married. Close by, a group of men were sitting together on rattan chairs, planters she judged by their khaki suits and wide-brimmed double felt hats, and they kept the deck-steward busy with their orders. They were talking loudly and laughing, for they had all drunk enough to make them somewhat foolishly hilarious, and they were evidently giving one of their number a send-off; but Mrs. Hamlyn could not tell which it was that was to be a fellow-passenger. The time was growing short. More passengers arrived, and then Mr. Jephson with dignity strolled up the gangway. He was a consul and was going home on leave. He had joined the ship at Shanghai and had immediately set about making himself agreeable to Mrs. Hamlyn. But just then she was disinclined for anything in the nature of a flirtation. She frowned as she thought of the reason which was taking her back to England. She would be spending Christmas at sea, far from anyone who cared two straws about her, and for a moment she felt a little twist at her heartstrings; it vexed her that a subject which she was so resolute to put away from her should so constantly intrude on her unwilling mind.

But a warning bell clanged loudly, and there was a general movement among the men who sat beside her.

'Well, if we don't want to be taken on we'd better be toddling,' said one of them.

They rose and walked towards the gangway. Now that they were all shaking hands she saw who it was that they had come to see the last of. There was nothing very interesting about the man on whom Mrs. Hamlyn's eyes rested, but because she had nothing better to do she gave him more than a casual glance. He was a big fellow, well over six feet high, broad and stout; he was dressed in a bedraggled suit of khaki drill and his hat was battered and shabby. His friends left him, but they bandied chaff from the quay, and Mrs. Hamlyn noticed that he had a strong Irish brogue; his voice was full, loud and hearty.

Mrs. Linsell had gone below and the doctor came and sat down beside Mrs. Hamlyn. They told one another their small adventures of the day. The bell sounded again and presently the ship slid away from the wharf. The Irishman waved a last farewell to his friends, and then sauntered towards the chair on which he had left papers and magazines. He nodded to the doctor.

'Is that someone you know?' asked Mrs. Hamlyn.

'I was introduced to him at the club before tiffin. His name is Gallagher. He's a planter.'

After the hubbub of the port and the noisy bustle of departure, the silence of the ship was marked and grateful. They steamed slowly past green-clad, rocky cliffs (the P. & O. anchorage was in a charming and secluded cove), and came out into the main harbour. Ships of all nations lay at anchor, a great multitude, passenger boats, tugs, lighters, tramps; and beyond, behind the break-water, you saw the crowded masts, a bare straight forest, of the native junks. In the soft light of the evening the busy scene was strangely touched with mystery, and you felt that all those vessels, their activity for the moment suspended, waited for some event of a peculiar significance.

Mrs. Hamlyn was a bad sleeper and when the dawn broke she was in the habit of going on deck. It rested her troubled heart to watch the last faint stars fade before the encroaching day, and at that early hour the glassy sea had often an immobility which seemed to make all earthly sorrows of little consequence. The

light was wan, and there was a pleasant shiver in the
air. But next morning, when she went to the end of the
promenade deck, she found that someone was up before
her. It was Mr. Gallagher. He was watching the low coast
of Sumatra which the sunrise like a magician seemed to
call forth from the dark sea. She was startled and a little
vexed, but before she could turn away he had seen her
and nodded.

'Up early,' he said. 'Have a cigarette?'

He was in pyjamas and slippers. He took his case from
his coat pocket and handed it to her. She hesitated. She
had on nothing but a dressing-gown and a little lace cap
which she had put over her tousled hair, and she knew
that she must look a sight; but she had her reasons for
scourging her soul.

'I suppose a woman of forty has no right to mind how
she looks,' she smiled, as though he must know what
vain thoughts occupied her. She took the cigarette. 'But
you're up early too.'

'I'm a planter. I've had to get up at five in the morning
for so many years that I don't know how I'm going to get
out of the habit.'

'You'll not find it will make you very popular at
home.'

She saw his face better now that it was not shadowed
by a hat. It was agreeable without being handsome. He
was of course much too fat, and his features which must
have been good enough when he was a young man were
thickened. His skin was red and bloated. But his dark
eyes were merry; and though he could not have been
less than five and forty his hair was black and thick.
He gave you an impression of great strength. He was a
heavy, ungraceful, commonplace man, and Mrs. Hamlyn,
except for the promiscuity of ship-board, would never
have thought it worth while to talk to him.

'Are you going home on leave?' she hazarded.

47

'No, I'm going home for good.'

His black eyes twinkled. He was of a communicative turn, and before it was time for Mrs. Hamlyn to go below in order to have her bath he had told her a good deal about himself. He had been in the Federated Malay States for twenty-five years, and for the last ten had managed an estate in Selantan. It was a hundred miles from anything that could be described as civilisation and the life had been lonely; but he had made money; during the rubber boom he had done very well, and with an astuteness which was unexpected in a man who looked so happy-go-lucky he had invested his savings in Government stock. Now that the slump had come he was prepared to retire.

'What part of Ireland do you come from?' asked Mrs. Hamlyn.

'Galway.'

Mrs. Hamlyn had once motored through Ireland and she had a vague recollection of a sad and moody town with great stone warehouses, deserted and crumbling, which faced the melancholy sea. She had a sensation of greenness and of soft rain, of silence and of resignation. Was it here that Mr. Gallagher meant to spend the rest of his life? He spoke of it with boyish eagerness. The thought of his vitality in that grey world of shadows was so incongruous that Mrs. Hamlyn was intrigued.

'Does your family live there?' she asked.

'I've got no family. My mother and father are dead. So far as I know I haven't a relation in the world.'

He had made all his plans, he had been making them for twenty-five years, and he was pleased to have someone to talk to of all these things that he had been obliged for so long only to talk to himself about. He meant to buy a house and he would keep a motor car. He was going to breed horses. He didn't much care about shooting; he had shot a lot of big game during his first years in the

F.M.S.; but now he had lost his zest. He didn't see why the beasts of the jungle should be killed; he had lived in the jungle so long. But he could hunt.

'Do you think I'm too heavy?' he asked.

Mrs. Hamlyn, smiling, looked him up and down with appraising eyes.

'You must weigh a ton,' she said.

He laughed. The Irish horses were the best in the world, and he'd always kept pretty fit. You had a devil of a lot of walking exercise on a rubber estate and he'd played a good deal of tennis. He'd soon get thin in Ireland. Then he'd marry. Mrs. Hamlyn looked silently at the sea coloured now with the tenderness of the sunrise. She sighed.

'Was it easy to drag up all your roots? Is there no one you regret leaving behind? I should have thought after so many years, however much you'd looked forward to going home, when the time came at last to go it must have given you a pang.'

'I was glad to get out. I was fed up. I never want to see the country again or anyone in it.'

One or two early passengers now began to walk round the deck and Mrs. Hamlyn, remembering that she was scantily clad, went below.

During the next day or two she saw little of Mr. Gallagher who passed his time in the smoking-room. Owing to a strike the ship was not touching at Colombo and the passengers settled down to a pleasant voyage across the Indian Ocean. They played deck games, they gossiped about one another, they flirted. The approach of Christmas gave them an occupation, for someone had suggested that there should be a fancy-dress dance on Christmas day, and the ladies set about making their dresses. A meeting was held of the first-class passengers to decide whether the second-class passengers should be invited, and notwithstanding the heat the discussion was animated. The ladies said that the second-class passengers would only feel ill-at-ease. On Christmas day it was to be expected that they would drink more than was good for them and unpleasantness might ensue. Everyone who spoke insisted that there was in his (or her) mind no idea of class distinction, no one would be so snobbish as to think there was any difference between first and second-class passengers as far as that went, but it would really be kinder to the second-class passengers not to put them in a false position. They would enjoy themselves much more if they had a party of their own in the second-class cabin. On the other hand, no one wanted to hurt their feelings, and of course one had to be more democratic nowadays (this was in reply to the wife of a missionary in China who said she had travelled on the P. & O. for thirty-five years and she had never heard of the second-class passengers being invited to a dance in the first-class saloon) and even though they wouldn't enjoy it, they might like to come. Mr. Gallagher, dragged unwillingly from the card-table, because it had been foreseen that the voting would be close, was asked his opinion by the consul. He was taking home in the second-class a man who had been employed on his estate. He raised his massive bulk from the couch on which he sat.

'As far as I'm concerned I've only got this to say: I've got the man who was looking after our engines with me. He's a rattling good fellow, and he's just as fit to come to your party as I am. But he won't come because I'm going to make him so drunk on Christmas day that by six o'clock he'll be fit for nothing but to be put to bed.'

Mr. Jephson, the consul, gave a distorted smile. On account of his official position, he had been chosen to preside at the meeting and he wished the matter to be taken seriously. He was a man who often said that if a thing was worth doing it was worth doing well.

'I gather from your observations,' he said, not without acidity, 'that the question before the meeting does not seem to you of great importance.'

'I don't think it matters a tinker's curse,' said Gallagher, with twinkling eyes.

Mrs. Hamlyn laughed. The scheme was at last devised to invite the second-class passengers, but to go to the captain privily and point out to him the advisability of withholding his consent to their coming into the first-class saloon. It was on the evening of the day on which this happened that Mrs. Hamlyn, having dressed for dinner, came on deck at the same time as Mr. Gallagher.

'Just in time for a cocktail, Mrs. Hamlyn,' he said jovially.

'I'd like one. To tell you the truth I need cheering up.'

'Why?' he smiled.

Mrs. Hamlyn thought his smile attractive, but she did not want to answer his question.

'I told you the other morning,' she answered cheerfully. 'I'm forty.'

'I never met a woman who insisted on the fact so much.'

They went into the lounge and the Irishman ordered a dry Martini for her and a gin pahit for himself. He had lived too long in the East to drink anything else.

'You've got hiccups,' said Mrs. Hamlyn.

'Yes, I've had them all afternoon,' he answered carelessly. 'It's rather funny, they came on just as we got out of sight of land.'

'I daresay they'll pass off after dinner.'

They drank, the second bell rang, and they went into the dining-saloon.

'You don't play bridge?' he said, as they parted.

'No.'

Mrs. Hamlyn did not notice that she saw nothing of Gallagher for two or three days. She was occupied with her own thoughts. They crowded upon her when she was sewing; they came between her and the novel with which she sought to cheat their insistence. She had hoped that as the ship took her further away from the scene of her unhappiness, the torment of her mind would be eased; but contrariwise, each day that brought her nearer England increased her distress. She looked forward with dismay to the bleak emptiness of the life that awaited her; and then, turning her exhausted wits from a prospect that made her flinch, she considered, as she had done she knew not how many times before, the situation from which she had fled.

She had been married for twenty years. It was a long time and of course she could not expect her husband to be still madly in love with her; she was not madly in love with him; but they were good friends and they understood one another. Their marriage, as marriages go, might very well have been looked upon as a success. Suddenly she discovered that he had fallen in love. She would not have objected to a flirtation, he had had those before, and she had chaffed him about them; he had not minded that, it somewhat flattered him, and they had laughed together at an inclination which was neither deep nor serious. But this was different. He was in love as passionately as a boy of eighteen. He was fifty-two. It was ridiculous. It was indecent. And he loved without sense of prudence: by the time the hideous fact was forced upon her all the foreigners in Yokohama knew it. After the first shock of astonished anger, for he was the last man from whom such a folly might have been expected, she tried to persuade herself that she could have understood, and so have forgiven, if he had fallen in love with a girl. Middle-aged men often make fools of themselves with flappers, and after twenty years in the Far East she knew that the fifties were the dangerous age for men. But he had no excuse. He was in love with a woman eight years older than herself. It was grotesque, and it made her, his wife, perfectly absurd. Dorothy Lacom was hard on fifty. He had known her for eighteen years, for Lacom, like her own husband, was a silk merchant in Yokohama. Year in, year out, they had seen one another three or four times a week, and once, when they happened to be in England together, had shared a house at the sea-side. But nothing! Not till a year ago had there been anything between them but a chaffing friendship. It was incredible. Of course Dorothy was a handsome woman; she had a good figure, over-developed, perhaps, but still comely; with bold black eyes and a red mouth and lovely hair; but all that she had had years before. She was forty-eight. Forty-eight!

Mrs. Hamlyn tackled her husband at once. At first he swore that there was not a word of truth in what she accused him of, but she had her proofs; he grew sulky; and at last he admitted what he could no longer deny. Then he said an astonishing thing.

'Why should you care?' he asked.

It maddened her. She answered him with angry scorn. She was voluble, finding in the bitterness of her heart wounding things to say. He listened to her quietly.

'I've not been a such a bad husband to you for the twenty years we've been married. For a long time now we've only been friends. I have a great deal of affection for you, and this hasn't altered it in the very smallest degree. I'm giving Dorothy nothing that I take away from you.'

'But what have you to complain of in me?'

'Nothing. No man could want a better wife.'

'How can you say that when you have the heart to treat me so cruelly?'

'I don't want to be cruel to you. I can't help myself.'

'But what on earth made you fall in love with her?'

'How can I tell? You don't think I wanted to, do you?'

'Couldn't you have resisted?'

'I tried. I think we both tried.'

'You talk as though you were twenty. Why, you're both middle-aged people. She's eight years older than I am. It makes me look such a perfect fool.'

He did not answer. She did not know what emotions seethed in her heart. Was it jealousy that seemed to clutch at her throat, anger, or was it merely wounded pride?

'I'm not going to let it go on. If only you and she were concerned I would divorce you, but there's her husband, and then there are the children. Good heavens, does it occur to you that if they were girls instead of boys she might be a grandmother by now?'

'Easily.'

'What a mercy that we have no children!'

He put out an affectionate hand as though to caress her, but she drew back with horror.

'You've made me the laughing stock of all my friends. For all our sakes I'm willing to hold my tongue, but only on the condition that everything stops now, at once, and for ever.'

He looked down and played reflectively with a Japanese knick-knack that was on the table.

'I'll tell Dorothy what you say,' he replied at last.

She gave him a little bow, silently, and walked past him out of the room. She was too angry to observe that she was somewhat melodramatic.

She waited for him to tell her the result of his interview with Dorothy Lacom, but he made no further reference to the scene. He was quiet, polite and silent; and at last she was obliged to ask him.

'Have you forgotten what I said to you the other day?' she inquired, frigidly.

'No. I talked to Dorothy. She wishes me to tell you that she is desperately sorry that she has caused you so much pain. She would like to come and see you, but she is afraid you wouldn't like it.'

'What decision have you come to?'

He hesitated. He was very grave, but his voice trembled a little.

'I'm afraid there's no use in our making a promise we shouldn't be able to keep.'

'That settles it then,' she answered.

'I think I should tell you that if you brought an action for divorce we should have to contest it. You would find it impossible to get the necessary evidence and you would lose your case.'

'I wasn't thinking of doing that. I shall go back to England and consult a lawyer. Nowadays these things can be managed fairly easily, and I shall throw myself on your generosity. I daresay you will enable me to get my freedom without bringing Dorothy Lacom into the matter.'

He sighed.

'It's an awful muddle, isn't it? I don't want you to divorce me, but of course I'll do anything I can to meet your wishes.'

'What on earth do you expect me to do?' she cried, her anger rising again. 'Do you expect me to sit still and be made a damned fool of?'

'I'm awfully sorry to put you in a humiliating position.' He looked at her with harassed eyes. 'I'm quite sure we didn't want to fall in love with one another. We're both of us very conscious of our age. Dorothy, as you say, is old enough to be a grandmother and I'm a baldish, stoutish gentleman of fifty-two. When you fall in love at twenty you think your love will last for ever, but at fifty you know so much, about life and about love, and you know that it will last so short a time.' His voice was low and rueful. It was as though before his mind's eye he saw the sadness of autumn and the leaves falling from the trees. He looked at her gravely. 'And at that age you feel that you can't afford to throw away the chance of happiness which a freakish destiny has given you. In five years it will certainly be over, and perhaps in six months. Life is rather drab and grey, and happiness is so rare. We shall be dead so long.'

It gave Mrs. Hamlyn a bitter sensation of pain to hear her husband, a matter-of-fact and practical man, speak in a strain which was quite new to her. He had gained on a sudden a wistful and tragic personality of which she knew nothing. The twenty years during which they had lived together had no power over him and she was helpless in face of his determination. She could do nothing but go, and now, resentfully determined to get the divorce with which she had threatened him, she was on her way to England.

The smooth sea, upon which the sun beat down so that it shone like a sheet of glass, was as empty and hostile as life in which there was no place for her. For three days no other craft had broken in upon the solitariness of that expanse. Now and again its even surface was scattered for the twinkling of an eye by the scurry of flying fish. The heat was so great that even the most energetic of passengers had given up deck-games, and now (it was after luncheon) such as were not resting in their cabins lay about on chairs. Linsell strolled towards her and sat down.

'Where's Mrs. Linsell?' asked Mrs. Hamlyn.

'Oh, I don't know. She's about somewhere.'

His indifference exasperated her. Was it possible that he did not see that his wife and the surgeon were falling in love with one another? Yet, not so very long ago, he must have cared. Their marriage had been romantic. They had become engaged when Mrs. Linsell was still at school and he little more than a boy. They must have been a charming, handsome pair, and their youth and their mutual love must have been touching. And now, after so short a time, they were tired of one another. It was heart-breaking. What had her husband said?

'I suppose you're going to live in London when you get home?' asked Linsell lazily, for something to say.

'I suppose so,' said Mrs. Hamlyn.

It was hard to reconcile herself to the fact that she had nowhere to go, and where she lived mattered not in the least to anyone alive. Some association of ideas made her think of Gallagher. She envied the eagerness with which he was returning to his native land, and she was touched, and at the same time amused, when she remembered the exuberant imagination he showed in describing the house he meant to live in and the wife he meant to marry. Her friends in Yokohama, apprised in confidence of her determination to divorce her husband, had assured her that she would marry again. She did not much want to enter a second time upon a state which had once so disappointed her, and besides, most men would think twice before they suggested marriage to a woman of forty. Mr. Gallagher wanted a buxom young person.

'Where is Mr. Gallagher?' she asked the submissive Linsell. 'I havent seen him for the last day or two.'

'Didn't you know? He's ill.'

'Poor thing. What's the matter with him?'

'He's got hiccups.'

Mrs. Hamlyn laughed.

'Hiccups don't make one ill, do they?'

'The surgeon is rather worried. He's tried all sorts of things, but he can't stop them.'

'How very odd.'

She thought no more about it, but next morning, chancing upon the surgeon, she asked him how Mr.

Gallagher was. She was surprised to see his boyish, cheerful face darken and grow perplexed.

'I'm afraid he's very bad, poor chap.'

'With hiccups?' she cried in amazement.

It was a disorder that really it was impossible to take seriously.

'You see, he can't keep any food down. He can't sleep. He's fearfully exhausted. I've tried everything I can think of.' He hesitated. 'Unless I can stop them soon – I don't quite know what'll happen.'

Mrs. Hamlyn was startled.

'But he's so strong. He seemed so full of vitality.'

'I wish you could see him now.'

'Would he like me to go and see him?'

'Come along.'

Gallagher had been moved from his cabin into the ship's hospital, and as they approached it they heard a loud hiccup. The sound, perhaps owing to its connection with insobriety, had in it something ludicrous. But Gallagher's appearance gave Mrs. Hamlyn a shock. He had lost flesh and the skin hung about his neck in loose folds; under the sunburn his face was pale. His eyes, before, full of fun and laughter, were haggard and tormented. His great body was shaken incessantly by the hiccups and now there was nothing ludicrous in the sound; to Mrs. Hamlyn, for no reason that she knew, it seemed strangely terrifying. He smiled when she came in.

'I'm sorry to see you like this,' she said.

'I shan't die of it, you know,' he gasped. 'I shall reach the green shores of Erin all right.'

There was a man sitting beside him and he rose as they entered.

'This is Mr. Pryce,' said the surgeon. 'He was in charge of the machinery on Mr. Gallagher's estate.'

Mrs. Hamlyn nodded. This was the second-class passenger to whom Gallagher had referred when they had discussed the party which was to be given on Christmas day. He was a very small man, but sturdy, with a pleasantly impudent countenance and an air of self-assurance.

'Are you glad to be going home?' asked Mrs. Hamlyn.

'You bet I am, lady,' he answered.

The intonation of the few words told Mrs. Hamlyn that he was a cockney and, recognising the cheerful, sensible, good-humoured and careless type, her heart warmed to him.

'You're not Irish?' she smiled.

'Not me, miss. London's my 'ome and I shan't be sorry to see it again, I can tell you.'

Mrs. Hamlyn never thought it offensive to be called miss.

'Well, sir, I'll be getting along,' he said to Gallagher, with the beginning of a gesture as though he were going to touch a cap which he hadn't got on.

Mrs. Hamlyn asked the sick man whether she could do anything for him and in a minute or two left him with the doctor. The little cockney was waiting outside the door.

'Can I speak to you a minute or two, miss?' he asked.

'Of course.'

The hospital cabin was aft and they stood, leaning against the rail, and looked down on the well-deck where lascars and stewards off duty were lounging about on the covered hatches.

'I don't know exactly 'ow to begin,' said Pryce, uncertainly, a serious look strangely changing his lively, puckered face. 'I've been with Mr. Gallagher for four years now and a better gentleman you wouldn't find in a week of Sundays.'

He hesitated again.

'I don't like it and that's the truth.'

'What don't you like?'

59

'Well, if you ask me 'e's for it, and the doctor don't know it. I told 'im, but 'e won't listen to a word I say.'

'You mustn't be too depressed, Mr. Pryce. Of course the doctor's young, but I think he's quite clever, and people don't die of hiccups, you know. I'm sure Mr. Gallagher will be all right in a day or two.'

'You know when it come on? Just as we was out of sight of land. She said 'e'd never see 'is 'ome.'

Mrs. Hamlyn turned and faced him. She stood a good three inches taller than he.

'What do you mean?'

'My belief is, it's a spell been put on 'im, if you understand what I mean. Medicine's going to do 'im no good. You don't know them Malay women like what I do.'

For a moment Mrs. Hamlyn was startled, and because she was startled she shrugged her shoulders and laughed.

'Oh, Mr. Pryce, that's nonsense.'

'That's what the doctor said when I told 'im. But you mark my words, 'e'll die before we see land again.'

The man was so serious that Mrs. Hamlyn, vaguely uneasy, was against her will impressed.

'Why should anyone cast a spell on Mr. Gallagher?' she asked.

'Well, it's a bit awkward speakin' of it to a lady.'

'Please tell me.'

Pryce was so embarrassed that at another time Mrs. Hamlyn would have had difficulty in concealing her amusement.

'Mr. Gallagher's lived a long time up-country, if you understand what I mean, and of course it's lonely, and you know what men are, miss.'

'I've been married for twenty years,' she replied, smiling.

'I beg your pardon, ma'am. The fact is he had a Malay girl living with him. I don't know 'ow long, ten or twelve years, I think. Well, when 'e made up 'is mind to come

'ome for good she didn't say nothing. She just sat there. He thought she'd carry on no end, but she didn't. Of course 'e provided for 'er all right, 'e gave 'er a little 'ouse for herself, an' 'e fixed it up so as so much should be paid 'er every month. 'E wasn't mean, I will say that for 'im, an' she knew all along as 'e'd be going some time. She didn't cry or anything. When 'e packed up all 'is things and sent them off, she just sat there an' watched 'em go. And when 'e sold 'is furniture to the Chinks she never said a word. He'd give 'er all she wanted. And when it was time for 'im to go so as to catch the boat she just kep' on sitting, on the steps of the bungalow, you know, and she just looked an' said nothing. He wanted to say good-bye to 'er, same as anyone would, an', would you believe it? she never even moved. "Aren't you going to say good-bye to me," he says. A rare funny look come over 'er face. And do you know what she says? "You go," she says; they 'ave a funny way of talking, them natives, not like we 'ave, "you go," she says, "but I tell you that you will never come to your own country. When the land sinks into the sea, death will come upon you, an' before them as goes with you sees the land again, death will have took you." It gave me quite a turn.'

'What did Mr. Gallagher say?' asked Mrs. Hamlyn.

'Oh, well, you know what 'e is. He just laughed. "Always merry and bright," 'e says and 'e jumps into the motor, an' off we go.'

Mrs. Hamlyn saw the bright and sunny road that ran through the rubber estates, with their trim green trees, carefully spaced, and their silence, and then wound its way up hill and down through the tangled jungle. The car raced on, driven by a reckless Malay, with its white passengers, past Malay houses that stood away from the road among the coconut trees, sequestered and taciturn, and through busy villages where the market-place was crowded with dark-skinned little people in

gay sarongs. Then towards evening it reached the trim,
modern town, with its clubs and its golf links, its
well-ordered resthouse, its white people, and its railway
station, from which the two men could take the train
to Singapore. And the woman sat on the steps of the
bungalow, empty till the new manager moved in, and
watched the road down which the car had panted,
watched the car as it sped on, and watched till at last
it was lost in the shadow of the night.

'What was she like?' Mrs. Hamlyn asked.

'Oh, well, to my way of thinking them Malay women
are all very much alike, you know,' Pryce answered. 'Of
course she wasn't so young any more, and you know
what they are, them natives, they run to fat something
terrible.'

'Fat?'

The thought, absurdly enough, filled Mrs. Hamlyn
with dismay.

'Mr. Gallagher was always one to do himself well, if
you understand what I mean.'

The idea of corpulence at once brought Mrs. Hamlyn
back to common sense. She was impatient with herself
because for an instant she had seemed to accept the little
cockney's suggestion.

'It's perfectly absurd, Mr. Pryce. Fat women can't throw
spells on people at a distance of a thousand miles. In fact
life is very difficult for a fat woman any way.'

'You can laugh, miss, but unless something's done, you
mark my words, the governor's for it. And medicine ain't
goin' to save him, not white man's medicine.'

'Pull yourself together, Mr. Pryce. This fat lady had no
particular grievance against Mr. Gallagher. As things are
done in the East he seems to have treated her very well.
Why should she wish him any harm?'

'We don't know 'ow they look at things. Why, a man
can live there for twenty years with one of them natives,

and d'you think 'e knows what's goin' on in that black heart of hers? Not 'im!'

She could not smile at his melodramatic language, for his intensity was impressive. And she knew, if anyone did, that the hearts of men, whether their skins are yellow or white or brown, are incalculable.

'But even if she felt angry with him, even if she hated him and wanted to kill him, what could she do?' It was strange that Mrs. Hamlyn with her questions was trying now, unconsciously, to reassure herself. 'There's no poison that could start working after six or seven days.'

'I never said it was poison.'

'I'm sorry, Mr. Pryce,' she smiled, 'but I'm not going to believe in a magic spell, you know.'

'You've lived in the East.'

'Off and on for twenty years.'

'Well, if you can say what they can do and what they can't, it's more than I can.' He clenched his fist and beat it on the rail with sudden, angry violence. 'I'm fed up with the bloody country. It's got on my nerves, that's what it is. We're no match for them, us white men, and that's a fact. If you'll excuse me I think I'll go an' 'ave a tiddley. I've got the jumps.'

He nodded abruptly and left her. Mrs. Hamlyn watched him, a sturdy, shuffling little man in shabby khaki, slither down the companion into the waist of the ship, walk across it with bent head, and disappear into the second-class saloon. She did not know why he left with her a vague uneasiness. She could not get out of her mind that picture of a stout woman, no longer young, in a sarong, a coloured jacket and gold ornaments, who sat on the steps of a bungalow looking at an empty road. Her heavy face was painted, but in her large, tearless eyes there was no expression. The men who drove in the car were like schoolboys going home for the holidays. Gallagher gave a sigh of relief. In the early morning, under the bright sky, his spirits bubbled. The future was like a sunny road that wandered through a wide-flung, wooded plain.

Later in the day Mrs. Hamlyn asked the doctor how his patient did. The doctor shook his head.

'I'm done. I'm at the end of my tether.' He frowned unhappily. 'It's rotten luck, striking a case like this. It would be bad enough at home, but on board ship . . .'

He was an Edinburgh man, but recently qualified, and he was taking this voyage as a holiday before settling down to practice. He felt himself aggrieved. He wanted to have a good time and, faced with this mysterious illness, he was worried to death. Of course he was inexperienced, but he was doing everything that could be done and it exasperated him to suspect that the passengers thought him an ignorant fool.

'Have you heard what Mr. Pryce thinks?' asked Mrs. Hamlyn.

'I never heard such rot. I told the captain and he's right up in the air. He doesn't want it talked about. He thinks it'll upset the passengers.'

'I'll be as silent as the grave.'

The surgeon looked at her sharply.

'Of course you don't believe that there can be any truth in nonsense of that sort?' he asked.

'Of course not.' She looked out at the sea which shone, blue and oily and still, all round them. 'I've lived in the East a long time,' she added. 'Strange things happen there.'

'This is getting on my nerves,' said the doctor.

Near them two little Japanese gentlemen were playing deck quoits. They were trim and neat in their tennis shirts, white trousers and buckram shoes. They looked very European, they even called the score to one another in English, and yet somehow to look at them filled Mrs. Hamlyn at that moment with a vague disquiet. Because they seemed to wear so easily a disguise there was about them something sinister. Her nerves too were on edge.

And presently, no one quite knew how, the notion spread through the ship that Gallagher was bewitched. While the ladies sat about on their deck-chairs, stitching away at the costumes they were making for the fancy-dress party on Christmas day, they gossiped about it in undertones, and the men in the smoking-room talked of it over their cocktails. A good many of the passengers had lived long in the East and from the recesses of their memory they produced strange and inexplicable stories. Of course it was absurd to think seriously that Gallagher was suffering from a malignant spell, such things were impossible, and yet this and that was a fact and no one had been able to explain it. The doctor had to confess that he could suggest no cause for Gallagher's condition, he was able to give a physiological explanation, but why these terrible spasms should have suddenly assailed him he did not say. Feeling vaguely to blame, he tried to defend himself.

'Why, it's the sort of case you might never come across in the whole of your practice,' he said. 'It's rotten luck.'

He was in wireless communication with passing ships, and suggestions for treatment came from here and there.

'I've tried everything they tell me,' he said irritably. 'The doctor of the Japanese boat advised adrenalin. How the devil does he expect me to have adrenalin in the middle of the Indian Ocean?'

There was something impressive in the thought of this ship speeding through a deserted sea, while to her from all parts came unseen messages. She seemed at that moment strangely alone and yet the centre of the world. In the lazaret the sick man, shaken by the cruel spasms, gasped for life. Then the passengers became conscious that the ship's course was altered, and they heard that the captain had made up his mind to put in at Aden.

Gallagher was to be landed there and taken to the hospital, where he could have attention which on board was impossible. The chief engineer received orders to force his engines. The ship was an old one and she throbbed with the greater effort. The passengers had grown used to the sound and feel of her engines, and now the greater vibration shook their nerves with a new sensation. It would not pass into each one's unconsciousness, but beat on their sensibilities so that each felt a personal concern. And still the wide sea was empty of traffic, so that they seemed to traverse an empty world. And now the uneasiness which had descended upon the ship, but which no one had been willing to acknowledge, became a definite malaise. The passengers grew irritable, and people quarrelled over trifles which at another time would have seemed insignificant. Mr. Jephson made his hackneyed jokes, but no one any longer repaid him with a smile. The Linsells had an altercation, and Mrs. Linsell was heard late at night walking round the deck with her husband, and uttering in a low, tense voice a stream of vehement reproaches. There was a violent scene in the smoking-room one night over a game of bridge, and the reconciliation which followed it was attended with general intoxication. People talked little of Gallagher, but he was seldom absent from their thoughts. They examined the route map. The doctor said now that Gallagher could not live more than three or four days, and they discussed acrimoniously what was the shortest time in which Aden could be reached. What happened to him after he was landed was no affair of theirs; they did not want him to die on board.

Mrs. Hamlyn saw Gallagher every day. With the suddenness with which after tropical rain in the spring you seem to see the herbage grow before your very eyes, she saw him go to pieces. Already his skin hung loosely on his bones, and his double chin was like the wrinkled wattle of a turkey-cock. His cheeks were sunken. You saw now how large his frame was, and through the sheet under which he lay his bony structure was like the skeleton of a prehistoric giant. For the most part he lay with his eyes closed, torpid with morphia, but shaken still with terrible spasms, and when now and again he opened his eyes they were preternaturally large; they looked at you vaguely, perplexed and troubled, from the depths of their bony sockets. But when, emerging from his stupor, he recognised Mrs. Hamlyn, he forced a gallant smile to his lips.

'How are you, Mr. Gallagher?' she said.

'Getting along, getting along. I shall be all right when we get out of this confounded heat. Lord, how I look forward to a dip in the Atlantic. I'd give anything for a good swim. I want to feel the cold grey sea of Galway beating against my chest.'

Then the hiccup shook him from the crown of his head to the sole of his foot. Mr. Pryce and the stewardess shared the care of him. The little cockney's face wore no longer its look of impudent gaiety, but instead was sullen.

'The captain sent for me yesterday,' he told Mrs. Hamlyn when they were alone. 'He gave me a rare talking to.'

'What about?'

'He said 'e wouldn't 'ave all this hoodoo stuff. He said it was frightening the passengers and I'd better keep a watch on me tongue or I'd 'ave 'im to reckon with. It's not my doing. I never said a word except to you and the doctor.'

'It's all over the ship.'

'I know it is. D'you think it's only me that's saying it? All them Lascars and the Chinese, they all know what's the matter with him. You don't think you can teach them much, do you? They know it ain't a natural illness.'

67

Mrs. Hamlyn was silent. She knew through the amahs of some of the passengers that there was no one on the ship, except the whites, who doubted that the woman whom Gallagher had left in distant Selantan was killing him with her magic. All were convinced that as they sighted the barren rocks of Arabia his soul would be parted from his body.

'The captain says if he hears of me trying any hanky-panky he'll confine me to my cabin for the rest of the voyage,' said Pryce, suddenly, a surly frown on his puckered face.

'What do you mean by hanky-panky?'

He looked at her for a moment fiercely as though she too were an object of the anger he felt against the captain.

'The doctor's tried every damned thing he knows, and he's wirelessed all over the place, and what good 'as 'e done? Tell me that. Can't 'e see the man's dying? There's only one way to save him now.'

'What do you mean?'

'It's magic what's killing 'im, and it's only magic what'll save him. Oh, don't you say it can't be done. I've seen it with me own eyes.' His voice rose, irritable and shrill. 'I've seen a man dragged from the jaws of death, as you might say, when they got in a *pawang*, what we call a witch-doctor, an' 'e did 'is little tricks. I seen it with me own eyes, I tell you.'

Mrs. Hamlyn did not speak. Pryce gave her a searching look.

'One of them Lascars on board, he's a witch-doctor, same as the *pawang* that we 'ave in the F.M.S. An' 'e says he'll do it. Only he must 'ave a live animal. A cock would do.'

'What do you want a live animal for?' Mrs. Hamlyn asked, frowning a little.

The cockney looked at her with quick suspicion.

'If you take my advice you won't know anything
about it. But I tell you what, I'm going to leave no
stone unturned to save my governor. An' if the captain
'ears of it and shuts me up in me cabin well, let 'im.'

At that moment Mrs. Linsell came up and Pryce with
his quaint gesture of salute left them. Mrs. Linsell
wanted Mrs. Hamlyn to fit the dress she had been
making herself for the fancy-dress ball, and on the way
down to the cabin she spoke to her anxiously of the
possibility that Mr. Gallagher might die on Christmas
day. They could not possibly have the dance if he did.
She had told the doctor that she would never speak to
him again if this happened, and the doctor had promised
her faithfully that he would keep the man alive over
Christmas day somehow.

'It would be nice for him, too,' said Mrs. Linsell.

'For whom?' asked Mrs. Hamlyn.

'For poor Mr. Gallagher. Naturally no one likes to die
on Christmas day. Do they?'

'I don't really know,' said Mrs. Hamlyn.

That night, after she had been asleep a little while,
she awoke weeping. It dismayed her that she should
cry in her sleep. It was as though then the weakness
of the flesh mastered her, and, her will broken, she were
defenceless against a natural sorrow. She turned over in
her mind, as so often before, the details of the disaster
which had so profoundly affected her; she repeated the
conversations with her husband, wishing she had said
this and blaming herself because she had said the other.
She wished with all her heart that she had remained in
comfortable ignorance of her husband's infatuation, and
asked herself whether she would not have been wiser to
pocket her pride and shut her eyes to the unwelcome
truth. She was a woman of the world, and she knew
too well how much more she lost in separating herself
from her husband than his love; she lost the settled

69

establishment and the assured position, the ample means and the support of a recognised background. She had known of many separated wives, living equivocally on smallish incomes, and knew how quickly their friends found them tiresome. And she was lonely. She was as lonely as the ship that throbbed her hasting way through an unpeopled sea, and lonely as the friendless man who lay dying in the ship's lazaret. Mrs. Hamlyn knew that her thoughts had got the better of her now and that she would not easily sleep again. It was very hot in her cabin. She looked at the time; it was between four and half-past; she must pass two mortal hours before broke the reassuring day.

She slipped into a kimono and went on deck. The night was sombre and although the sky was unclouded no stars were visible. Panting and shaking, the old ship under full steam lumbered through the darkness. The silence was uncanny. Mrs. Hamlyn with bare feet groped her way slowly along the deserted deck. It was so black that she could see nothing. She came to the end of the promenade deck and leaned against the rail. Suddenly she started and her attention was fixed, for on the lower deck she caught a fitful glow. She leaned forward cautiously. It was a little fire, and she saw only the glow because the naked backs of men, crouched round, hid the flame. At the edge of the circle she divined, rather than saw, a stocky figure in pyjamas. The rest were natives, but this was a European. It must be Pryce and she guessed immediately that some dark ceremony of exorcism was in progress. Straining her ears she heard a low voice muttering a string of secret words. She began to tremble. She was aware that they were too intent upon their business to think that anyone was watching them, but she dared not move. Suddenly, rending the sultry silence of the night like a piece of silk violently torn in two, came the crowing of a cock. Mrs. Hamlyn almost shrieked. Mr. Pryce was trying to save the life of his friend and master by a sacrifice to the strange gods of the East. The voice went on, low and insistent. Then in the dark circle there was a movement, something was happening, she knew not what; there was a cluck-cluck from the cock, angry and frightened, and then a strange, indescribable sound; the magician was cutting the cock's throat; then silence; there were vague doings that she could not follow, and in a little while it looked as though someone were stamping out the fire. The figures she had dimly seen were dissolved in the night and all once more was still. She heard again the regular throbbing of the engines.

Mrs. Hamlyn stood still for a little while, strangely shaken, and then walked slowly along the deck. She found a chair and lay down in it. She was trembling still. She could only guess what had happened. She did not know how long she lay there, but at last she felt that the dawn was approaching. It was not yet day, and it was no longer night. Against the darkness of the sky she could now see the ship's rail. Then she saw a figure come towards her. It was a man in pyjamas.

'Who's that?' she cried nervously.

'Only the doctor,' came a friendly voice.

'Oh! What are you doing here at this time of night?'

'I've been with Gallagher.' He sat down beside her and lit a cigarette. 'I've given him a good strong hypodermic and he's quiet now.'

'Has he been very ill?'

'I thought he was going to pass out. I was watching him, and suddenly he started up on his bed and began to talk Malay. Of course I couldn't understand a thing. He kept on saying one word over and over again.'

'Perhaps it was a name, a woman's name.'

'He wanted to get out of bed. He's a damned powerful man even now. By George, I had a struggle with him. I was afraid he'd throw himself overboard. He seemed to think someone was calling him.'

'When was that?' asked Mrs. Hamlyn, slowly.

'Between four and half-past. Why?'

'Nothing.'

She shuddered.

Later in the morning when the ship's life was set upon its daily round, Mrs. Hamlyn passed Pryce on the deck, but he gave her a brief greeting and walked on with quickly averted gaze. He looked tired and overwrought. Mrs. Hamlyn thought again of that fat woman, with golden ornaments in her thick, black hair, who sat on the steps of the deserted bungalow and looked at the road which ran through the trim lines of the rubber trees.

It was fearfully hot. She knew now why the night had been so dark. The sky was no longer blue, but a dead, level white; its surface was too even to give the effect of cloud; it was as though in the upper air the heat hung like a pall. There was no breeze and the sea, as colourless as the sky, was smooth and shining like the dye in a dyer's vat. The passengers were listless; when they walked round the deck they panted, and beads of sweat broke out on their foreheads. They spoke in undertones. Something uncanny and disquieting brooded over the ship, and they could not bring themselves to laugh. A feeling of resentment arose in their hearts; they were alive and well, and it exasperated them that, so near, a man should be dying and by the fact (which was after all no concern of theirs) so mysteriously affect them. A planter in the smoking-room over a gin sling said brutally what most of them felt, though none had confessed.

'Well, if he's going to peg out,' he said, 'I wish he'd hurry up and get it over. It gives me the creeps.'

The day was interminable. Mrs. Hamlyn was thankful when the dinner hour arrived. So much time, at all events, was passed. She sat at the doctor's table.

'When do we reach Aden?' she asked.

'Some time tomorrow. The captain says we shall sight land between five and six in the morning.'

She gave him a sharp look. He stared at her for a moment, then dropped his eyes and reddened. He remembered that the woman, the fat woman sitting on the bungalow steps, had said that Gallagher would never see the land. Mrs. Hamlyn wondered whether he, the sceptical, matter-of-fact young doctor, was wavering at last. He frowned a little and then, as though he sought to pull himself together, looked at her once more.

'I shan't be sorry to hand over my patient to the hospital people at Aden, I can tell you,' he said.

Next day was Christmas eve. When Mrs. Hamlyn awoke from a troubled sleep the dawn was breaking. She looked out of her porthole and saw that the sky was clear and silvery; during the night the haze had melted, and the morning was brilliant. With a lighter heart she went on deck. She walked as far forward as she could go. A late star twinkled palely close to the horizon. There was a shimmer on the sea as though a loitering breeze passed playful fingers over its surface. The light was exquisitely soft, tenuous like a budding wood in spring, and crystalline so that it reminded you of the bubbling of water in a mountain brook. She turned to look at the sun rising rosy in the east, and saw coming towards her the doctor. He wore his uniform; he had not been to bed all night; he was dishevelled and he walked, with bowed shoulders, as though he were dog-tired. She knew at once that Gallagher was dead. When he came up to her she saw that he was crying. He looked so young then that her heart went out to him. She took his hand.

'You poor dear,' she said. 'You're tired out.'

'I did all I could,' he said. 'I wanted so awfully to save him.'

His voice shook and she saw that he was almost hysterical.

'When did he die?' she asked.

He closed his eyes, trying to control himself, and his lips trembled.

'A few minutes ago.'

Mrs. Hamlyn sighed. She found nothing to say. Her gaze wandered across the calm, dispassionate and ageless sea. It stretched on all sides of them as infinite as human sorrow. But on a sudden her eyes were held, for there, ahead of them, on the horizon was something which looked like a precipitous and massy cloud. But its outline was too sharp to be a cloud's. She touched the doctor on the arm.

'What's that?'

He looked at it for a moment and under his sunburn she saw him grow white.

'Land.'

Once more Mrs. Hamlyn thought of the fat Malay woman who sat silently on the steps of Gallagher's bungalow. Did she know?

They buried him when the sun was high in the heavens. They stood on the lower deck and on the hatches, the first and second-class passengers, the white stewards and the European officers. The missionary read the burial service.

'*Man that is born of woman hath but a short time to live, and is full of misery. He cometh up, and is cut down, like a flower; he fleeth as it were a shadow, and never continueth in one stay.*'

Pryce looked down at the deck with knit brows. His teeth were tight clenched. He did not grieve, for his heart was hot with anger. The doctor and the consul stood side by side. The consul bore to a nicety the expression of an official regret, but the doctor, clean-shaven now, in his neat fresh uniform and his gold braid, was pale

and harassed. From him Mrs. Hamlyn's eyes wandered
to Mrs. Linsell. She was pressed against her husband,
weeping, and he was holding her hand tenderly. Mrs.
Hamlyn did not know why this sight singularly affected
her. At that moment of grief, her nerves distraught, the
little woman went by instinct to the protection and
support of her husband. But then Mrs. Hamlyn felt a
little shudder pass through her and she fixed her eyes
on the seams in the deck, for she did not want to see
what was toward. There was a pause in the reading.
There were various movements. One of the officers gave
an order. The missionary's voice continued.

*'Forasmuch as it has pleased Almighty God of his
great mercy to take unto himself the soul of our dear
brother here departed: we therefore commend his body
to the deep, to be turned into corruption, looking for
the resurrection of the body when the sea shall give up
its dead.'*

Mrs. Hamlyn felt the hot tears flow down her cheeks.
There was a dull splash. The missionary's voice went
on.

When the service was finished the passengers scattered;
the second-class passengers returned to their quarters
and a bell rang to summon them to luncheon. But
the first-class passengers sauntered aimlessly about the
promenade deck. Most of the men made for the smoking-
room and sought to cheer themselves with whiskies and
sodas and with gin slings. But the consul put up a notice
on the board outside the dining-saloon summoning the
passengers to a meeting. Most of them had an idea
for what purpose it was called, and at the appointed
hour they assembled. They were more cheerful than
they had been for a week and they chattered with a
gaiety which was only subdued by a mannerly reserve.
The consul, an eye-glass in his eye, said that he had
gathered them together to discuss the question of the

fancy-dress dance on the following day. He knew they all had the deepest sympathy for Mr. Gallagher and he would have proposed that they should combine to send an appropriate message to the deceased's relatives; but his papers had been examined by the purser and no trace could be found of any relative or friend with whom it was possible to communicate. The late Mr. Gallagher appeared to be quite alone in the world. Meanwhile he (the consul) ventured to offer his sincere sympathy to the doctor who, he was quite sure, had done everything that was possible in the circumstances.

'Hear, hear,' said the passengers.

They had all passed through a very trying time, proceeded the consul, and to some it might seem that it would be more respectful to the deceased's memory if the fancy-dress ball were postponed till New Year's eve. This, however, he told them frankly was not his view, and he was convinced that Mr. Gallagher himself would not have wished it. Of course it was a question for the majority to decide. The doctor got up and thanked the consul and the passengers for the kind things that had been said of him, it had of course been a very trying time, but he was authorised by the captain to say that the captain expressly wished all the festivities to be carried out on Christmas day as though nothing had happened. He (the doctor) told them in confidence that the captain felt the passengers had got into a rather morbid state, and thought it would do them all good if they had a jolly good time on Christmas day. Then the missionary's wife rose and said they mustn't think only of themselves; it had been arranged by the Entertainment Committee that there should be a Christmas tree for the children, immediately after the first-class passengers' dinner, and the children had been looking forward to seeing everyone in fancy-dress; it would be too bad to disappoint them; she yielded to no one in her respect for the dead, and she sympathised with anyone who felt too sad to think of dancing just then, her own heart was very heavy, but she did feel it would be merely selfish to give way to a feeling which could do no good to anyone. Let them think of the little ones. This very much impressed the passengers. They wanted to forget the brooding terror which had hung over the boat for so many days, they were alive and they wanted to enjoy themselves; but they had an uneasy notion that it would be decent to exhibit a certain grief. It was quite another matter if they could do as they wished from altruistic motives. When the consul called for a show of hands everyone, but Mrs. Hamlyn and one old lady who was rheumatic, held up an eager arm.

'The ayes have it,' said the consul. 'And I venture to congratulate the meeting on a very sensible decision.'

It was just going to break up when one of the planters got on his feet and said he wished to offer a suggestion. Under the circumstances didn't they all think it would be as well to invite the second-class passengers? They had all come to the funeral that morning. The missionary jumped up and seconded the motion. The events of the last few days had drawn them all together, he said, and in the presence of death all men were equal. The consul again addressed them. This matter had been discussed at a previous meeting, and the conclusion had been reached that it would be pleasanter for the second-class passengers to have their own party, but circumstances alter cases, and he was distinctly of opinion that their previous decision should be reversed.

'Hear, hear,' said the passengers.

A wave of democratic feeling swept over them and the motion was carried by acclamation. They separated light-heartedly, they felt charitable and kindly. Everyone stood everyone else drinks in the smoking-room.

And so, on the following evening, Mrs. Hamlyn put

on her fancy-dress. She had no heart for the gaiety before her, and for a moment had thought of feigning illness, but she knew no one would believe her, and was afraid to be thought affected. She was dressed as Carmen and she could not resist the vanity of making herself as attractive as possible. She darkened her eyelashes and rouged her cheeks. The costume suited her. When the bugle sounded and she went into the saloon she was received with flattering surprise. The consul (always a humourist) was dressed as a ballet-girl and was greeted with shouts of delighted laughter. The missionary and his wife, self-conscious but pleased with themselves, were very grand as Manchus. Mrs. Linsell, as Columbine, showed all that was possible of her very pretty legs. Her husband was an Arab sheik and the doctor was a Malay sultan.

A subscription had been collected to provide champagne at dinner and the meal was hilarious. The company had provided crackers in which were paper hats of various shapes and these the passengers put on. There were paper streamers too which they threw at one another and little balloons which they beat from one to the other across the room. They laughed and shouted. They were very gay. No one could say that they were not having a good time. As soon as dinner was finished they went into the saloon where the Christmas tree, with candles lit, was ready, and the children were brought in, shrieking with delight, and given presents. Then the dance began. The second-class passengers stood about shyly round the part of the deck reserved for dancing and occasionally danced with one another.

'I'm glad we had them,' said the consul, dancing with Mrs. Hamlyn. 'I'm all for democracy, and I think they're very sensible to keep themselves to themselves.'

But she noticed that Pryce was not to be seen, and when an opportunity presented asked one of the second-class passengers where he was.

'Blind to the world,' was the answer. 'We put him to bed in the afternoon and locked him up in his cabin.'

The consul claimed her for another dance. He was very facetious. Suddenly Mrs. Hamlyn felt that she could not bear it any more, the noise of the amateur band, the consul's jokes, the gaiety of the dancers. She knew not why, but the merriment of those people passing on their ship through the night and the solitary sea affected her on a sudden with horror. When the consul released her she slipped away and, with a look to see that no one had noticed her, ascended the companion to the boat deck. Here everything was in darkness. She walked softly to a spot where she knew she would be safe from all intrusion. But she heard a faint laugh and she caught sight in a hidden corner of a Columbine and a Malay sultan. Mrs. Linsell and the doctor had resumed already the flirtation which the death of Gallagher had interrupted.

Already all those people had put out of their minds with a kind of ferocity the thought of that poor lonely man who had so strangely died in their midst. They felt no compassion for him, but resentment rather, because on his account they had been ill-at-ease. They seized upon life avidly. They made their jokes, they flirted, they gossiped. Mrs. Hamlyn remembered what the consul had said, that among Mr. Gallagher's papers no letters could be found, not the name of a single friend to whom the news of his death might be sent, and she knew not why this seemed to her unbearably tragic. There was something mysterious in a man who could pass through the world in such solitariness. When she remembered how he had come on deck in Singapore, so short a while since, in such rude health, full of vitality, and his arrogant plans for the future, she was seized with dismay. Those words of the burial service filled her with a solemn awe: *Man that is born of a woman hath but a short time to live, and is full of misery. He cometh up, and is cut down, like a flower . . .* Year in, year out, he had made his plans for the future, he wanted to live so much and he had so much to live for, and then just when he stretched out his hand – oh, it was pitiful; it made all the other distresses of the world of small account. Death with its mystery was the only thing that really mattered. Mrs. Hamlyn leaned over the rail and looked at the starry sky. Why did people make themselves unhappy? Let them weep for the death of those they loved, death was terrible always, but for the rest, was it worth while to be wretched, to harbour malice, to be vain and uncharitable? She thought again of herself and her husband and the woman he so strangely loved. He too had said that we live to be happy so short a time and we are so long dead. She pondered long and intently, and suddenly, as summer lightning flashes across the darkness of the night, she made a discovery which filled her with tremulous surprise; for she found that in her heart was no longer anger with her husband nor jealousy of her rival. A notion dawned on some remote horizon of her consciousness and like the morning sun suffused her soul with a tender, blissful glow. Out of the tragedy of that unknown Irishman's death, she gathered elatedly the courage for a desperate resolution. Her heart beat quickly, she was impatient to carry it into effect. A passion for self-sacrifice seized her.

The music had stopped, the ball was over; most of the passengers would have gone to bed and the rest would be in the smoking-room. She went down to her cabin and met no one on the way. She took her writing pad and wrote a letter to her husband.

My dear. It is Christmas day and I want to tell you that my heart is filled with kindly thoughts towards both of you. I have been foolish and

unreasonable. I think we should allow those we
care for to be happy in their own way, and we
should care for them enough not to let it make us
unhappy. I want you to know that I grudge you
none of the joy that has so strangely come into your
life. I am no longer jealous, nor hurt, nor vindictive.
Do not think I shall be unhappy or lonely. If ever
you feel that you need me, come to me, and I will
welcome you with a cheerful spirit and without
reproach or ill-will. I am most grateful for all the
years of happiness and of tenderness that you gave
me, and in return I wish to offer you an affection
which makes no claim on you and is, I hope,
utterly disinterested. Think kindly of me and be
happy, happy, happy.

She signed her name and put the letter into an envelope. Though it would not go till they reached Port Said
she wanted to place it at once in the letter-box. When she
had done this, beginning to undress, she looked at herself
in the glass. Her eyes were shining and under her rouge
her colour was bright. The future was no longer desolate,
but bright with a fair hope. She slipped into bed and fell
at once into a sound and dreamless sleep.

The Door of Opportunity

They got a first-class carriage to themselves. It was lucky, because they were taking a good deal in with them, Alban's suit-case and a hold-all, Anne's dressing-case and her hat-box. They had two trunks in the van, containing what they wanted immediately, but all the rest of their luggage Alban had put in the care of an agent who was to take it up to London and store it till they had made up their minds what to do. They had a lot, pictures and books, curios that Alban had collected in the East, his guns and saddles. They had left Sondurah for ever. Alban, as was his way, tipped the porter generously and then went to the bookstall and bought papers. He bought 'The New Statesman' and 'The Nation', and 'The Tatler' and 'The Sketch,' and the last number of 'The London Mercury'. He came back to the carriage and threw them on the seat.

'It's only an hour's journey,' said Anne.

'I know, but I wanted to buy them. I've been starved so long. Isn't it grand to think that to-morrow morning we shall have to-morrow's "Times", and "The Express" and "The Mail"?'

She did not answer and he turned away, for he saw coming towards them two persons, a man and his wife, who had been fellow-passengers from Singapore.

'Get through the customs all right?' he cried to them cheerily.

The man seemed not to hear, for he walked straight on, but the woman answered.

'Yes, they never found the cigarettes.'

She saw Anne, gave her a friendly little smile, and passed on. Anne flushed.

'I was afraid they'd want to come in here,' said Alban. 'Let's have the carriage to ourselves if we can.'

She looked at him curiously.

'I don't think you need worry,' she answered. 'I don't think anyone will come in.'

He lit a cigarette and lingered at the carriage door. On his face was a happy smile. When they had passed through the Red Sea and found a sharp wind in the Canal, Anne had been surprised to see how much the men who had looked presentable enough in the white ducks in which she had been accustomed to see them, were changed when they left them off for warmer clothes. They looked like nothing on earth then. Their ties were awful and their shirts all wrong. They wore grubby flannel trousers and shabby old golf-coats that had too obviously been bought off the nail, or blue serge suits that betrayed the provincial tailor. Most of the passengers had got off at Marseilles, but a dozen or so, either because after a long period in the East they thought the trip through the Bay would do them good, or, like themselves, for economy's sake, had gone all the way to Tilbury, and now several of them walked along the platform. They wore solar topis or double-brimmed terais, and heavy greatcoats, or else shapeless soft hats or bowlers, not too well brushed, that looked too small for them. It was a shock to see them. They looked suburban and a trifle second-rate. But Alban had already a London look. There was not a speck of dust on his smart greatcoat, and his black Homburg hat looked brand-new. You would never have guessed that he had not been home for three years. His collar fitted closely round his neck and his foulard tie was neatly tied. As Anne looked at him she could not but think how good-looking he was. He was just under six feet tall, and slim, and he wore his clothes well, and his clothes were well cut. He had fair hair, still thick, and blue eyes and the faintly yellow skin common to men of that complexion after they have lost the pink-and-white freshness of early youth. There was no colour in his cheeks. It was a fine head, well-set on rather a long neck, with a somewhat prominent Adam's apple; but you were more impressed with the distinction than with the beauty of his face. It was because his features were so regular, his nose so straight, his brow so broad that he photographed so well. Indeed, from his photographs you would have thought him extremely handsome. He was not that, perhaps because his eyebrows and his eyelashes were pale, and his lips thin, but he looked very intellectual. There was refinement in his face and a spirituality that was oddly moving. That was how you thought a poet should look; and when Anne became engaged to him she told her girl friends who asked her about him that he looked like Shelley. He turned to her now with a little smile in his blue eyes. His smile was very attractive.

'What a perfect day to land in England!'

It was October. They had steamed up the Channel on a grey sea under a grey sky. There was not a breath of wind. The fishing boats seemed to rest on the placid water as though the elements had for ever forgotten their old hostility. The coast was incredibly green, but with a bright cosy greenness quite unlike the luxuriant, vehement verdure of Eastern jungles. The red towns they passed here and there were comfortable and homelike. They seemed to welcome the exiles with a smiling friendliness. And when they drew into the estuary of the Thames they saw the rich levels of Essex and in a little while Chalk Church on the Kentish shore, lonely in the midst of weather-beaten trees, and beyond it the woods of Cobham. The sun, red in a faint mist, set on the marshes, and night fell. In the station the arc-lamps shed a light that spotted the darkness with cold hard patches. It was good to see the porters lumbering about in their grubby uniforms and the stationmaster fat and important in his bowler hat. The stationmaster blew a whistle and waved his arm. Alban stepped into the carriage and seated himself in the corner opposite to Anne. The train started.

'We're due in London at six-ten,' said Alban. 'We ought to get to Jermyn Street by seven. That'll give us an hour to bath and change and we can get to the Savoy for dinner by eight-thirty. A bottle of pop to-night, my pet, and a slap-up dinner.' He gave a chuckle. 'I heard the Strouds and the Maundys arranging to meet at the Trocadero Grill-Room.'

He took up the papers and asked if she wanted any of them. Anne shook her head.

'Tired?' he smiled.

'No.'

'Excited?'

In order not to answer she gave a little laugh. He began to look at the papers, starting with the publishers' advertisements, and she was conscious of the intense satisfaction it was to him to feel himself through them once more in the middle of things. They had taken in those same papers in Sondurah, but they arrived six weeks old, and though they kept them abreast of what was going on in the world that interested them both, they emphasised their exile. But these were fresh from the Press. They smelt different. They had a crispness that was almost voluptuous. He wanted to read them all at once. Anne looked out of the window. The country was dark, and she could see little but the lights of their carriage reflected on the glass, but very soon the town encroached upon it, and then she saw little sordid houses, mile upon mile of them, with a light in a window here and there, and the chimneys made a dreary pattern against the sky. They

85

passed through Barking and East Ham and Bromley—it was silly that the name on the platform as they went through the station should give her such a tremor—and then Stepney. Alban put down his papers.

'We shall be there in five minutes now.'

He put on his hat and took down from the racks the things the porter had put in them. He looked at her with shining eyes and his lips twitched. She saw that he was only just able to control his emotion. He looked out of the window, too, and they passed over brightly lighted thoroughfares, close packed with tram-cars, buses and motor-vans, and they saw the streets thick with people. What a mob! The shops were all lit up. They saw the hawkers with their barrows at the curb.

'London,' he said.

He took her hand and gently pressed it. His smile was so sweet that she had to say something. She tried to be facetious.

'Does it make you feel all funny inside?'

'I don't know if I want to cry or if I want to be sick.'

Fenchurch Street. He lowered the window and waved his arm for a porter. With a grinding of brakes the train came to a standstill. A porter opened the door and Alban handed him out one package after another. Then in his polite way, having jumped out, he gave his hand to Anne to help her down to the platform. The porter went to fetch a barrow and they stood by the pile of their luggage. Alban waved to two passengers from the ship who passed them. The man nodded stiffly.

'What a comfort it is that we shall never have to be civil to those awful people any more,' said Alban lightly.

Anne gave him a quick glance. He was really incomprehensible. The porter came back with his barrow, the luggage was put on and they followed him to collect their trunks. Alban took his wife's arm and pressed it.

'The smell of London. By God, it's grand.'

He rejoiced in the noise and the bustle, and the crowd of people who jostled them; the radiance of the arc-lamps and the black shadows they cast, sharp but full-toned, gave him a sense of elation. They got out into the street and the porter went off to get them a taxi. Alban's eyes glittered as he looked at the buses and the policemen trying to direct the confusion. His distinguished face bore a look of something like inspiration. The taxi came. Their luggage was stowed away and piled up beside the driver, Alban gave the porter half-a-crown, and they drove off. They turned down Gracechurch Street and in Cannon Street were held up by a block in the traffic. Alban laughed out loud.

'What's the matter?' said Anne.

'I'm so excited.'

They went along the Embankment. It was relatively quiet there. Taxis and cars passed them. The bells of the trams were music in his ears. At Westminster Bridge they cut across Parliament Square and drove through the green silence of St. James's Park. They had engaged a room at a hotel just off Jermyn Street. The reception clerk took them upstairs and a porter brought up their luggage. It was a room with twin beds and a bathroom.

'This looks all right,' said Alban. 'It'll do us till we can find a flat or something.'

He looked at his watch.

'Look here, darling, we shall only fall over one another if we try to unpack together. We've got oodles of time and it'll take you longer to get straight and dress than me. I'll clear out. I want to go to the club and see if there's any mail for me. I've got my dinner-jacket in my suit-case and it'll only take me twenty minutes to have a bath and dress. Does that suit you?'

'Yes. That's all right.'

'I'll be back in an hour.'

'Very well.'

He took out of his pocket the little comb he always carried and passed it through his long fair hair. Then he put on his hat. He gave himself a glance in the mirror.

'Shall I turn on the bath for you?'

'No, don't bother.'

'All right. So long.'

He went out.

When he was gone Anne took her dressing-case and her hat-box and put them on the top of her trunk. Then she rang the bell. She did not take off her hat. She sat down and lit a cigarette. When a servant answered the bell she asked for the porter. He came. She pointed to the luggage.

'Will you take those things and leave them in the hall for the present. I'll tell you what to do with them presently.'

'Very good, ma'am.'

She gave him a florin. He took the trunk out and the other packages and closed the door behind him. A few tears slid down Anne's cheeks, but she shook herself; she dried her eyes and powdered her face. She needed all her calm. She was glad that Alban had conceived the idea of going to his club. It made things easier and gave her a little time to think them out.

Now that the moment had come to do what she had for weeks determined, now that she must say the terrible things she had to say, she quailed. Her heart sank. She knew exactly what she meant to say to Alban, she had made up her mind about that long ago, and had said the very words to herself a hundred times, three or four times a day every day of the long journey from Singapore, but she was afraid that she would grow confused. She dreaded an argument. The thought of a scene made her feel slightly sick. It was something at all events to have an hour in which to collect herself. He would say she was heartless and cruel and unreasonable. She could not help it.

'No, no, no,' she cried aloud.

She shuddered with horror. And all at once she saw herself again in the bungalow, sitting as she had been sitting when the whole thing started. It was getting on towards tiffin time and in a few minutes Alban would be back from the office. It gave her pleasure to reflect that it was an attractive room for him to come back to, the large verandah which was their parlour, and she knew that though they had been there eighteen months he was still alive to the success she had made of it. The jalousies were drawn now against the midday sun and the mellowed light filtering through them gave an impression of cool silence. Anne was house-proud, and though they were moved from district to district according to the exigencies of the Service and seldom stayed anywhere very long, at each new post she started with new enthusiasm to make their house cosy and charming. She was very modern. Visitors were surprised because there were no knick-knacks. They were taken aback by the bold colour of her curtains and could not at all make out the tinted reproductions of pictures by Marie Laurencin and Gauguin in silvered frames which were placed on the walls with such cunning skill. She was conscious that few of them quite approved and the good ladies of Port Wallace and Pemberton thought such arrangements odd, affected and out of place; but this left her calm. They would learn. It did them good to get a bit of a jolt. And now she looked round the long, spacious verandah with the complacent sigh of the artist satisfied with his work. It was gay. It was bare. It was restful. It refreshed the spirit and gently excited the fancy. Three immense bowls of yellow cannas completed the colour scheme. Her eyes lingered for a moment on the book-shelves filled with books; that was another thing that disconcerted the colony, all the books they had, and strange books too, heavy they thought them for the most part; and she gave them a little affectionate look as though they were living things. Then she gave the piano a glance. A piece of music was still open on the rack, it was something of Debussy, and Alban had been playing it before he went to the office.

Her friends in the colony had condoled with her when Alban was appointed D.O. at Daktar, for it was the most isolated district in Sondurah. It was connected with the town which was the headquarters of the government neither by telegraph nor telephone. But she liked it. They had been there for some time and she hoped they would remain till Alban went home on leave in another twelve months. It was as large as an English county, with a long coast-line, and the sea was dotted with little islands. A broad, winding river ran through it and on each side of this stretched hills densely covered with virgin forest. The station, a good way up the river, consisted of a row of Chinese shops and a native village nestling amid coconut trees, the District Office, the D.O.'s bungalow, the Clerk's quarters and the barracks. Their only neighbours were the manager of a rubber estate a few miles up the river and the manager and his assistant, Dutchmen both, of a timber camp on one of the river's tributaries. The rubber estate's launch went up and down twice a month and was their only means of regular communication with the outside world. But though they were lonely they were not dull. Their days were full. Their ponies waited for them at dawn and they rode while the day was still fresh and in the bridle-paths through the jungle lingered the mystery of the tropical night. They came back, bathed, changed and had breakfast, and Alban went to the office. Anne spent the morning writing letters and working. She had fallen in love with the country from the first day she arrived in it and had taken pains to master the common language spoken. Her imagination was inflamed by the stories she heard of love and jealousy and death. She was told romantic tales of a time that was only just past. She sought to steep herself in the lore of those strange people. Both she and Alban read a great deal. They had for the country a considerable library and new books came from London by nearly every mail. Little that was noteworthy escaped them. Alban was fond of playing the piano. For an amateur he played very well. He had studied rather seriously, and he had an agreeable touch and a good ear; he could read music with ease, and it was always a pleasure to Anne to sit by him and follow the score when he tried something new. But their great delight was to tour the district. Sometimes they would be away for a fortnight at a time. They would go down the river in a prahu and then sail from one little island to another, bathe in the sea, and fish, or else row upstream till it grew shallow and the trees on either bank were so close to one another that you only saw a slim strip of sky between. Here the boatmen had to pole and they would spend the night in a native house. They bathed in a river pool so clear that you could see the sand shining silver at the bottom; and the spot was so lovely, so peaceful and remote, that you felt you could stay there for ever. Sometimes, on the other hand, they would tramp for days along the jungle paths, sleeping under canvas, and notwithstanding the mosquitoes that tormented them and the leeches that sucked their blood, enjoy every moment. Whoever slept so well as on a camp bed? And then there was the gladness of getting back, the delight in the comfort of the well-ordered establishment, the mail that had arrived with letters from home and all the papers, and the piano.

Alban would sit down to it then, his fingers itching to feel the keys, and in what he played, Stravinsky,

Ravel, Darius Miehaud, she seemed to feel that he put in something of his own, the sounds of the jungle at night, dawn over the estuary, the starry nights and the crystal clearness of the forest pools.

Sometimes the rain fell in sheets for days at a time. Then Alban worked at Chinese. He was learning it so that he could communicate with the Chinese of the country in their own language, and Anne did the thousand-and-one things for which she had not had time before. Those days brought them even more closely together; they always had plenty to talk about, and when they were occupied with their separate affairs they were pleased to feel in their bones that they were near to one another. They were wonderfully united. The rainy days that shut them up within the walls of the bungalow made them feel as if they were one body in face of the world.

On occasion they went to Port Wallace. It was a change, but Anne was always glad to get home. She was never quite at her ease there. She was conscious that none of the people they met liked Alban. They were very ordinary people, middle-class and suburban and dull, without any of the intellectual interests that made life so full and varied to Alban and her, and many of them were narrow-minded and ill-natured; but since they had to pass the better part of their lives in contact with them, it was tiresome that they should feel so unkindly towards Alban. They said he was conceited. He was always very pleasant with them, but she was aware that they resented his cordiality. When he tried to be jovial they said he was putting on airs, and when he chaffed them they thought he was being funny at their expense.

Once they stayed at Government House, and Mrs. Hannay, the Governor's wife, who liked her, talked to her about it. Perhaps the Governor had suggested that she should give Anne a hint.

'You know, my dear, it's a pity your husband doesn't try to be more come-hither with people. He's very intelligent; don't you think it would be better if he didn't let others see he knows it quite so clearly? My husband said to me only yesterday: of course I know Alban Torel is the cleverest young man in the Service, but he does manage to put my back up more than anyone I know. I am the Governor, but when he talks to me he always gives me the impression that he looks upon me as a damned fool.'

The worst of it was that Anne knew how low an opinion Alban had of the Governor's parts.

'He doesn't mean to be superior,' Anne answered, smiling. 'And he really isn't in the least conceited. I think it's only because he has a straight nose and high cheek-bones.'

'You know, they don't like him at the club. They call him Powder-Puff Percy.'

Anne flushed. She had heard that before and it made her very angry. Her eyes filled with tears.

'I think it's frightfully unfair.'

Mrs. Hannay took her hand and gave it an affectionate little squeeze.

'My dear, you know I don't want to hurt your feelings. Your husband can't help rising very high in the Service. He'd make things so much easier for himself if he were a little more human. Why doesn't he play football?'

'It's not his game. He's always only too glad to play tennis.'

'He doesn't give that impression. He gives the impression that there's no one here who's worth his while to play with.'

'Well, there isn't,' said Anne, stung.

Alban happened to be an extremely good tennis-player. He had played a lot of tournaments in England and Anne knew that it gave him a grim satisfaction to knock those

93

beefy, hearty men all over the court. He could make the best of them look foolish. He could be maddening on the tennis court and Anne was aware that sometimes he could not resist the temptation.

'He does play to the gallery, doesn't he?' said Mrs. Hannay.

'I don't think so. Believe me, Alban has no idea he isn't popular. As far as I can see he's always pleasant and friendly with everybody.'

'It's then he's most offensive,' said Mrs. Hannay dryly.

'I know people don't like us very much,' said Anne, smiling a little. 'I'm very sorry, but really I don't know what we can do about it.'

'Not you, my dear,' cried Mrs. Hannay. 'Everybody adores you. That's why they put up with your husband. My dear, who could help liking you?'

'I don't know why they should adore me,' said Anne.

But she did not say it quite sincerely. She was deliberately playing the part of the dear little woman and within her she bubbled with amusement. They disliked Alban because he had such an air of distinction, and because he was interested in art and literature; they did not understand these things and so thought them unmanly; and they disliked him because his capacity was greater than theirs. They disliked him because he was better bred than they. They thought him superior; well, he was superior, but not in the sense they meant. They forgave her because she was an ugly little thing. That was what she called herself, but she wasn't that, or if she was it was with an ugliness that was most attractive. She was like a little monkey, but a very sweet little monkey and very human. She had a neat figure. That was her best point. That and her eyes. They were very large, of a deep brown, liquid and shining; they were full of fun, but they could be tender on occasion with a charming sympathy.

She was dark, her frizzy hair was almost black, and her skin was swarthy; she had a small fleshy nose, with large nostrils, and much too big a mouth. But she was alert and vivacious. She could talk with a show of real interest to the ladies of the colony about their husbands and their servants and their children in England, and she could listen appreciatively to the men who told her stories that she had often heard before. They thought her a jolly good sort. They did not know what clever fun she made of them in private. It never occurred to them that she thought them narrow, gross and pretentious. They found no glamour in the East because they looked at it vulgarly with material eyes. Romance lingered at their threshold and they drove it away like an importunate beggar. She was aloof. She repeated to herself Landor's line:

'Nature I loved, and next to nature, art.'

She reflected on her conversation with Mrs. Hannay, but on the whole it left her unconcerned. She wondered whether she should say anything about it to Alban; it had always seemed a little odd to her that he should be so little aware of his unpopularity; but she was afraid that if she told him of it he would become self-conscious. He never noticed the coldness of the men at the club. He made them feel shy and therefore uncomfortable. His appearance there caused a sort of awkwardness, but he, happily insensible, was breezily cordial to all and sundry. The fact was that he was strangely unconscious of other people. She was in a class by herself, she and a little group of friends they had in London, but he could never quite realise that the people of the colony, the government officials and the planters and their wives, were human beings. They were to him like pawns in a game. He laughed with them, chaffed them, and was amiably tolerant of them; with a chuckle Anne told herself that he was rather like the master of a preparatory school taking little boys out on a picnic and anxious to give them a good time.

She was afraid it wasn't much good telling Alban. He was incapable of the dissimulation which, she happily realised, came so easily to her. What was one to do with these people? The men had come out to the colony as lads from second-rate schools, and life had taught them nothing. At fifty they had the outlook of hobbledehoys. Most of them drank a great deal too much. They read nothing worth reading. Their ambition was to be like everybody else. Their highest praise was to say that a man was a damned good sort. If you were interested in the things of the spirit you were a prig. They were eaten up with envy of one another and devoured by petty jealousies. And the women, poor things, were obsessed by petty rivalries. They made a circle that was more provincial than any in the smallest town in England. They were prudish and spiteful. What did it matter if they did not like Alban? They would have to put up with him because his ability was so great. He was clever and energetic. They could not say that he did not do his work well. He had been successful in every post he had occupied. With his sensitiveness and his imagination he understood the native mind and he was able to get the natives to do things that no one in his position could. He had a gift for languages, and he spoke all the local dialects. He not only knew the common tongue that most of the government officials spoke, but was acquainted with the niceties of the language and on occasion could make use of a ceremonial speech that flattered and impressed the chiefs. He had a gift for organisation. He was not afraid of responsibility. In due course he was bound to be made a Resident. Alban had some interest in England; his father was a brigadier-general killed in the war, and though he had no private means he had influential friends. He spoke of them with pleasant irony.

'The great advantage of democratic government,' he said, 'is that merit, with influence to back it, can be pretty sure of receiving its due reward.'

Alban was so obviously the ablest man in the service that there seemed no reason why he should not eventually be made Governor. Then, thought Anne, his air of superiority, of which they complained, would be in place. They would accept him as their master and he would know how to make himself respected and obeyed. The position she foresaw did not dazzle her. She accepted it as a right. It would be fun for Alban to be Governor and for her to be the Governor's wife. And what an opportunity! They were sheep, the government servants and the planters; when Government House was the seat of culture they would soon fall into line. When the best way to the Governor's favour was to be intelligent, intelligence would become the fashion. She and Alban would cherish the native arts and collect carefully the memorials of a vanished past. The country would make an advance it had never dreamed of. They would develop it, but along lines of order and beauty. They would instil into their subordinates a passion for that beautiful land and a loving interest in these romantic races. They would make them realise what music meant. They would cultivate literature. They would create beauty. It would be the golden age.

Suddenly she heard Alban's footstep. Anne awoke from her day-dream. All that was far away in the future. Alban was only a District Officer yet and what was important was the life they were living now. She heard Alban go into the bath-house and splash water over himself. In a minute he came in. He had changed into a shirt and shorts. His fair hair was still wet.

'Tiffin ready?' he asked.

'Yes.'

He sat down at the piano and played the piece that he

had played in the morning. The silvery notes cascaded coolly down the sultry air. You had an impression of a formal garden with great trees and elegant pieces of artificial water and of leisurely walks bordered with pseudo-classical statues. Alban played with an exquisite delicacy. Lunch was announced by the head boy. He rose from the piano. They walked into the dining-room hand in hand. A punkah lazily fanned the air. Anne gave the table a glance. With its bright-coloured table-cloth and the amusing plates it looked very gay.

'Anything exciting at the office this morning?' she asked.

'No, nothing much. A buffalo case. Oh, and Prynne has sent along to ask me to go up to the estate. Some coolies have been damaging the trees and he wants me to come along and look into it.'

Prynne was manager of the rubber estate up the river and now and then they spent a night with him. Sometimes when he wanted a change he came down to dinner and slept at the D.O.'s bungalow. They both liked him. He was a man of five-and-thirty, with a red face, with deep furrows in it, and very black hair. He was quite uneducated, but cheerful and easy, and being the only Englishman within two days' journey they could not but be friendly with him. He had been a little shy of them at first. News spreads quickly in the East and long before they arrived in the district he heard that they were highbrows. He did not know what he would make of them. He probably did not know that he had charm, which makes up for many more commendable qualities, and Alban with his almost feminine sensibilities was peculiarly susceptible to this. He found Alban much more human than he expected, and of course Anne was stunning. Alban played ragtime for him, which he would not have done for the Governor, and played dominoes with him. When Alban was making his first tour of the district with Anne, and suggested that they would like to spend a couple of nights on the estate, he had thought it as well to warn him that he lived with a native woman and had two children by her. He would do his best to keep them out of Anne's sight, but he could not send them away, there was nowhere to send them. Alban laughed.

'Anne isn't that sort of woman at all. Don't dream of hiding them. She loves children.'

Anne quickly made friends with the shy, pretty little native woman and soon was playing happily with the children. She and the girl had long confidential chats. The children took a fancy to her. She brought them lovely toys from Port Wallace. Prynne, comparing her smiling tolerance with the disapproving acidity of the other white women of the colony, described himself as knocked all of a heap. He could not do enough to show his delight and gratitude.

'If all highbrows are like you,' he said, 'give me highbrows every time.'

He hated to think that in another year they would leave the district for good and the chances were that, if the next D.O. was married, his wife would think it dreadful that, rather than live alone, he had a native woman to live with him and, what was more, was much attached to her.

But there had been a good deal of discontent on the estate of late. The coolies were Chinese and infected with communist ideas. They were disorderly. Alban had been obliged to sentence several of them for various crimes to terms of imprisonment.

'Prynne tells me that as soon as their term is up he's going to send them all back to China and get Javanese instead,' said Alban. 'I'm sure he's right. They're much more amenable.'

'You don't think there's going to be any serious trouble?'

'Oh, no. Prynne knows his job and he's a pretty determined fellow. He wouldn't put up with any nonsense and with me and our policemen to back him up I don't imagine they'll try any monkey tricks.' He smiled. 'The iron hand in the velvet glove.'

The words were barely out of his mouth when a sudden shouting arose. There was a commotion and the sound of steps. Loud voices and cries.

'Tuan, Tuan.'

'What the devil's the matter?'

Alban sprang from his chair and went swiftly on to the verandah. Anne followed him. At the bottom of the steps was a group of natives. There was the sergeant, and three or four policemen, boatmen and several men from the kampong.

'What is it?' called Alban.

Two or three shouted back in answer. The sergeant pushed others aside and Alban saw lying on the ground a man in a shirt and khaki shorts. He ran down the steps. He recognised the man as the assistant manager of Prynne's estate. He was a half-caste. His shorts were covered with blood and there was clotted blood all over one side of his face and head. He was unconscious.

'Bring him up here,' called Anne.

Alban gave an order. The man was lifted up and carried on to the verandah. They laid him on the floor and Anne put a pillow under his head. She sent for water and for the medicine-chest in which they kept things for emergency.

'Is he dead?' asked Alban.

'No.'

'Better try to give him some brandy.'

The boatmen brought ghastly news. The Chinese coolies had risen suddenly and attacked the manager's office. Prynne was killed and the assistant manager, Oakley by name, had escaped only by the skin of his teeth. He had come upon the rioters when they were looting the office, he had seen Prynne's body thrown out of the window, and had taken to his heels. Some of the Chinese saw him and gave chase. He ran for the river and was wounded as he jumped into the launch. The launch managed to put off before the Chinese could get on board and they had come down-stream for help as fast as they could go. As they went they saw flames rising from the office buildings. There was no doubt that the coolies had burned down everything that would burn.

Oakley gave a groan and opened his eyes. He was a little, dark-skinned man, with flattened features and thick coarse hair. His great native eyes were filled with terror.

'You're all right,' said Anne. 'You're quite safe.'

He gave a sigh and smiled. Anne washed his face and swabbed it with antiseptics. The wound on his head was not serious.

'Can you speak yet?' said Alban.

'Wait a bit,' she said. 'We must look at his leg.'

Alban ordered the sergeant to get the crowd out of the verandah. Anne ripped up one leg of the shorts. The material was clinging to the coagulated wound.

'I've been bleeding like a pig,' said Oakley.

It was only a flesh wound. Alban was clever with his fingers, and though the blood began to flow again they stanched it. Alban put on a dressing and a bandage. The sergeant and a policeman lifted Oakley on to a long chair. Alban gave him a brandy and soda, and soon he felt strong enough to speak. He knew no more than the boatmen had already told. Prynne was dead and the estate was in flames.

'And the girl and the children?' asked Anne.

'I don't know.'

'Oh, Alban.'

'I must turn out the police. Are you sure Prynne is dead?'

'Yes, sir. I saw him.'

'Have the rioters got fire-arms?'

'I don't know, sir.'

'How d'you mean, you don't know?' Alban cried irritably. 'Prynne had a gun, hadn't he?'

'Yes, sir.'

'There must have been more on the estate. You had one, didn't you? The head overseer had one.'

The half-caste was silent. Alban looked at him sternly.

'How many of those damned Chinese are there?'

'A hundred and fifty.'

Anne wondered that he asked so many questions. It seemed waste of time. The important thing was to collect coolies for the transport up-river, prepare the boats and issue ammunition to the police.

'How many policemen have you got, sir?' asked Oakley.

'Eight and the sergeant.'

'Could I come too? That would make ten of us. I'm sure I shall be all right now I'm bandaged.'

'I'm not going,' said Alban.

'Alban, you must,' cried Anne. She could not believe her ears.

'Nonsense. It would be madness. Oakley's obviously useless. He's sure to have a temperature in a few hours. He'd only be in the way. That leaves nine guns. There are a hundred and fifty Chinese and they've got fire-arms and all the ammunition in the world.'

'How d'you know?'

'It stands to reason they wouldn't have started a show like this unless they had. It would be idiotic to go.'

Anne stared at him with open mouth. Oakley's eyes were puzzled.

'What are you going to do?'

'Well, fortunately we've got the launch. I'll send it to Port Wallace with a request for reinforcements.'

'But they won't be here for two days at least.'

'Well, what of it? Prynne's dead and the estate burned to the ground. We couldn't do any good by going up now. I shall send a native to reconnoitre so that we can find out exactly what the rioters are doing.' He gave Anne his charming smile. 'Believe me, my pet, the rascals won't lose anything by waiting a day or two for what's coming to them.'

Oakley opened his mouth to speak, but perhaps he hadn't the nerve. He was a half-caste assistant manager and Alban, the D.O., represented the power of the Government. But the man's eyes sought Anne's and she thought she read in them an earnest and personal appeal.

'But in two days they're capable of committing the most frightful atrocities,' she cried. 'It's quite unspeakable what they may do.'

'Whatever damage they do they'll pay for. I promise you that.'

'Oh, Alban, you can't sit still and do nothing. I beseech you to go yourself at once.'

'Don't be so silly. I can't quell a riot with eight policemen and a sergeant. I haven't got the right to take a risk of that sort. We'd have to go in boats. You don't think we could get up unobserved. The lalang along the banks is perfect cover and they could just take pot shots at us as we came along. We shouldn't have a chance.'

'I'm afraid they'll only think it weakness if nothing is done for two days, sir,' said Oakley.

'When I want your opinion I'll ask for it,' said Alban acidly. 'So far as I can see when there was danger the only thing you did was to cut and run. I can't persuade myself that your assistance in a crisis would be very valuable.'

The half-caste reddened. He said nothing more. He looked straight in front of him with troubled eyes.

'I'm going down to the office,' said Alban. 'I'll just write a short report and send it down the river by launch at once.'

He gave an order to the sergeant who had been standing all this time stiffly at the top of the steps. He saluted and ran off. Alban went into a little hall they had to get his topi. Anne swiftly followed him.

'Alban, for God's sake listen to me a minute,' she whispered.

'I don't want to be rude to you, darling, but I am pressed for time. I think you'd much better mind your own business.'

'You can't do nothing, Alban. You must go. Whatever the risk.'

'Don't be such a fool,' he said angrily.

He had never been angry with her before. She seized his hand to hold him back.

'I tell you I can do no good by going.'

'You don't know. There's the woman and Prynne's children. We must do something to save them. Let me come with you. They'll kill them.'

'They've probably killed them already.'

'Oh, how can you be so callous! If there's a chance of saving them it's your duty to try.'

'It's my duty to act like a reasonable human being. I'm not going to risk my life and my policemen's for the sake of a native woman and her half-caste brats. What sort of a damned fool do you take me for?'

'They'll say you were afraid.'

'Who?'

'Everyone in the colony.'

He smiled disdainfully.

'If you only knew what a complete contempt I have for the opinion of everyone in the colony.'

She gave him a long searching look. She had been married to him for eight years and she knew every expression of his face and every thought in his mind. She stared into his blue eyes as if they were open windows. She suddenly went quite pale. She dropped his hand and turned away. Without another word she went back on to the verandah. Her ugly little monkey face was a mask of horror.

Alban went to his office, wrote a brief account of the facts, and in a few minutes the motor launch was pounding down the river.

The next two days were endless. Escaped natives brought them news of happenings on the estate. But from their excited and terrified stories it was impossible to get an exact impression of the truth. There had been a good deal of bloodshed. The head overseer had been killed. They brought wild tales of cruelty and outrage. Anne could hear nothing of Prynne's woman and the two children. She shuddered when she thought of what might have been their fate. Alban collected as many natives as he could. They were armed with spears and swords. He commandeered boats. The situation was serious, but he kept his head. He felt that he had done all that was possible and nothing remained but for him to carry on normally. He did his official work. He played the piano a great deal. He rode with Anne in the early morning. He appeared to have forgotten that they had had the first serious difference of opinion in the whole of their married life. He took it that Anne had accepted the wisdom of his decision. He was as amusing, cordial and gay with her as he had always been. When he spoke of the rioters it was with grim irony: when the time came to settle matters a good many of them would wish they had never been born.

'What'll happen to them?' asked Anne.

'Oh, they'll hang.' He gave a shrug of distaste. 'I hate

having to be present at executions. It always makes me feel rather sick.'

He was very sympathetic to Oakley, whom they had put to bed and whom Anne was nursing. Perhaps he was sorry that in the exasperation of the moment he had spoken to him offensively, and he went out of his way to be nice to him.

Then on the afternoon of the third day, when they were drinking their coffee after luncheon, Alban's quick ears caught the sound of a motor boat approaching. At the same moment a policeman ran up to say that the government launch was sighted.

'At last,' cried Alban.

He bolted out of the house. Anne raised one of the jalousies and looked out at the river. Now the sound was quite loud and in a moment she saw the boat come round the bend. She saw Alban on the landing-stage. He got into a prahu and as the launch dropped her anchor he went on board. She told Oakley that the reinforcements had come.

'Will the D.O. go up with them when they attack?' he asked her.

'Naturally,' said Anne coldly.

'I wondered.'

Anne felt a strange feeling in her heart. For the last two days she had had to exercise all her self-control not to cry. She did not answer. She went out of the room.

A quarter of an hour later Alban returned to the bungalow with the captain of constabulary who had been sent with twenty Sikhs to deal with the rioters. Captain Stratton was a little red-faced man with a red moustache and bow legs, very hearty and dashing, whom she had met often at Port Wallace.

'Well, Mrs. Torel, this is a pretty kettle of fish,' he cried, as he shook hands with her, in a loud jolly voice. 'Here I am, with my army all full of pep and ready for a scrap.

Up, boys, and at 'em. Have you got anything to drink in this benighted place?'

'Boy,' she cried, smiling.

'Something long and cool and faintly alcoholic, and then I'm ready to discuss the plan of campaign.'

His breeziness was very comforting. It blew away the sullen apprehension that had seemed ever since the disaster to brood over the lost peace of the bungalow. The boy came in with a tray and Stratton mixed himself a stengah. Alban put him in possession of the facts. He told them clearly, briefly and with precision.

'I must say I admire you,' said Stratton. 'In your place I should never have been able to resist the temptation to take my eight cops and have a whack at the blighters myself.'

'I thought it was a perfectly unjustifiable risk to take.'

'Safety first, old boy, eh, what?' said Stratton jovially. 'I'm jolly glad you didn't. It's not often we get the chance of a scrap. It would have been a dirty trick to keep the whole show to yourself.'

Captain Stratton was all for steaming straight up the river and attacking at once, but Alban pointed out to him the inadvisability of such a course. The sound of the approaching launch would warn the rioters. The long grass at the river's edge offered them cover and they had enough guns to make a landing difficult. It seemed useless to expose the attacking force to their fire. It was silly to forget that they had to face a hundred and fifty desperate men and it would be easy to fall into an ambush. Alban expounded his own plan. Stratton listened to it. He nodded now and then. The plan was evidently a good one. It would enable them to take the rioters on the rear, surprise them, and in all probability finish the job without a single casualty. He would have been a fool not to accept it.

'But why didn't you do that yourself?' asked Stratton.

'With eight men and a sergeant?'

Stratton did not answer.

'Anyhow it's not a bad idea and we'll settle on it. It gives us plenty of time, so with your permission, Mrs. Torel, I'll have a bath.'

They set out at sunset, Captain Stratton and his twenty Sikhs, Alban with his policemen and the natives he had collected. The night was dark and moonless. Trailing behind them were the dug-outs that Alban had gathered together and into which after a certain distance they proposed to transfer their force. It was important that no sound should give warning of their approach. After they had gone for about three hours by launch they took to the dug-outs and in them silently paddled up stream. They reached the border of the vast estate and landed. Guides led them along a path so narrow that they had to march in single file. It had been long unused and the going was heavy. They had twice to ford a stream. The path led them circuitously to the rear of the coolie lines, but they did not wish to reach them till nearly dawn and presently Stratton gave the order to halt. It was a long cold wait. At last the night seemed to be less dark; you did not see the trunks of the trees, but were vaguely sensible of them against its darkness. Stratton had been sitting with his back to a tree. He gave a whispered order to a sergeant and in a few minutes the column was once more on the march. Suddenly they found themselves on a road. They formed fours. The dawn broke and in the ghostly light the surrounding objects were wanly visible. The column stopped on a whispered order. They had come in sight of the coolie lines. Silence reigned in them. The column crept on again and again halted. Stratton, his eyes shining, gave Alban a smile.

'We've caught the blighters asleep.'

He lined up his men. They inserted cartridges in

their guns. He stepped forward and raised his hand. The carbines were pointed at the coolie lines.

'Fire.'

There was a rattle as the volley of shots rang out. Then suddenly there was a tremendous din and the Chinese poured out, shouting and waving their arms, but in front of them, to Alban's utter bewilderment, bellowing at the top of his voice and shaking his fist at them, was a white man.

'Who the hell's that?' cried Stratton.

A very big, very fat man, in khaki trousers and a singlet, was running towards them as fast as his fat legs would carry him and as he ran shaking both fists at them and yelling:

'*Smerige flikkers*! *Verlockte ploerten*!'

'My God, it's Van Hasseldt,' said Alban.

This was the Dutch manager of the timber camp which was situated on a considerable tributary of the river about twenty miles away.

'What the hell do you think you're doing?' he puffed as he came up to them.

'How the hell did you get here?' asked Stratton in turn.

He saw that the Chinese were scattering in all directions and gave his men instructions to round them up. Then he turned again to Van Hasseldt.

'What's it mean?'

'Mean? Mean?' shouted the Dutchman furiously. 'That's what I want to know. You and your damned policemen. What do you mean by coming here at this hour in the morning and firing a damned volley. Target practice? You might have killed me. Idiots!'

'Have a cigarette,' said Stratton.

'How did you get here, Van Hasseldt?' asked Alban again, very much at sea. 'This is the force they've sent from Port Wallace to quell the riot.'

'How did I get here? I walked. How did you think I got here? Riot be damned. I quelled the riot. If that's what you came for you can take your damned policemen home again. A bullet came within a foot of my head.'

'I don't understand,' said Alban.

'There's nothing to understand,' spluttered Van Hasseldt, still fuming. 'Some coolies came to my estate and said the Chinks had killed Prynne and burned the bally place down, so I took my assistant and my head overseer and a Dutch friend I had staying with me and came over to see what the trouble was.'

Captain Stratton opened his eyes wide.

'Did you just stroll in as if it was a picnic?' he asked.

'Well, you don't think after all the years I've been in this country I'm going to let a couple of hundred Chinks put the fear of God into me? I found them all scared out of their lives. One of them had the nerve to pull a gun on me and I blew his bloody brains out. And the rest surrendered. I've got the leaders tied up. I was going to send a boat down to you this morning to come up and get them.'

Stratton stared at him for a minute and then burst into a shout of laughter. He laughed till the tears ran down his face. The Dutchman looked at him angrily, then began to laugh too; he laughed with the big belly laugh of a very fat man and his coils of fat heaved and shook. Alban watched them sullenly. He was very angry.

'What about Prynne's girl and the kids?' he asked.

'Oh, they got away all right.'

It just showed how wise he had been not to let himself be influenced by Anne's hysteria. Of course the children had come to no harm. He never thought they would.

Van Hasseldt and his little party started back for the timber camp, and as soon after as possible Stratton embarked his twenty Sikhs and leaving Alban with his sergeant and his policemen to deal with the situation departed for Port Wallace. Alban gave him a brief report for the Governor. There was much for him to do. It looked as though he would have to stay for a considerable time; but since every house on the estate had been burned to the ground and he was obliged to install himself in the coolie lines he thought it better that Anne should not join him. He sent her a note to that effect. He was glad to be able to reassure her of the safety of poor Prynne's girl. He set to work at once to make his preliminary enquiry. He examined a host of witnesses. But a week later he received an order to go to Port Wallace at once. The launch that brought it was to take him and he was able to see Anne on the way down for no more than an hour. Alban was a trifle vexed.

'I don't know why the Governor can't leave me to get things straight without dragging me off like this. It's extremely inconvenient.'

'Oh, well, the Government never bothers very much about the convenience of its subordinates, does it?' smiled Anne.

'It's just red-tape. I would offer to take you along, darling, only I shan't stay a minute longer than I need. I want to get my evidence together for the Sessions Court as soon as possible. I think in a country like this it's very important that justice should be prompt.'

When the launch came in to Port Wallace one of the harbour police told him that the harbour-master had a chit for him. It was from the Governor's secretary and informed him that His Excellency desired to see him as soon as convenient after his arrival. It was ten in the morning. Alban went to the club, had a bath and shaved, and then in clean ducks, his hair neatly brushed, he called a rickshaw and told the boy to take him to the Governor's office. He was at once shown in to the secretary's room. The secretary shook hands with him.

'I'll tell H.E. you're here,' he said. 'Won't you sit down?'

The secretary left the room and in a little while came back.

'H.E. will see you in a minute. Do you mind if I get on with my letters?'

Alban smiled. The secretary was not exactly come-hither. He waited, smoking a cigarette, and amused himself with his own thoughts. He was making a good job of the preliminary enquiry. It interested him. Then an orderly came in and told Alban that the Governor was ready for him. He rose from his seat and followed him into the Governor's room.

'Good morning, Torel.'

'Good morning, sir.'

The Governor was sitting at a large desk. He nodded to Alban and motioned to him to take a seat. The Governor was all grey. His hair was grey, his face, his eyes; he looked as though the tropical suns had washed the colour out of him; he had been in the country for thirty years and had risen one by one through all the ranks of the Service; he looked tired and depressed. Even his voice was grey. Alban liked him because he was quiet; he did not think him clever, but he had an unrivalled knowledge of the country, and his great experience was a very good substitute for intelligence. He looked at Alban for a full moment without speaking and the odd idea came to Alban that he was embarrassed. He very nearly gave him a lead.

'I saw Van Hasseldt yesterday,' said the Governor suddenly.

'Yes, sir?'

'Will you give me your account of the occurrences at the Alud Estate and of the steps you took to deal with them.'

Alban had an orderly mind. He was self-possessed. He

marshalled his facts well and was able to state them with precision. He chose his words with care and spoke them fluently.

'You had a sergeant and eight policemen. Why did you not immediately go to the scene of the disturbance?'

'I thought the risk was unjustifiable.'

A thin smile was outlined on the Governor's grey face.

'If the officers of this Government had hesitated to take unjustifiable risks it would never have become a province of the British Empire.'

Alban was silent. It was difficult to talk to a man who spoke obvious nonsense.

'I am anxious to hear your reasons for the decision you took.'

Alban gave them coolly. He was quite convinced of the rightness of his action. He repeated, but more fully, what he had said in the first place to Anne. The Governor listened attentively.

'Van Hasseldt, with his manager, a Dutch friend of his, and a native overseer, seems to have coped with the situation very efficiently,' said the Governor.

'He had a lucky break. That doesn't prevent him from being a damned fool. It was madness to do what he did.'

'Do you realise that by leaving a Dutch planter to do what you should have done yourself, you have covered the Government with ridicule?'

'No, sir.'

'You've made yourself a laughing-stock in the whole colony.'

Alban smiled.

'My back is broad enough to bear the ridicule of persons to whose opinion I am entirely indifferent.'

'The utility of a Government official depends very largely on his prestige, and I'm afraid his prestige is likely to be inconsiderable when he lies under the stigma of cowardice.'

Alban flushed a little.

'I don't quite know what you mean by that, sir.'

'I've gone into the matter very carefully. I've seen Captain Stratton, and Oakley, poor Prynne's assistant, and I've seen Van Hasseldt. I've listened to your defence.'

'I didn't know that I was defending myself, sir.'

'Be so good as not to interrupt me. I think you committed a grave error of judgment. As it turns out the risk was very small, but whatever it was, I think you should have taken it. In such matters promptness and firmness are essential. It is not for me to conjecture what motive led you to send for a force of constabulary and do nothing till they came. I am afraid, however, that I consider that your usefulness in the Service is no longer very great.'

Alban looked at him with astonishment.

'But would you have gone under the circumstances?' he asked him.

'I should.'

Alban shrugged his shoulders.

'Don't you believe me?' rapped out the Governor.

'Of course I believe you, sir. But perhaps you will allow me to say that if you had been killed the colony would have suffered an irreparable loss.'

The Governor drummed on the table with his fingers. He looked out of the window and then looked again at Alban. When he spoke it was not unkindly.

'I think you are unfitted by temperament for this rather rough-and-tumble life, Torel. If you'll take my advice you'll go home. With your abilities I feel sure that you'll soon find an occupation much better suited to you.'

'I'm afraid I don't understand what you mean, sir.'

'Oh, come, Torel, you're not stupid. I'm trying to make

things easy for you. For your wife's sake as well as for your own I do not wish you to leave the colony with the stigma of being dismissed from the Service for cowardice. I'm giving you the opportunity of resigning.'

'Thank you very much, sir. I'm not prepared to avail myself of the opportunity. If I resign I admit that I committed an error and that the charge you make against me is justified. I don't admit it.'

'You can please yourself. I have considered the matter very carefully and I have no doubt about it in my mind. I am forced to discharge you from the Service. The necessary papers will reach you in due course. Meanwhile you will return to your post and hand over to the officer appointed to succeed you on his arrival.'

'Very good, sir,' replied Alban, a twinkle of amusement in his eyes. 'When do you desire me to return to my post?'

'At once.'

'Have you any objection to my going to the club and having tiffin before I go?'

The Governor looked at him with surprise. His exasperation was mingled with an unwilling admiration.

'Not at all. I'm sorry, Torel, that this unhappy incident should have deprived the Government of a servant whose zeal has always been so apparent and whose tact, intelligence and industry seemed to point him out in the future for very high office.'

'Your Excellency does not read Schiller, I suppose. You are probably not acquainted with his celebrated line: *mit der Dummheit kämpfen die Götter selbst vergebens*.'

'What does it mean?'

'Roughly: against stupidity the gods themselves battle in vain.'

'Good-morning.'

With his head in the air, a smile on his lips, Alban left the Governor's office. The Governor was human, and he had the curiosity to ask his secretary later in the day if Alban Torel had really gone to the club.

'Yes, sir. He had tiffin there.'

'It must have wanted some nerve.'

Alban entered the club jauntily and joined the group of men standing at the bar. He talked to them in the breezy, cordial tone he always used with them. It was designed to put them at their ease. They had been discussing him ever since Stratton had come back to Port Wallace with his story, sneering at him and laughing at him, and all that had resented his supercili-ousness, and they were the majority, were triumphant because his pride had had a fall. But they were so taken aback at seeing him now, so confused to find him as confident as ever, that it was they who were embarrassed.

One man, though he knew perfectly, asked him what he was doing in Port Wallace.

'Oh, I came about the riot on the Alud Estate. H.E. wanted to see me. He does not see eye to eye with me about it. The silly old ass has fired me. I'm going home as soon as he appoints a D.O. to take over.'

There was a moment of awkwardness. One, more kindly disposed than the others, said:

'I'm awfully sorry.'

Alban shrugged his shoulders.

'My dear fellow, what can you do with a perfect damned fool? The only thing is to let him stew in his own juice.'

When the Governor's secretary had told his chief as much of this as he thought discreet, the Governor smiled.

'Courage is a queer thing. I would rather have shot myself than go to the club just then and face all those fellows.'

A fortnight later, having sold to the incoming D.O. all

the decorations that Anne had taken so much trouble about, with the rest of their things in packing-cases and trunks, they arrived at Port Wallace to await the local steamer that was to take them to Singapore. The padre's wife invited them to stay with her, but Anne refused; she insisted that they should go to the hotel. An hour after their arrival she received a very kind little letter from the Governor's wife asking her to go and have tea with her. She went. She found Mrs. Hannay alone, but in a minute the Governor joined them. He expressed his regret that she was leaving and told her how sorry he was for the cause.

'It's very kind of you to say that,' said Anne, smiling gaily, 'but you mustn't think I take it to heart. I'm entirely on Alban's side. I think what he did was absolutely right and if you don't mind my saying so I think you've treated him most unjustly.'

'Believe me, I hated having to take the step I took.'

'Don't let's talk about it,' said Anne.

'What are your plans when you get home?' asked Mrs. Hannay.

Anne began to chat brightly. You would have thought she had not a care in the world. She seemed in great spirits at going home. She was jolly and amusing and made little jokes. When she took leave of the Governor and his wife she thanked them for all their kindness. The Governor escorted her to the door.

The next day but one, after dinner, they went on board the clean and comfortable little ship. The padre and his wife saw them off. When they went into their cabin they found a large parcel on Anne's bunk. It was addressed to Alban. He opened it and saw that it was an immense powder-puff.

'Hullo, I wonder who sent us this,' he said, with a laugh. 'It must be for you, darling.'

Anne gave him a quick look. She went pale. The

brutes! How could they be so cruel? She forced herself to smile.

'It's enormous, isn't it? I've never seen such a large powder-puff in my life.'

But when he had left the cabin and they were out at sea, she threw it passionately overboard.

And now, now that they were back in London and Sondurah was nine thousand miles away, she clenched her hands as she thought of it. Somehow, it seemed the worst thing of all. It was so wantonly unkind to send that absurd object to Alban, Powder-Puff Percy; it showed such a petty spite. Was that their idea of humour? Nothing had hurt her more and even now she felt that it was only by holding on to herself that she could prevent herself from crying. Suddenly she started, for the door opened and Alban came in. She was still sitting in the chair in which he had left her.

'Hullo, why haven't you dressed?' He looked about the room. 'You haven't unpacked.'

'No.'

'Why on earth not?'

'I'm not going to unpack. I'm not going to stay here. I'm leaving you.'

'What are you talking about?'

'I've stuck it out till now. I made up my mind I would till we got home. I set my teeth, I've borne more than I thought it possible to bear, but now it's finished. I've done all that could be expected of me. We're back in London now and I can go.'

He looked at her in utter bewilderment.

'Are you mad, Anne?'

'Oh, my God, what I've endured! The journey to Singapore, with all the officers knowing, and even the Chinese stewards. And at Singapore, the way people looked at us at the hotel, and the sympathy I had to put up with, the bricks they dropped and their embarrassment when they realised what they'd done. My God, I could have killed them. That interminable journey home. There wasn't a single passenger on the ship who didn't know. The contempt they had for you and the kindness they went out of their way to show me. And you so self-complacent and so pleased with yourself, seeing nothing, feeling nothing. You must have the hide of a rhinoceros. The misery of seeing you so chatty and agreeable. Pariahs, that's what we were. You seemed to ask them to snub you. How can anyone be so shameless?'

She was flaming with passion. Now that at last she need not wear the mask of indifference and pride that she had forced herself to assume she cast aside all reserve and all self-control. The words poured from her trembling lips in a virulent stream.

'My dear, how can you be so absurd?' he said good-naturedly, smiling. 'You must be very nervous and high-strung to have got such ideas in your head. Why didn't you tell me? You're like a country bumpkin who comes to London and thinks everyone is staring at him. Nobody bothered about us and if they did what on earth did it matter? You ought to have more sense than to bother about what a lot of fools say. And what do you imagine they were saying?'

'They were saying you'd been fired.'

'Well, that was true,' he laughed.

'They said you were a coward.'

'What of it?'

'Well, you see, that was true too.'

He looked at her for a moment reflectively. His lips tightened a little.

'And what makes you think so?' he asked acidly.

'I saw it in your eyes, that day the news came, when you refused to go to the estate and I followed you into the hall when you went to fetch your topi. I begged you to go, I felt that whatever the danger you must take it, and suddenly I saw the fear in your eyes. I nearly fainted with the horror.'

'I should have been a fool to risk my life to no purpose. Why should I? Nothing that concerned me was at stake. Courage is the obvious virtue of the stupid. I don't attach any particular importance to it.'

'How do you mean that nothing that concerned you was at stake? If that's true then your whole life is a sham. You've given away everything you stood for, everything we both stand for. You've let all of us down. We did set ourselves up on a pinnacle, we did think ourselves better than the rest of them because we loved literature and art and music, we weren't content to live a life of ignoble jealousies and vulgar tittletattle, we did cherish the things of the spirit, and we loved beauty. It was our food and drink. They laughed at us and sneered at us. That was inevitable. The ignorant and the common naturally hate and fear those who are interested in things they don't understand. We didn't care. We called them Philistines. We despised them and we had a right to despise them. Our justification was that we were better and nobler and wiser and braver than they were. And you weren't better, you weren't nobler, you weren't braver. When the crisis came you slunk away like a whipped cur with his tail between his legs. You of all people hadn't the right to be a coward. They despise *us* now and they have the right to despise us. Us and all we stood for. Now they can say that art and beauty are all rot; when it comes to a pinch people like us always let you down. They never stopped looking for a chance to turn and rend us and you gave it to them. They can say that they always expected it. It's a triumph for them. I used to be furious because they called you Powder-Puff Percy. Did you know they did?'

'Of course. I thought it very vulgar, but it left me entirely indifferent.'

'It's funny that their instinct should have been so right.'

'Do you mean to say you've been harbouring this against me all these weeks? I should never have thought you capable of it.'

'I couldn't let you down when everyone was against you. I was too proud for that. Whatever happened I swore to myself that I'd stick to you till we got home. It's been torture.'

'Don't you love me any more?'

'Love you? I loathe the very sight of you.'

'Anne.'

'God knows I loved you. For eight years I worshipped the ground you trod on. You were everything to me. I believed in you as some people believe in God. When I saw the fear in your eyes that day, when you told me that you weren't going to risk your life for a kept woman and her half-caste brats, I was shattered. It was as though someone had wrenched my heart out of my body and trampled on it. You killed my love there and then, Alban. You killed it stone-dead. Since then when you've kissed me I've had to clench my hands so as not to turn my face away. The mere thought of anything else makes me feel physically sick. I loathe your complacence and your frightful insensitiveness. Perhaps I could have forgiven it if it had been just a moment's weakness and if afterwards you'd been ashamed. I should have been miserable, but I think my love was so great that I should only have felt pity for you. But you're incapable of shame. And now I believe in nothing. You're only a silly, pretentious, vulgar poseur. I would rather be the wife of a second-rate planter so long as he had the common human virtues of a man than the wife of a fake like you.'

He did not answer. Gradually his face began to discompose. Those handsome, regular features of his horribly distorted and suddenly he broke out into loud sobs. She gave a little cry.

'Don't, Alban, don't.'

'Oh, darling, how can you be so cruel to me? I adore you. I'd give my whole life to please you. I can't live without you.'

She put out her arms as though to ward off a blow.

'No, no, Alban, don't try to move me. I can't. I must go. I can't live with you any more. It would be frightful. I can never forget. I must tell you the truth, I have only contempt for you and repulsion.'

He sank down at her feet and tried to cling to her knees. With a gasp she sprang up and he buried his head in the empty chair. He cried painfully with sobs that tore his chest. The sound was horrible. The tears streamed from Anne's eyes and, putting her hands to her ears to shut out that dreadful, hysterical sobbing, blindly stumbling she rushed to the door and ran out.

The Buried Talent

When Convers arrived at Penang and the Resident, coming to meet him, told him that a culvert on the line to Bangkok had been swept away by a flood so that unless he flew he would not be able to go for three or four days, he received the news with equanimity. He decided to wait till the line was repaired. The Resident asked him to stay with him, but with proper expressions of civility Convers chose rather to go to the hotel.

He was now having breakfast on the verandah of his room and he looked forward to spending a lazy day wandering about the pleasant town. He frowned slightly when a letter was brought in to him. On the evening of his arrival he had attended a large and dull dinner party at the Residency and on the day following another at the Club. He guessed that the letter was an invitation to a party of the same nature and he wondered whether there was any means by which he could politely refuse it. But though it was an invitation it was not of the sort he expected. The letter began abruptly.

> *I hardly know how to address you. I'm not quite sure if it's fitting to address His Britannic Majesty's Minister Plenipotentiary to the King of Siam as Teddie and I'm not quite sure if now you're so grand you will want to know an obscure doctor's wife whom you have not seen or heard of for more than twenty years.*

Convers interrupted his reading.
'Who the devil is this?'

He looked at the signature: Blanche MacArdle. It meant nothing to him at all. He went on.

> *I see that you are at Penang and if I know anything of the P.W.D. they won't get the trains running for at least three days, and I am wondering if for old times' sake you would come over to dinner and spend the night. It will only take you a couple of hours to get here by car. Considering the difficulties one has to contend with, I have a rather nice garden. It might amuse you to see what one can do in the East if one tries. I should like to talk to you about poor Charmian.*

Then of course he remembered. It gave him quite a turn. He didn't know much anatomy, but he felt that there was a loose string in his heart, dangling there, and someone had just given it a painful tug. The letter went on to say if he would telegraph, a car would be sent for him and would bring him back next day. Convers got up from his chair, went into the room and wrote out a telegram.

> GREATLY REGRET. ABSOLUTELY IMPOSSIBLE. CONVERS.

Then he came back and proceeded to finish his breakfast.

It was useless to renew an acquaintance that had ceased so many years ago. What was the sense of reviving painful memories and probing old wounds that had long been healed? Blanche must be a middle-aged woman by now. MacArdle? He had forgotten that this was the name of the man she married. He remembered him vaguely, a tall, big-boned solemn Scot; he smiled when he thought how Charmian and he had begged her not to marry him. What young fools they were then! And Charmian was dead.

Of course Blanche had done the wise thing and the right thing. Convers wondered what she looked like now. He wondered if she were as tidy as ever. She was a handsome creature, in those days, with fine eyes and a good profile, and in her bearing, although she could not have been more than twenty-four, something already of the tragedy queen. And what had become of the magnificent contralto? When quite unexpectedly she told them that she was giving up her singing to marry, and was going to the F.M.S. with Andrew, he remembered how Charmian and he had besought her not to throw away the glorious instrument that nature had given her. Charmian had wept. There was nothing so rare as a contralto and at the Conservatoire they held out to Blanche hopes of a splendid career. It was already decided that she should make her début in Gluck's *Orfeo*.

It was strange how it all came back to him, the memory of the past, and poor dead Charmian; he had scarcely thought of her for years. What a success she had had and in what shame ended! Convers read Blanche's letter again.

He remembered the room in a pension that he had lived in—he was learning French for his examination—and the studio that Blanche and Charmian had in a street that led out of the Boulevard Raspail, and the Closerie des Lilas, which was their favourite café. Good heavens, how it all came back! After all, why shouldn't he go to see Blanche? He wondered whether she had kept in touch with Charmian after her marriage. For a moment his thoughts lingered with the dead singer; he gave a sigh.

He had been married for nineteen years, happily married, and he had two sons of whom he was proud; after falling out of love with Charmian he had fallen in love again before falling in love with his wife; but thinking it over calmly it seemed to him that his love for Charmian, wretched as it had made him, was unique.

It had a spiritual quality, a sort of idealistic eagerness, that transfused sensual desire with some beauty not of this earth.

'I've never loved anyone as I loved Charmian,' he pondered, but he was no sooner conscious of the reflection than he felt a warm, grateful glow as he thought of his wife. He smiled affectionately in her absent eyes.

He returned to his room, tore up the telegraph form and wrote another.

> WILL COME TO DINE AND SLEEP TONIGHT. DON'T BOTHER ABOUT CAR. HIRING. TEDDIE.

His diplomatic career had taken him to several of the capitals of Europe, to Brazil and to Guatemala, but he had never been East and he viewed the passing scene with pleasure. But he saw it with the eyes of his head only; at the back of his mind—more vivid than the interminable plantations of rubber trees and the Malay villages, half hidden by fruit trees, that he drove through—he saw the streets of Paris, noisy, crowded and romantic, and Montparnasse, with its prim air of a town in the provinces and yet with an alertness that set the blood racing through one's veins. The world then was thrilling, and you could not walk down those wide, leisurely streets without a feeling that at every turn the unexpected awaited you. Anything was possible. Art was the only thing that mattered and everyone was young.

He had come from his own respectable pension near the Bois de Boulogne to a party given in his studio by an American painter, and there had met Blanche and Charmian. They were both studying singing and presently their host asked them to sing. Blanche sang some old Gaelic songs and her rich contralto gave them a lovely sadness. Then Charmian sang the great soprano aria from the *Marriage of Figaro*. She had a voice of exquisite purity, not very powerful, but of great sweetness. She was a lovely creature, with a very white skin, a little straight nose and large shining eyes. But it was not her voice nor her beauty that most captivated you; it was an urge of youth, a charming gay exuberance that seemed to shed a material radiance. She seemed to pour life forth as a lamp pours light.

Teddie Convers, a good-looking boy then, in Paris for the first time in his life, fell in love with her at first sight. He sought her society and Charmian seemed to like his. But she knew a good many people on the other side of the river and was often engaged; then Blanche and he would dine together and talk about her by the hour. Sometimes the three of them would go to Versailles and once they spent an enchanting holiday in the Forest of Fontainebleau.

Blanche, older than either of them and of a more serious nature, was in charge of Charmian and kept a watchful eye over her, but she liked the clean young Englishman and felt that Charmian was safe with him. Life was free and easy in the Latin Quarter. None of them had any money, but they enjoyed their work, they enjoyed their play and they were happy.

Of course they had their moments of difficulty, Charmian was careless and extravagant, and when she wanted something the last thing that occurred to her was that she could not afford it. One could not imagine what would have happened if Blanche had not been there. She pinched and saved. Charmian laughed at her prudence, but accepted whatever Blanche did for her with light-hearted insouciance. She managed to make it seem the most enchanting thing in the world to be privileged to do her a service.

Once Convers told Blanche that he thought her the most unselfish woman he had ever known.

'Because of what I do for Charmian?' she smiled. 'It makes me so happy. I love her.'

'Why aren't you jealous of me?'

'Because you love her too? Of course you love her. I should hate you if you didn't. We shall never either of us ever meet anyone quite like her. I think she's going to be one of the great singers of the world. I've got a feeling that some day we shall see that to have known her was the great experience of our lives.'

'You know we're not lovers, don't you?'

'Of course.'

He flushed. He was only twenty-two.

'I think I love her too much for that.'

'I know.'

It was a comfort to him that she understood and did not think him ridiculous. Common friends took it for granted that Charmian was his mistress; it did not dawn on them that his passion for her had a quality that made the thought of sexual union an offence. Charmian had a flower-like beauty that he felt it would be desecration to touch; her purity was so exquisite that it gave him a sort of mystical elation. He asked her to marry him and naturally she refused; she wanted her freedom, her career came before everything. He was prepared to wait. He thought he would love her to the end of time, and he had a kind of inner conviction that one day she would consent to be his wife. He adored her as the saint adores his God.

And now leaning back in the car that sped along the straight road, smoking a pipe, a middle-aged man with grey hair and a keen, intelligent face, he remembered that ecstatic feeling with precision and he was glad to have had it. He had gone through many experiences since then, he had loved, married and begotten children, he had made a success of his career and could look forward to greater success to come, but that ecstasy was a possession that neither time nor circumstance could take away from him. It had given him the sense of immortality.

But at last he was obliged to leave Paris. The second language he was taking for his examination was Spanish, and he was to spend some months in Seville. Charmian promised to write to him. They made plans for her and Blanche to come down and see him at Easter.

It was just then, on the eve of his departure, that Blanche broke the surprising news that she was giving up her career as a singer to marry the big Scotsman who had come over to Paris now and then to see her and whom they knew she refused to marry every time he came. She was going with him to Singapore as soon as they were married. It seemed a terrible thing that with such a glorious voice and the possibility of a great future she should bury herself in a distant country. But after all it was her business and the thought of leaving Charmian made Convers too unhappy for him to bother himself very much with other people's concerns.

Charmian saw him off at the station and she wept bitterly at parting from him. It was he who had to console her by telling her that the time would soon pass and they would be reunited. When the train steamed out of the station his heart was heavy and his eyes were blurred with tears. But his love, and the feeling he had that Charmian loved him also, filled him with a deep serenity. His mind busied itself with the future. He did not know that he was never to see her again.

But now they arrived at a considerable town. The chauffeur stopped in front of a large white handsome bungalow and Convers got out. A big stout woman with grey hair came down the steps with outstretched hands.

'Teddie,' she cried.

It was a shock to him. He would never have recognised her and in order to cover his confusion assumed an effusive cordiality.

'How do you do?' he cried. 'By George, I am glad to see you. What a long time!'

She had still the handsome dark eyes that he remembered, but a heavy jowl and bags under the eyes; her skin was coarse and sallow. She wore a sort of tea-gown, in white silk, and on her ample bosom hung three or four strings of coloured beads. She was an old woman.

'Come in,' she said, 'and I'll give you a drink. I want you to see the garden before it gets dark. Andrew is out. I told him not to come in till dinner so that we could have a good talk.'

She led him into a large sitting-room—overcrowded with furniture, among which he noticed a grand piano—and gave him a whisky and soda.

'I can't tell you how thrilled I was when I saw that you were the new Minister to Siam. At first I wasn't quite sure if Sir Edward Convers and Teddie Convers were one and the same. You see I never thought of you but as a dear little boy just down from Oxford. But then I thought it must be the same. Ought I to call you Sir Edward?'

'Only if you want to make me feel a damned fool.'

'You've got on, haven't you? I suppose you'll be an ambassador next.'

'If I'm lucky.'

She took him into the garden, and as gardeners will, talked to him of this that did well in that climate and of the other that wasn't worth the trouble it cost you. It was a small coconut plantation, a square plot of land fenced in, and Blanche had left the regular lines of tall trees undisturbed; she had sown grass and mown it. Along the fences were flowering shrubs; and here and there, seemingly at haphazard, grew clumps of cannas, yellow or flame-coloured. It was exquisitely romantic. Artifice and nature were combined to make a pattern that appealed to the eye and the fancy. The ordered beauty caught the heart with an ecstasy that was almost pain. Then as the light was failing they went and sat on the verandah that overlooked the garden. They made themselves comfortable in long chairs and the boy brought out whisky and soda and a bucket of ice.

'You must be very happy here,' said Convers.

'You're married, aren't you?'

'Yes.'

'Have you any children?'

'Two boys.'

'I envy you that. I never had any children. Will your wife join you in Bangkok?'

'Of course. I'm lost without her. She didn't come with me only because she thought she ought to stay with the boys till they went back to school.'

'I always imagined you'd make a very good husband.'

'It's not difficult to be a good husband when you've got a wife like mine.'

'That sounds as though you were very fond of her.'

'She's a very nice woman.'

'How long have you been married?'

'Nineteen years.'

'I've been married twenty-six.'

'I know.'

She gave a little laugh and he glanced at her, for there was in her laugh a harshness that surprised him. He smiled good-naturedly.

'My dear, I was twenty-two when I was in love with Charmian. You wouldn't have wished me to cherish a hopeless passion for her all my life. I suppose there are people who fall in love only once in their lives, but I think they must be exceptional.'

Blanche turned to him with a smile full of friendliness.

'And yet how indignant you'd have been if anyone had told you that your love for Charmian would die away and in three or four years you'd marry somebody else and live happily ever after!'

'I shouldn't have been indignant, I should just have

thought it ridiculous. Whoever loved that didn't think his love would last for ever?'

'It seems rather sad that a passion that was so pure, so intense, so beautiful, should die and leave not a trace behind.'

'Oh, but that isn't so. My love for Charmian was unique in my life. It is an imperishable and lovely memory. All the bitterness I endured is forgotten and I remember only the happiness it gave me. If it didn't sound so pretentious I'd say it enriched my soul.'

They were silent for a while. They thought of that beautiful, gifted creature who attained such heights and ended so tragically. The world moves quickly nowadays and the singer whom half the world so ecstatically applauded is forgotten. But here and there you can still find elderly people who remember Charmian's début in Brussels.

She had changed her good English name of Pelter to that of Pelletier. She made her first appearance in *Thaïs* and the Belgian public went mad over her. She was young and beautiful, she acted well, and her voice, though not very powerful, had a springtime purity and a sweetness that were enchanting. She was never a great artist, but nature endowed her with wonderful gifts and there was a spontaneity in her singing, a deep sincerity in her acting, that disarmed critical opinion.

The following season saw her début in Paris and her success far surpassed expectation. She was launched on the path of glory. But it is a dangerous path and it cannot be trod too warily. Charmian was weak. She squandered her gifts with a spendthrift's improvidence. She would not listen to the counsels of prudence. She was determined to wrest from life every possibility it afforded. She became notorious for her extravagance, the beauty of her clothes, the splendour of her jewels and the magnificence of her establishment. Rich men were glad to satisfy her whims and she flung their money away with the indifference of a wanton child.

She behaved as though her voice were an instrument that could be treated without concern and as though her radiant beauty were imperishable. Things began to go wrong. Now and then she gave a performance so bad that she was hissed. Once the curtain at the Opéra-Comique had to be lowered because she was too drunk to finish the scene. Her voice lost its silvery tone. She put on weight. The fall was as rapid as had been the ascent.

Although so much money had passed through her hands she was overwhelmed with debts. She fell ill. There was a spectacular sale of her effects. Two or three years more went by and she began to sing in second-rate companies at watering places and seaside resorts. Her voice was but a shadow of what it once had been. She continued to pursue pleasure with the same mad frenzy. She fell upon men who exploited and robbed her.

She sank lower and lower till at last she was glad to get engagements in provincial music halls of a doubtful character where she sold herself to coarse and vulgar men for a hundred francs. Any money she could get hold of she spent on drink and drugs. At last even this means of earning failed her.

She was fished out one morning from the harbour at Toulon with a knife thrust in her back. Her death gave the papers some welcome copy; her past triumphs were recalled and industrious journalists traced the course of her final degradation. The last few months of her life had been passed in sordid squalor. She was forty-three when she died.

Blanche sighed. The night had fallen. The fronds of the coconut trees made a florid pattern against the starry sky and in the garden the fire-flies, swaying deliberately upon the still air, were like the wavering lights of fairy boats that rose and fell on an unquiet, invisible sea. After the heat of the day the coolness was very grateful.

'Did you never see her again after you left Paris?'

'Never. At first I wrote to her every day and now and then she sent me an untidy scrawl in answer.'

'She never came down to Seville after all?'

'No. At the last minute she sent a wire to say she couldn't. I'd been looking forward to it so much, the disappointment shattered me. When I passed through Paris I couldn't find her. She'd left the studio and the concierge didn't know where she'd gone. I went back to London. I met new people, I had new experiences. I was very young.'

'You fell in love with somebody else.'

'Yes.'

'Did you never have the curiosity to go and hear her sing when she was at the height of her fame?'

'No. I didn't want to revive the old dead feeling. After all it would have been madness. I knew then how she was living. I'd loved her too much to be able to suffer the idea of the rich South American who provided all the luxury I'd heard about. I was older then. I didn't think she'd have much use for an obscure clerk in the Foreign Office. I wanted to keep my recollection undisturbed.'

'And you've done that notwithstanding all that happened afterwards?'

'Yes. My love for Charmian was a perfect thing. I shall always be thankful for it.'

Blanche sighed.

'I suppose it never occurred to you to ask yourself why I threw over the career that seemed open to me and sacrificed my ambition to marry a doctor and come out to the Far East. You weren't much interested in me, were you? I was the prim, prudish Scotswoman who was always in the way. You thought me rather absurd because I tidied up and kept accounts and tried not to run into debt. I'll tell you why I married Andrew. I was afraid.'

Convers did not speak. He waited for her to go on.

'We'd known one another all our lives. He'd asked me to marry him a score of times. He was a good fellow, I knew I could trust him, but I wanted to be a great singer, I wanted fame, and I wanted to lead a full and various life. I knew I had a good voice; of course I was a contralto, but voice for voice mine was finer than Charmian's. I was prepared to work like the devil to make the most of it. In my mind's eye I saw vast audiences held spellbound by the wonder of my singing and I heard the thunder of their applause. I know I should have realised my ambition.'

'I think you would.'

'I adored Charmian. I adored her beauty, I adored her careless gaiety. She was everything that I could have wished to be. I knew she was wilful and loved pleasure, but I was convinced there was no harm in her. My character was stronger than hers and I made up my mind to watch over her and guide her. I was as ambitious for her as I was for myself. When she told me there was a chance of her making her début in Brussels I was as excited as she was.

'I couldn't help boasting about it to one of the girls who were studying with us. She sniggered. I thought she was jealous and I was rather short with her. She lost her temper. She said that if Charmian got this engagement it would be for her looks rather than for her voice. I snapped back at her and we had a row. She said Charmian had been to bed with half the students at the Conservatoire; I don't know what she didn't say. Of course I didn't believe a word of it. I went straight to Charmian. I expected her to be as indignant as I was, but she only giggled; I was so taken aback by her attitude that for a moment I was beside myself.

'She didn't seem to realise the awfulness of the stories

that were being told of her. She came up and kissed me and told me not to be an old prude. Then it all came out. She confessed everything, without shame, without reluctance, with a brazen callousness that horrified me. She simply could not understand my horror. I cried with shame for her and it only made her laugh. She mocked me. She sneered at my coldness; she said I would never become a great singer until I let myself go. She called me a constipated virgin.

'I thought I knew every thought in her heart and now I realised there was an abyss between us. She said she wasn't prepared to wait for her chance, she wanted it now; a rich Belgian had promised to get her into the Opera at Brussels and she wasn't going to be such a fool as to miss the opportunity. Of course she would have to pay him his price. Well, what of it? She asked me if I thought one got anything without paying for it. I had a sudden revulsion of feeling for all that world of singers and musicians and impressarios.

'You see, although I was horrified, I saw her standpoint, I was young then and not bad-looking; men now and then had tried to be familiar with me, I wondered whether the time would come when I should go the way she had gone. It was such an easy way. I was frightened. And I was angry that she'd made such a fool of me. I think I had some sort of crazy feeling that by sacrificing everything I cared for I was revenging myself on her. I wired for Andrew and when he came told him that I was ready to marry him.'

Blanche gave a ghostly laugh and turned to Convers.

'You'll hardly believe it, but almost my first thought then was of you. I was as sorry for you as I was for myself. I couldn't bear that this first great love of yours, so pure and ideal, should suffer that awful shock. You were to go in a fortnight. I knew nothing would come of it and I wanted you to believe in her to the end.'

'That was kind of you.'

'Except for you I should have left her at once. On your account we pretended that we were as great friends as ever.'

'You pretended very well.'

'After she'd seen you off she came back to the studio and we parted for ever. My luggage was packed and Andrew was waiting to take me to the station. I was very sad. I loved her still. When I said goodbye to her I couldn't help crying. I know how weak she was. The last thing I said to her was, "Mark my words, it'll end badly"; she smiled and kissed me and answered, "I shall have had my fling."'

But at that moment came the sound of a heavy tread in the sitting-room, a voice called, and Dr. MacArdle thumped out on to the verandah.

'What are you sitting in pitch-darkness for?' he cried in a loud cheerful tone.

He turned on the electric light and Convers, getting out of his long chair to greet his host, found his hand heartily grasped by a big stout man with a great deal of curly white hair and a white beard. With his red cheeks he looked the picture of jovial health. The dour silent Scot that Convers remembered had turned into a chatty old fellow with a pleasant word for everybody. He carried his bedside manner into ordinary life and you felt it was his willing mission to cheer and encourage the ailing.

'Glad to see you, sir,' he cried. 'This is a real treat for my mem. You've worn well, upon my word. We're none of us so young as we used to be. Well, you're no end of a swell now, it appears, and I'm just what I was thirty years ago. Still, we mustn't complain. Dinner's ready, my dear. Would Sir Edward like to wash his hands before the cocktails come in?'

'I don't think you need call him Sir Edward.'

The doctor laughed aloud as though he or she had made a joke.

Presently they sat down to dinner. Andrew talked of Siam and asked Convers questions about the previous posts he had filled. He talked about the Federated Malay States and about rubber. He was well-informed. He liked to hear himself speak. He was obviously a good fellow, competent, jolly, who liked his life and was satisfied with what it had given him. It was plain too that he had the greatest admiration for his wife.

'You shall hear her sing after dinner,' he said. 'Her voice is better than ever.'

'What nonsense you talk, Andrew,' Blanche smiled good-naturedly.

'It's a fact. I'm not a bad doctor, though I say it myself, but I'm known from Penang to Singapore as Mrs MacArdle's husband. She's in demand, I can tell you and if I didn't put my foot down she'd be gallivanting about the country from one year's end to the other. Why, they'll come to hear her from fifty miles around. D'you know she collected over two thousand pounds for the Red Cross during the war?'

They lingered over their coffee and presently Blanche sat down at the piano. She sang that great aria from *Orfeo* which it had once been her ambition to sing at Covent Garden. Her low notes were as magnificent as ever, but the high ones were harsh and strained. She sang two or three more songs. Then Andrew looked at his watch.

'I'm afraid I must leave you. I've got a patient to go and see.' He turned to Convers. 'If I'm not back before you turn in I'll see you in the morning.'

'All right.'

When he had left them Convers asked:

'Do you ever sing those old Scottish songs that you used to sing? D'you remember you sang them the first time I ever saw you?'

'I haven't sung them for years.'

She looked through her music and found the book. She

sat down again at the piano and tentatively began an accompaniment. They were tunes gathered among the peasantry of the Northern Highlands and arranged by a sensitive musician. She sang one and then another. They had the melancholy of primitive music and in that warm silent night these songs of women wailing for their men killed in battle and of maids mourning their faithless lovers had a grave plaintiveness that was deeply moving. They did not seem out of place in that distant country; you felt that this music born amid mists and barren mountains had a subtle relation with the land of palm trees and wide rivers. There was a tragic quality in Blanche's voice that gave them a troubling and enigmatic significance. You listened with a feeling of awe for you knew not what and you seemed carried back to ages long ago.

'Let's go into the garden,' said Blanche suddenly.

She got up from the piano and went out. Convers followed her. The moon had risen and in its light the garden was like a closed garden of a king's palace in the *Arabian Nights*. The coconut trees in their regular lines had a hieratic solemnity. Night-flowering shrubs scented the air with a heavy perfume. With silent steps on the close-cut grass they walked down the central avenue.

'Do you know that Charmian wrote to me two days before she died?' Blanche said suddenly. 'I'd read in the paper of her horrible end and it was a shock to me when I recognised her writing. I'd never had a line from her since we'd parted that evening in Paris after you'd gone to Spain. It was written on a common sheet of paper with the name of some café in Toulon and it was in a flimsy, cheap envelope.'

'Did she know your address?'

'It had been sent to my old home in Scotland. It's a miracle I ever got it.'

'What did she say?'

Blanche stopped and even though it was night he could see that she was frightfully pale.

'It was only one line, with her name at the bottom. *It's been worth it.* That's all.'

'I wonder if it was true.'

'I'm sure it was true. But how strange that she should write to me after all those years and how horrible that I should get it when she was dead. It was like a voice from the dead. It's haunted me ever since.'

'Yes, it is strange.'

'I'm glad that she never forgot me entirely. I wonder what was in her mind.'

'Perhaps she was drunk.'

'I don't believe it. I believe that she had a presentiment that her end was near. I think she looked back on her life and she thought of her triumph and her fame, and the love she'd inspired and the love she'd suffered, and her fall, her shame, her disgrace, and she was glad to have lived it all. And she wanted me to know, because I'd run away, because I'd buried my talent in the ground, because I'd made nothing of the gift God have given me and had crept shivering with fear into a hole where I could be safe.'

'I don't see how you can say that you buried your talent in the ground. You've given pleasure to a great many people. And what about those two thousand pounds that Andrew says you made for the Red Cross?'

'What is that?' she cried with a bitterness that startled Convers. 'I've sung cheap ballads to people who could appreciate nothing else. I've sung in drawing-rooms after dinner to people who wanted to play bridge. D'you remember what my voice was like twenty-four years ago?'

'But you've been happy here. You've had the love of your husband.'

'Oh, yes, I've been happy. I'm fond of Andrew. I've

been comfortable. My life has been a sober jog-trot. Dull, mediocre, aimless. And that brief note of Charmian's asks me a question all the time. It asks me: Can you say as much, can *you* say it's been worth it? And the answer is No. I made a mistake. I oughtn't to have hesitated at the risk. I was a coward to throw my chance away. And now it's too late. I'm almost an old woman and life has given me nothing. By my own fault. Oh, I know all about those years of degeneration, but even they were life; she *lived* and I've existed; when I look back on her life with its glory and its shame I know it was worth it. In my respectability, in my security, I envy her.'

'Even when you think of her pitiful, shameful end?'

'Even then. Do you remember what Elizabeth said about Mary Stuart? "The Queen of Scots hath a bonny bairn and I am but a barren stock." I look back on *my* life and see nothing but the waste of a great opportunity. At the Day of Judgement, if there is one, it would not be so strange if Charmian found more mercy than I. Oh, the bitterness of those words: too late!'

A sob broke from her and he knew she was weeping. He was deeply moved, but he was silent for he knew no words of consolation. What was there for him to say that would give her back the lost years? She turned to him suddenly and held out her hand.

'Good night. I'm sorry to have made a nuisance of myself. I won't see you in the morning. Goodbye.'

Her voice was strangled with her tears. She touched his hand and walked towards the house. When she came to the verandah the light fell on her and she climbed the steps, a large heavy woman in her ample draperies, with the weariness of one who has lost hope.

Next day, on his return to Penang, Convers heard that the line was repaired and in the evening he started for Bangkok. During the journey he thought much of Blanche and Charmian. He was a man of intelligence and he had some knowledge of the world. He smiled when he thought of himself, whom Blanche had looked upon as an absurd and callow youth, now giving her good advice. During a halt of the train he wrote a letter to her. He reminded her how ephemeral was the glory of the stage and how heart-rending its disappointments. He tried to make her see that there was beauty also in the normal life of ordinary people. Was it not Marcus Aurelius who had said that our life was what our thoughts made it? He said a number of wise and sensible things and he ended up with these words:

> *My dear, don't think me unsympathetic when I tell you that regret is meaningless. You couldn't have done anything but what you did. You think you could have acted differently because you've forgotten what sort of a woman you were then. Let's come down to brass tacks: now, twenty-five years later, you wished you had consented when some man wanted to become your lover, you've forgotten that then the mere thought of it filled you with physical repulsion.*
>
> *It wasn't only your mind that kept you pure, it was your nerves. The virtuous woman deceives herself when she thinks she could have been a light one if she had wished. They say every woman is a rake at heart. Nonsense. You resisted the temptations to which poor Charmian succumbed not because you were any better than she, don't think that for a minute; you resisted because there was no temptation. Only a harlot can be a harlot.*

He posted the letter at a wayside station. The reply

reached him a few day later. It was from Andrew MacArdle. It ran as follows:

Your letter came too late. Blanche killed herself last night.

Before the Party

Mrs. Skinner liked to be in good time. She was already dressed, in black silk as befitted her age and the mourning she wore for her son-in-law, and now she put on her toque. She was a little uncertain about it, since the egrets' feathers which adorned it might very well arouse in some of the friends she would certainly meet at the party acid expostulations; and of course it was shocking to kill those beautiful white birds, in the mating season too, for the sake of their feathers; but there they were, so pretty and stylish, and it would have been silly to refuse them, and it would have hurt her son-in-law's feelings. He had brought them all the way from Borneo and he expected her to be so pleased with them. Kathleen had made herself rather unpleasant about them, she must wish she hadn't now, after what had happened, but Kathleen had never really liked Harold. Mrs. Skinner, standing at her dressing-table, placed the toque on her head, it was after all the only nice hat she had, and put in a pin with a large jet knob. If anybody spoke to her about the ospreys she had her answer.

'I know it's dreadful,' she would say, 'and I wouldn't dream of buying them, but my poor son-in-law brought them back the last time he was home on leave.'

That would explain her possession of them and excuse their use. Everyone had been very kind. Mrs. Skinner took a clean handkerchief from a drawer and sprinkled a little *Eau de Cologne* on it. She never used scent, and she had always thought it rather fast, but *Eau de Cologne* was so refreshing. She was very nearly ready now, and her eyes wandered out of the window behind her looking-glass. Canon Heywood had a beautiful day for his garden-party. It was warm and the sky was blue; the trees had not yet lost the fresh green of the spring. She smiled as she saw her little granddaughter in the strip of garden behind the house busily raking her very own flower-bed. Mrs. Skinner wished Joan were not quite so pale, it was a mistake to have kept her so long in the tropics; and she was so grave for her age, you never saw her run about; she played quiet games of her own invention and watered her garden. Mrs. Skinner gave the front of her dress a little pat, took up her gloves, and went down-stairs.

Kathleen was at the writing-table in the window busy with lists she was making, for she was honorary secretary of the Ladies' Golf Club, and when there were competitions had a good deal to do. But she too was ready for the party.

'I see you've put on your jumper after all,' said Mrs. Skinner.

They had discussed at luncheon whether Kathleen should wear her jumper or her black chiffon. The jumper was black and white, and Kathleen thought it rather smart, but it was hardly mourning. Millicent, however, was in favour of it.

'There's no reason why we should all look as if we'd just come from a funeral,' she said. 'Harold's been dead eight months.'

To Mrs. Skinner it seemed rather unfeeling to talk like that. Millicent was strange since her return from Borneo.

'You're not going to leave off your weeds yet, darling?' she asked.

Millicent did not give a direct answer.

'People don't wear mourning in the way they used,' she said. She paused a little and when she went on there was a tone in her voice which Mrs. Skinner thought quite peculiar. It was plain that Kathleen noticed it too, for she gave her sister a curious look. 'I'm sure Harold wouldn't wish me to wear mourning for him indefinitely.'

'I dressed early because I wanted to say something to Millicent,' said Kathleen in reply to her mother's observation.

'Oh?'

Kathleen did not explain. But she put her lists aside and with knitted brows read for the second time a letter from a lady who complained that the committee had most unfairly marked down her handicap from twenty-four to eighteen. It requires a good deal of tact to be Honorary Secretary to a ladies' golf club. Mrs. Skinner began to put on her new gloves. The sun-blinds kept the room cool and dark. She looked at the great wooden hornbill, gaily painted, which Harold had left in her safekeeping; and it seemed a little odd and barbaric to her, but he had set much store on it. It had some religious significance and Canon Heywood had been greatly struck by it. On the wall, over the sofa, were Malay weapons, she forgot what they were called, and here and there on occasional tables pieces of silver and brass which Harold at various times had sent to them. She had liked Harold and involuntarily her eyes sought his photograph which stood on the piano with photographs of her two daughters, her grandchild, her sister and her sister's son.

'Why, Kathleen, where's Harold's photograph?' she asked.

Kathleen looked round. It no longer stood in its place.

'Someone's taken it away,' said Kathleen.

Surprised and puzzled, she got up and went over to the piano. The photographs had been rearranged so that no gap should show.

'Perhaps Millicent wanted to have it in her bedroom,' said Mrs. Skinner.

'I should have noticed it. Besides, Millicent has several photographs of Harold. She keeps them locked up.'

Mrs. Skinner had thought it very peculiar that her daughter should have no photographs of Harold in her room. Indeed she had spoken of it once, but Millicent had made no reply. Millicent had been strangely silent since she came back from Borneo, and had not encouraged the sympathy Mrs. Skinner would have been so willing to show her. She seemed unwilling to speak of her great loss. Sorrow took people in different ways. Her husband had said the best thing was to leave her alone. The thought of him turned her ideas to the party they were going to.

'Father asked if I thought he ought to wear a top-hat,' she said. 'I said I thought it was just as well to be on the safe side.'

It was going to be quite a grand affair. They were having ices, strawberry and vanilla, from Boddy, the confectioner, but the Heywoods were making the iced coffee at home. Everyone would be there. They had been asked to meet the Bishop of Hong-Kong, who was staying with the Canon, an old college friend of his, and he was going to speak on the Chinese missions. Mrs. Skinner, whose daughter had lived in the East for eight years and whose son-in-law had been Resident of a district in Borneo, was in a flutter of interest. Naturally it meant more to her than to people who had never had anything to do with the Colonies and that sort of thing.

'What can they know of England who only England know?' as Mr. Skinner said.

He came into the room at that moment. He was a lawyer, as his father had been before him, and he had offices in Lincoln's Inn Fields. He went up to London every morning and came down every evening. He was only able to accompany his wife and daughters to the Canon's garden-party, because the Canon had very wisely chosen a Saturday to have it on. Mr. Skinner looked very well in his tail-coat and pepper-and-salt trousers. He was not exactly dressy, but he was neat. He looked like a respectable family solicitor, which indeed he was; his firm never touched work that was not perfectly above board, and if a client went to him with some trouble that was not quite nice, Mr. Skinner would look grave.

'I don't think this is the sort of case that we very much care to undertake,' he said. 'I think you'd do better to go elsewhere.'

He drew towards him his writing-block and scribbled a name and address on it. He tore off a sheet of paper and handed it to his client.

'If I were you I think I would go and see these people. If you mention my name I believe they'll do anything they can for you.'

Mr. Skinner was clean-shaven and very bald. His pale lips were tight and thin, but his blue eyes were shy. He had no colour in his cheeks and his face was much lined.

'I see you've put on your new trousers,' said Mrs. Skinner.

'I thought it would be a good opportunity,' he answered. 'I was wondering if I should wear a buttonhole.'

'I wouldn't, father,' said Kathleen. 'I don't think it's awfully good form.'

'A lot of people will be wearing them,' said Mrs. Skinner.

'Only clerks and people like that,' said Kathleen. 'The Heywoods have had to ask everybody, you know. And besides, we are in mourning.'

'I wonder if there'll be a collection after the Bishop's address,' said Mr. Skinner.

'I should hardly think so,' said Mrs. Skinner.

'I think it would be rather bad form,' agreed Kathleen.

'It's as well to be on the safe side,' said Mr. Skinner. 'I'll give for all of us. I was wondering if ten shillings would be enough or if I must give a pound.'

'If you give anything I think you ought to give a pound, father,' said Kathleen.

'I'll see when the time comes. I don't want to give less than anyone else, but on the other hand I see no reason to give more than I need.'

Kathleen put away her papers in the drawer of the writing-table and stood up. She looked at her wrist-watch.

'Is Millicent ready?' asked Mrs. Skinner.

'There's plenty of time. We're only asked at four, and I don't think we ought to arrive much before half-past. I told Davis to bring the car round at four-fifteen.'

Generally Kathleen drove the car, but on grand occasions like this Davis, who was the gardener, put on his uniform and acted as chauffeur. It looked better when you drove up, and naturally Kathleen didn't much want to drive herself when she was wearing her new jumper. The sight of her mother forcing her fingers one by one into her new gloves reminded her that she must put on her own. She smelt them to see if any odour of the cleaning still clung to them. It was very slight. She didn't believe anyone would notice.

At last the door opened and Millicent came in. She wore her widow's weeds. Mrs. Skinner never could get used to them, but of course she knew that Millicent must wear them for a year. It was a pity they didn't suit her; they suited some people. She had tried on Millicent's bonnet once, with its white band and long veil, and thought she looked very well in it. Of course she hoped dear Alfred would survive her, but if he didn't she would never go out of weeds. Queen Victoria never had. It was different for Millicent; Millicent was a much younger woman; she was only thirty-six; it was very sad to be a widow at thirty-six. And there wasn't much chance of her marrying again. Kathleen wasn't very likely to marry now, she was thirty-five; last time Millicent and

Harold had come home she had suggested that they should have Kathleen to stay with them; Harold had seemed willing enough, but Millicent said it wouldn't do. Mrs. Skinner didn't know why not. It would give her a chance. Of course they didn't want to get rid of her, but a girl ought to marry, and somehow all the men they knew at home were married already. Millicent said the climate was trying. It was true she was a bad colour. No one would think now that Millicent had been the prettier of the two. Kathleen had fined down as she grew older, of course some people said she was too thin, but now that she had cut her hair, with her cheeks red from playing golf in all weathers, Mrs. Skinner thought her quite pretty. No one could say that of poor Millicent; she had lost her figure completely; she had never been tall, and now that she had filled out she looked stocky. She was a good deal too fat; Mrs. Skinner supposed it was due to the tropical heat that prevented her from taking exercise. Her skin was sallow and muddy; and her blue eyes, which had been her best feature, had gone quite pale.

'She ought to do something about her neck,' Mrs. Skinner reflected. 'She's becoming dreadfully jowly.'

She had spoken of it once or twice to her husband. He remarked that Millicent wasn't as young as she was; that might be, but she needn't let herself go altogether. Mrs. Skinner made up her mind to talk to her daughter seriously, but of course she must respect her grief, and she would wait till the year was up. She was just as glad to have this reason to put off a conversation the thought of which made her slightly nervous. For Millicent was certainly changed. There was something sullen in her face which made her mother not quite at home with her. Mrs. Skinner liked to say aloud all the thoughts that passed through her head, but Millicent when you made a remark (just to say something, you know) had an awkward habit of not answering, so that you wondered whether she had heard. Sometimes Mrs. Skinner found it so irritating, that not to be quite sharp with Millicent she had to remind herself that poor Harold had only been dead eight months.

The light from the window fell on the widow's heavy face as she advanced silently, but Kathleen stood with her back to it. She watched her sister for a moment.

'Millicent, there's something I want to say to you,' she said. 'I was playing golf with Gladys Heywood this morning?'

'Did you beat her?' asked Millicent.

Gladys Heywood was the Canon's only unmarried daughter.

'She told me something about you which I think you ought to know.'

Millicent's eyes passed beyond her sister to the little girl watering flowers in the garden.

'Have you told Annie to give Joan her tea in the kitchen, mother?' she said.

'Yes, she'll have it when the servants have theirs.'

Kathleen looked at her sister coolly.

'The Bishop spent two or three days at Singapore on his way home,' she went on. 'He's very fond of travelling. He's been to Borneo, and he knows a good many of the people that you know.'

'He'll be interested to see you, dear,' said Mrs. Skinner. 'Did he know poor Harold?'

'Yes, he met him at Kuala Solor. He remembers him very well. He says he was shocked to hear of his death.'

Millicent sat down and began to put on her black gloves. It seemed strange to Mrs. Skinner that she received these remarks with complete silence.

'Oh, Millicent,' she said, 'Harold's photo has disappeared. Have you taken it?'

'Yes, I put it away.'

'I should have thought you'd like to have it out.'

Once more Millicent said nothing. It really was an exasperating habit.

Kathleen turned slightly in order to face her sister.

'Millicent, why did you tell us that Harold died of fever?'

The widow made no gesture, she looked at Kathleen with steady eyes, but her sallow skin darkened with a flush. She did not reply.

'What *do* you mean, Kathleen?' asked Mr. Skinner, with surprise.

'The Bishop says that Harold committed suicide.'

Mrs. Skinner gave a startled cry, but her husband put out a deprecating hand.

'Is it true, Millicent?'

'It is.'

'But why didn't you tell us?'

Millicent paused for an instant. She fingered idly a piece of Brunei brass which stood on the table by her side. That too had been a present from Harold.

'I thought it better for Joan that her father should be thought to have died of fever. I didn't want her to know anything about it.'

'You've put us in an awfully awkward position,' said Kathleen, frowning a little. 'Gladys Heywood said she thought it rather nasty of me not to have told her the truth. I had the greatest difficulty in getting her to believe that I knew absolutely nothing about it. She said her father was rather put out. He says, after all the years we've known one another, and considering that he married you, and the terms we've been on, and all that, he does think we might have had confidence in him. And at all events, if we didn't want to tell him the truth we needn't have told him a lie.'

'I must say I sympathise with him there,' said Mr. Skinner, acidly.

'Of course I told Gladys that we weren't to blame. We only told them what you told us.'

'I hope it didn't put you off your game,' said Millicent.

'Really, my dear, I think that is a most improper observation,' exclaimed her father.

He rose from his chair, walked over to the empty fireplace, and from force of habit stood in front of it with parted coat-tails.

'It was my business,' said Millicent, 'and if I chose to keep it to myself I didn't see why I shouldn't.'

'It doesn't look as if you had any affection for your mother if you didn't even tell her,' said Mrs. Skinner.

Millicent shrugged her shoulders.

'You might have known it was bound to come out,' said Kathleen.

'Why? I didn't expect that two gossiping old parsons would have nothing else to talk about than me.'

'When the Bishop said he'd been to Borneo it's only natural that the Heywoods should ask him if he knew you and Harold.'

'And that's neither here nor there,' said Mr. Skinner. 'I think you should certainly have told us the truth, and we could have decided what was the best thing to do. As a solicitor I can tell you that in the long run it only makes things worse if you attempt to hide them.'

'Poor Harold,' said Mrs. Skinner, and the tears began to trickle down her raddled cheeks. 'It seems dreadful. He was always a good son-in-law to me. Whatever induced him to do such a dreadful thing?'

'The climate.'

'I think you'd better give us all the facts, Millicent,' said her father.

'Kathleen will tell you.'

Kathleen hesitated. What she had to say really was rather dreadful. It seemed terrible that such things should happen to a family like theirs.

'The Bishop says he cut his throat.'

Mrs. Skinner gasped and she went impulsively up to her bereaved daughter. She wanted to fold her in her arms.

'My poor child,' she sobbed.

But Millicent withdrew herself.

'Please don't fuss me, mother. I really can't stand being mauled about.'

'Really, Millicent,' said Mr. Skinner, with a frown.

He did not think she was behaving very nicely.

Mrs. Skinner dabbed her eyes carefully with her handkerchief and with a sigh and a little shake of the head returned to her chair. Kathleen fidgetted with the long chain she wore round her neck.

'It does seem rather absurd that I should have to be told the details of my brother-in-law's death by a friend. It makes us all look such fools. The Bishop wants very much to see you, Millicent; he wants to tell you how much he feels for you.' She paused, but Millicent did not speak. 'He says that Millicent had been away with Joan and when she came back she found poor Harold lying dead on his bed.'

'It must have been a great shock,' said Mr. Skinner.

Mrs. Skinner began to cry again, but Kathleen put her hand gently on her shoulder.

'Don't cry, mother,' she said. 'It'll make your eyes red and people will think it so funny.'

They were all silent while Mrs. Skinner, drying her eyes, made a successful effort to control herself. It seemed very strange to her that at this very moment she should be wearing in her toque the ospreys that poor Harold had given her.

'There's something else I ought to tell you,' said Kathleen.

Millicent looked at her sister again, without haste, and her eyes were steady, but watchful. She had the look of a person who is waiting for a sound which he is afraid of missing.

'I don't want to say anything to wound you, dear,' Kathleen went on, 'but there's something else and I think you ought to know it. The Bishop says that Harold drank.'

'Oh, my dear, how dreadful!' cried Mrs. Skinner. 'What a shocking thing to say. Did Gladys Heywood tell you? What did you say?'

'I said it was entirely untrue.'

'This is what comes of making secrets of things,' said Mr. Skinner, irritably. 'It's always the same. If you try and hush a thing up all sorts of rumours get about which are ten times worse than the truth.'

'They told the Bishop in Singapore that Harold had killed himself while he was suffering from *delirium tremens*. I think for all our sakes you ought to deny that, Millicent.'

'It's such a dreadful thing to have said about anyone who's dead,' said Mrs. Skinner. 'And it'll be so bad for Joan when she grows up.'

'But what is the foundation of this story, Millicent?' asked her father. 'Harold was always very abstemious.'

'Here,' said the widow.

'Did he drink?'

'Like a fish.'

The answer was so unexpected, and the tone so sardonic, that all three of them were startled.

'Millicent, how can you talk like that of your husband when he's dead?' cried her mother, clasping her neatly gloved hands. 'I can't understand you. You've been so strange since you came back. I could never have believed that a girl of mine could take her husband's death like that.'

'Never mind about that, mother,' said Mr. Skinner. 'We can go into all that later.'

He walked to the window and looked out at the sunny little garden, and then walked back into the room. He took his pince-nez out of his pocket and, though he had no intention of putting them on, wiped them with his handkerchief. Millicent looked at him and in her eyes, unmistakably, was a look of irony which was quite cynical. Mr. Skinner was vexed. He had finished his week's work and he was a free man till Monday morning. Though he had told his wife that this garden-party was a great nuisance and he would much sooner have tea quietly in his own garden, he had been looking forward to it. He did not care very much about Chinese missions, but it would be interesting to meet the Bishop. And now this! It was not the kind of thing he cared to be mixed up in; it was most unpleasant to be told on a sudden that his son-in-law was a drunkard and a suicide. Millicent was thoughtfully smoothing her white cuffs. Her coolness irritated him; but instead of addressing her he spoke to his younger daughter.

'Why don't you sit down, Kathleen? Surely there are plenty of chairs in the room.'

Kathleen drew forward a chair and without a word seated herself. Mr. Skinner stopped in front of Millicent and faced her.

'Of course I see why you told us Harold had died of fever. I think it was a mistake, because that sort of thing is bound to come out sooner or later. I don't know how far what the Bishop has told the Heywoods coincides with the facts, but if you will take my advice you will tell us everything as circumstantially as you can, then we can see. We can't hope that it will go no further now that Canon Heywood and Gladys know. In a place like this people are bound to talk. It will make it easier for all of us if we at all events know the exact truth.'

Mrs. Skinner and Kathleen thought he put the matter very well. They waited for Millicent's reply. She had listened with an impassive face; that sudden flush had disappeared and it was once more, as usual, pasty and sallow.

'I don't think you'll much like the truth if I tell it you,' she said.

'You must know that you can count on our sympathy and understanding,' said Kathleen gravely.

Millicent gave her a glance and the shadow of a smile flickered across her set mouth. She looked slowly at the three of them. Mrs. Skinner had an uneasy impression that she looked at them as though they were mannequins at a dressmaker's. She seemed to live in a different world from theirs and to have no connection with them.

'You know, I wasn't in love with Harold when I married him,' she said reflectively.

Mrs. Skinner was on the point of making an exclamation when a rapid gesture of her husband, barely indicated, but after so many years of married life perfectly significant, stopped her. Millicent went on. She spoke with a level voice, slowly, and there was little change of expression in her tone.

'I was twenty-seven, and no one else seemed to want to marry me. It's true he was forty-four, and it seemed rather old, but he had a very good position, hadn't he? I wasn't likely to get a better chance.'

Mrs. Skinner felt inclined to cry again, but she remembered the party.

'Of course I see now why you took his photograph away,' she said dolefully.

'Don't, mother,' exclaimed Kathleen.

It had been taken when he was engaged to Millicent and was a very good photograph of Harold. Mrs. Skinner had always thought him quite a fine man. He was heavily built, tall and perhaps a little too fat, but he held himself well, and his presence was imposing. He was inclined to be bald, even then, but men did go bald very early nowadays, and he said that topees, sun-helmets, you know, were very bad for the hair. He had a small dark moustache, and his face was deeply burned by the sun. Of course his best feature was his eyes; they were brown and large, like Joan's. His conversation was interesting. Kathleen said he was pompous, but Mrs. Skinner didn't think him so, she didn't mind it if a man laid down the law; and when she saw, as she very soon did, that he was attracted by Millicent she began to like him very much. He was always very attentive to Mrs. Skinner, and she listened as though she were really interested when he spoke of his district, and told her of the big game he had killed. Kathleen said he had a pretty good opinion of himself, but Mrs. Skinner came of a generation which accepted without question the good opinion that men had of themselves. Millicent saw very soon which way the wind blew, and though she said nothing to her mother, her mother knew that if Harold asked her she was going to accept him.

Harold was staying with some people who had been thirty years in Borneo and they spoke well of the country. There was no reason why a woman shouldn't live there comfortably; of course the children had to come home when they were seven; but Mrs. Skinner thought it unnecessary to trouble about that yet. She asked Harold to dine, and she told him they were always in to tea. He seemed to be at a loose end, and when his visit to his old friends was drawing to a close, she told him they would be very much pleased if he would come and spend a fortnight with them. It was towards the end of this that Harold and Millicent became engaged. They had a very pretty wedding, they went to Venice for their honeymoon, and then they started for the East. Millicent wrote from various ports at which the ship touched. She seemed happy.

'People were very nice to me at Kuala Solor,' she said.

Kuala Solor was the chief town of the state of Sembulu. 'We stayed with the Resident and everyone asked us to dinner. Once or twice I heard men ask Harold to have a drink, but he refused; he said he had turned over a new leaf now he was a married man. I didn't know why they laughed. Mrs. Gray, the Resident's wife, told me they were all so glad Harold was married. She said it was dreadfully lonely for a bachelor on one of the outstations. When we left Kuala Solor Mrs. Gray said good-bye to me so funnily that I was quite surprised. It was as if she was solemnly putting Harold in my charge.'

They listened to her in silence. Kathleen never took her eyes off her sister's impassive face; but Mr. Skinner stared straight in front of him at the Malay arms, krises and parangs, which hung on the wall above the sofa on which his wife sat.

'It wasn't till I went back to Kuala Solor a year and a half later, that I found out why their manner had seemed so odd.' Millicent gave a queer little sound like the echo of a scornful laugh. 'I knew then a good deal that I hadn't known before. Harold came to England that time in order to marry. He didn't much mind who it was. Do you remember how we spread ourselves out to catch him, mother? We needn't have taken so much trouble.'

'I don't know what you mean, Millicent,' said Mrs. Skinner, not without acerbity, for the insinuation of scheming did not please her. 'I saw he was attracted by you.'

Millicent shrugged her heavy shoulders.

'He was a confirmed drunkard. He used to go to bed every night with a bottle of whisky and empty it before morning. The Chief Secretary told him he'd have to resign unless he stopped drinking. He said he'd give him one more chance. He could take his leave then and go to England. He advised him to marry so that when he got back he'd have someone to look after him. Harold married me because he wanted a keeper. They took bets in Kuala Solor on how long I'd make him stay sober.'

'But he was in love with you,' Mrs. Skinner interrupted. 'You don't know how he used to speak to me about you, and at that time you're speaking of, when you went to Kuala Solor to have Joan, he wrote me such a charming letter about you.'

Millicent looked at her mother again and a deep colour dyed her sallow skin. Her hands, lying on her lap, began to tremble a little. She thought of those first months of her married life. The Government launch took them to the mouth of the river, and they spent the night at the bungalow which Harold said jokingly was their seaside residence. Next day they went up stream in a prahu. From the novels she had read she expected the rivers of Borneo to be dark and strangely sinister, but the sky was blue, dappled with little white clouds, and the green of the mangroves and the nipahs, washed by the flowing water, glistened in the sun. On each side stretched the pathless jungle, and in the distance, silhouetted against the sky, was the rugged outline of a mountain. The air in the early morning was fresh and buoyant. She seemed to enter upon a friendly, fertile land, and she had a sense of spacious freedom. They watched the banks for monkeys sitting on the branches of the tangled trees, and once Harold pointed out something that looked like a log and said it was a crocodile. The Assistant Resident, in ducks and a topee, was at the landing-stage to meet them, and a dozen trim little soldiers were lined up to do them honour. The Assistant Resident was introduced to her. His name was Simpson.

'By Jove, sir,' he said to Harold, 'I'm glad to see you back. It's been deuced lonely without you.'

The Resident's bungalow, surrounded by a garden in which grew wildly all manner of gay flowers, stood on the top of a low hill. It was a trifle shabby and the furniture was sparse, but the rooms were cool and of generous size.

'The kampong is down there,' said Harold, pointing.

Her eyes followed his gesture, and from among the coconut trees rose the beating of a gong. It gave her a queer little sensation in the heart.

Though she had nothing much to do the days passed easily enough. At dawn a boy brought them their tea and they lounged about the verandah, enjoying the fragrance of the morning (Harold in a singlet and a sarong, she in a dressing-gown) till it was time to dress for breakfast. Then Harold went to his office and she spent an hour or two learning Malay. After tiffin he went back to his office while she slept. A cup of tea revived them both, and they went for a walk or played golf on the nine-hole links which Harold had made on a level piece of cleared jungle below the bungalow. Night fell at six and Mr. Simpson came along to have a drink. They chatted till their late dinner hour, and sometimes Harold and Mr. Simpson played chess. The balmy evenings were enchanting. The fireflies turned the bushes just below the verandah into coldly-sparkling, tremulous beacons, and flowering trees scented the air with sweet odours. After dinner they read the papers which had left London six weeks before and presently went to bed. Millicent enjoyed being a married woman, with a house of her own, and she was pleased with the native servants, in their gay sarongs, who went about the bungalow, with bare feet, silent but friendly. It gave her a pleasant sense of importance to be the wife of the Resident. Harold impressed her by the fluency with which he spoke the language, by his air of command, and by his dignity. She went into the court-house now and then to hear him try cases. The multifariousness of his duties and the competent way in which he performed them aroused her respect. Mr. Simpson told her that Harold understood the natives as well as any man in the country. He had the combination of firmness, tact and good humour, which was essential in dealing with that timid, revengeful and suspicious race. Millicent began to feel a certain admiration for her husband.

They had been married nearly a year when two English naturalists came to stay with them for a few days on their way to the interior. They brought a pressing recommendation from the Governor, and Harold said he wanted to do them proud. Their arrival was an agreeable change. Millicent asked Mr. Simpson to dinner (he lived at the Fort and only dined with them on Sunday nights) and after dinner the men sat down to play bridge. Millicent left them presently and went to bed, but they were so noisy that for some time she could not get to sleep. She did not know at what hour she was awakened by Harold staggering into the room. She kept silent. He made up his mind to have a bath before getting into bed; the bath-house was just below their room, and he went down the steps that led to it. Apparently he slipped, for there was a great clatter, and he began to swear. Then he was violently sick. She heard him sluice the buckets of water over himself and in a little while, walking very cautiously this time, he crawled up the stairs and slipped into bed. Millicent pretended to be asleep. She was disgusted. Harold was drunk. She made up her mind to speak about it in the morning. What would the naturalists think of him? But in the morning Harold was so dignified that she hadn't quite the determination to refer to the matter. At eight Harold and she, with their two guests, sat down to breakfast. Harold looked round the table.

'Porridge,' he said. 'Millicent, your guests might manage a little Worcester Sauce for breakfast, but I don't think they'll much fancy anything else. Personally I shall content myself with a whisky and soda.'

The naturalists laughed, but shamefacedly.

'Your husband's a terror,' said one of them.

'I should not think I had properly performed the duties of hospitality if I sent you sober to bed on the first night of your visit,' said Harold, with his round, stately way of putting things.

Millicent, smiling acidly, was relieved to think that her guests had been as drunk as her husband. The next evening she sat up with them and the party broke up at a reasonable hour. But she was glad when the strangers went on with their journey. Their life resumed its placid course. Some months later Harold went on a tour of inspection of his district and came back with a bad attack of malaria. This was the first time she had seen the disease of which she had heard so much, and when he recovered it did not seem strange to her that Harold was very shaky. She found his manner peculiar. He would come back from the office and stare at her with glazed eyes; he would stand on the verandah, swaying slightly, but still dignified, and make long harangues about the political situation in England; losing the thread of his discourse, he would look at her with an archness which his natural stateliness made somewhat disconcerting and say:

'Pulls you down dreadfully, this confounded malaria. Ah, little woman, you little know the strain it puts upon a man to be an empire builder.'

She thought that Mr. Simpson began to look worried, and once or twice, when they were alone, he seemed on the point of saying something to her which his shyness at the last moment prevented. The feeling grew so strong that it made her nervous, and one evening when Harold, she knew not why, had remained later than usual at the office she tackled him.

'What have you got to say to me, Mr. Simpson?' she broke out suddenly.

He blushed and hesitated.

'Nothing. What makes you think I have anything in particular to say to you?'

Mr. Simpson was a thin, weedy youth of four and twenty, with a fine head of waving hair which he took great pains to plaster down very flat. His wrists were swollen and scarred with mosquito bites. Millicent looked at him steadily.

'If it's something to do with Harold don't you think it would be kinder to tell me frankly?'

He grew scarlet now. He shuffled uneasily on his rattan chair. She insisted.

'I'm afraid you'll think it awful cheek,' he said at last. 'It's rotten of me to say anything about my chief behind his back. Malaria's a rotten thing, and after one's had a bout of it one feels awfully down and out.'

He hesitated again. The corners of his mouth sagged as if he were going to cry. To Millicent he seemed like a little boy.

'I'll be as silent as the grave,' she said with a smile, trying to conceal her apprehension. 'Do tell me.'

'I think it's a pity your husband keeps a bottle of whisky at the office. He's apt to take a nip more often than he otherwise would.'

Mr. Simpson's voice was hoarse with agitation. Millicent felt a sudden coldness shiver through her. She controlled herself, for she knew that she must not frighten the boy if she were to get out of him all there was to tell. He was unwilling to speak. She pressed him, wheedling, appealing to his sense of duty, and at last she began to cry. Then he told her that Harold had been drunk more or less for the last fortnight, the natives were talking about it, and they said that soon he would be as bad as he had been before his marriage. He had been in the habit of drinking a good deal too much then, but details of that time, notwithstanding all her attempts, Mr. Simpson resolutely declined to give her.

'Do you think he's drinking now?' she asked.

'I don't know.'

Millicent felt herself on a sudden hot with shame and anger. The Fort, as it was called because the rifles and the ammunition were kept there, was also the court-house. It stood opposite the Resident's bungalow in a garden of its own. The sun was just about to set and she did not need a hat. She got up and walked across. She found Harold sitting in the office behind the large hall in which he administered justice. There was a bottle of whisky in front of him. He was smoking cigarettes and talking to three or four Malays who stood in front of him listening with obsequious and at the same time scornful smiles. His face was red.

The natives vanished.

'I came to see what you were doing,' she said.

He rose, for he always treated her with elaborate politeness, and lurched. Feeling himself unsteady he assumed an elaborate stateliness of demeanour.

'Take a seat, my dear, take a seat. I was detained by press of work.'

She looked at him with angry eyes.

'You're drunk,' she said.

He stared at her, his eyes bulging a little, and a haughty look gradually traversed his large and fleshy face.

'I haven't the remotest idea what you mean,' he said.

She had been ready with a flow of wrathful expostulation, but suddenly she burst into tears. She sank into a chair and hid her face. Harold looked at her for an instant, then the tears began to trickle down his own cheeks; he came towards her with outstretched arms and fell heavily on his knees. Sobbing, he clasped her to him.

'Forgive me, forgive me,' he said. 'I promise you it shall not happen again. It was that damned malaria.'

'It's so humiliating,' she moaned.

He wept like a child. There was something very touching

in the self-abasement of that big dignified man. Presently Millicent looked up. His eyes, appealing and contrite, sought hers.

'Will you give me your word of honour that you'll never touch liquor again?'

'Yes, yes. I hate it.'

It was then she told him that she was with child. He was overjoyed.

'That is the one thing I wanted. That'll keep me straight.'

They went back to the bungalow. Harold bathed himself and had a nap. After dinner they talked long and quietly. He admitted that before he married her he had occasionally drunk more than was good for him; in outstations it was easy to fall into bad habits. He agreed to everything that Millicent asked. And during the months before it was necessary for her to go to Kuala Solor for her confinement, Harold was an excellent husband, tender, thoughtful, proud and affectionate; he was irreproachable. A launch came to fetch her, she was to leave him for six weeks, and he promised faithfully to drink nothing during her absence. He put his hands on her shoulders.

'I never break a promise,' he said in his dignified way. 'But even without it, can you imagine that while you are going through so much, I should do anything to increase your troubles?'

Joan was born. Millicent stayed at the Resident's and Mrs. Gray, his wife, a kindly creature of middle age, was very good to her. The two women had little to do during the long hours they were alone but to talk, and in course of time Millicent learnt everything there was to know of her husband's alcoholic past. The fact which she found most difficult to reconcile herself to, was that Harold had been told that the only condition upon which he would be allowed to keep his post was that he should bring back a wife. It caused in her a dull feeling of resentment. And when she discovered what a persistent drunkard he had been, she felt vaguely uneasy. She had a horrid fear that during her absence he would not have been able to resist the craving. She went home with her baby and a nurse. She spent a night at the mouth of the river and sent a messenger in a canoe to announce her arrival. She scanned the landing-stage anxiously as the launch approached it. Harold and Mr. Simpson were standing there. The trim little soldiers were lined up. Her heart sank, for Harold was swaying slightly, like a man who seeks to keep his balance on a rolling ship, and she knew he was drunk.

It wasn't a very pleasant home-coming. She had almost forgotten her mother and father and her sister who sat there silently listening to her. Now she roused herself and became once more aware of their presence. All that she spoke of seemed very far away.

'I knew that I hated him then,' she said. 'I could have killed him.'

'Oh, Millicent, don't say that,' cried her mother. 'Don't forget that he's dead, poor man.'

Millicent looked at her mother, and for a moment a scowl darkened her impassive face. Mr. Skinner moved uneasily.

'Go on,' said Kathleen.

'When he found out that I knew all about him he didn't bother very much more. In three months he had another attack of D.T.'s.'

'Why didn't you leave him?' said Kathleen.

'What would have been the good of that? He would have been dismissed from the service in a fortnight. Who was to keep me and Joan? I had to stay. And when he was sober I had nothing to complain of. He wasn't in the least in love with me, but he was fond of me; I hadn't married him because I was in love with him, but because I wanted to be married. I did everything I could to keep the liquor from him; I managed to get Mr. Gray to prevent whisky being sent from Kuala Solor, but he got it from the Chinese. I watched him as a cat watches a mouse. He was too cunning for me. In a little while he had another outbreak. He neglected his duties. I was afraid complaints would be made. We were two days from Kuala Solor and that was our safeguard, but I suppose something was said, for Mr. Gray wrote a private letter of warning to me. I showed it to Harold. He stormed and blustered, but I saw he was frightened, and for two or three months he was quite sober. Then he began again. And so it went on till our leave became due.

'Before we came to stay here I begged and prayed him to be careful. I didn't want any of you to know what sort of a man I had married. All the time he was in England he was all right and before we sailed I warned him. He'd grown to be very fond of Joan, and very proud of her, and she was devoted to him. She always liked him better than she liked me. I asked him if he wanted to have his child grow up, knowing that he was a drunkard, and I found out that at last I'd got a hold on him. The thought terrified him. I told him that *I* wouldn't allow it, and if he ever let Joan see him drunk I'd take her away from him at once. Do you know, he grew quite pale when I said it. I fell on my knees that night and thanked God, because I'd found a way of saving my husband.

'He told me that if I would stand by him he would have another try. We made up our minds to fight the thing together. And he tried so hard. When he felt as though he *must* drink he came to me. You know he was inclined to be rather pompous; with me he was so humble, he was like a child; he depended on me. Perhaps he didn't love me when he married me, but he loved me then, me and Joan. I'd hated him, because of the humiliation, because when he was drunk and tried to be dignified and impressive he was loathsome; but now I got a strange feeling in my heart. It wasn't love, but it was a queer, shy tenderness. He was something more than my husband, he was like a child that I'd carried under my heart for long and weary months. He was so proud of me and you know, I was proud too. His long speeches didn't irritate me any more, and I only thought his stately ways rather funny and charming. At last we won. For two years he never touched a drop. He lost his craving entirely. He was even able to joke about it.

'Mr. Simpson had left us then and we had another young man called Francis.

' "I'm a reformed drunkard you know, Francis," Harold said to him once. "If it hadn't been for my wife I'd have been sacked long ago. I've got the best wife in the world, Francis."

'You don't know what it meant to hear him say that. I felt that all I'd gone through was worth while. I was so happy.'

She was silent. She thought of the broad, yellow and turbid river on whose banks she had lived so long. The egrets, white and gleaming in the tremulous sunset, flew down the stream in a flock, flew low and swift, and scattered. They were like a ripple of snowy notes, sweet and pure and spring-like, which an unseen hand drew forth, a divine arpeggio, from an unseen harp. They fluttered along between the green banks, wrapped in the shadows of evening, like the happy thoughts of a contented mind.

'Then Joan fell ill. For three weeks we were very anxious. There was no doctor nearer than Kuala Solor and we had to put up with the treatment of a native dispenser. When she grew well again I took her down to the mouth of the river in order to give her a breath of sea air. We stayed there a week. It was the first time I had been separated from Harold since I went away to have Joan. There was a fishing village, on piles, not far from us, but really we were quite alone. I thought a great deal about Harold, so tenderly, and all at once I knew that I loved him. I was so glad when the prahu came to fetch us back, because I wanted to tell him. I thought it would mean a good deal to him. I can't tell you how happy I was. As we rowed up stream the headman told me that Mr. Francis had had to go up country to arrest a woman who had murdered her husband. He had been gone a couple of days.

'I was surprised that Harold was not on the landing-stage to meet me; he was always very punctilious about that sort of thing; he used to say that husband and wife should treat one another as politely as they treated acquaintances; and I could not imagine what business had prevented him. I walked up the little hill on which the bungalow stood. The ayah brought Joan behind me. The bungalow was strangely silent. There seemed to be no servants about, and I could not make it out; I wondered if Harold hadn't expected me so soon and was out. I went up the steps. Joan was thirsty and the ayah took her to the servants quarters to give her something to drink. Harold was not in the sitting-room. I called him, but there was no answer. I was disappointed because I should have liked him to be there. I went into our bedroom. Harold wasn't out after all; he was lying on the bed asleep. I was really very much amused, because he always pretended he never slept in the afternoon. He said it was an unnecessary habit that we white people got into. I went up to the bed softly. I thought I would have a joke with him. I opened the mosquito curtains. He was lying on his back, with nothing on but a sarong, and there was an empty whisky bottle by his side. He was drunk.

'It had begun again. All my struggles for so many

years were wasted. My dream was shattered. It was all hopeless. I was seized with rage.'

Millicent's face grew once again darkly red and she clenched the arms of the chair she sat in.

'I took him by the shoulders and shook him with all my might. "You beast," I cried, "you beast." I was so angry I don't know what I did, I don't know what I said. I kept on shaking him. You don't know how loathsome he looked, that large fat man, half naked; he hadn't shaved for days, and his face was bloated and purple. He was breathing heavily. I shouted at him, but he took no notice. I tried to drag him out of bed, but he was too heavy. He lay there like a log. "Open your eyes," I screamed. I shook him again. I hated him. I hated him all the more because for a week I'd loved him with all my heart. He'd let me down. He'd let me down. I wanted to tell him what a filthy beast he was. I could make no impression on him. "You shall open your eyes," I cried. I was determined to make him look at me.'

The widow licked her dry lips. Her breath seemed hurried. She was silent.

'If he was in that state I should have thought it best to have let him go on sleeping,' said Kathleen.

'There was a parang on the wall by the side of the bed. You know how fond Harold was of curios.'

'What's a parang?' said Mrs. Skinner.

'Don't be silly, mother,' he husband replied irritably. 'There's one on the wall immediately behind you.'

He pointed to the Malay sword on which for some reason his eyes had been unconsciously resting. Mrs. Skinner drew quickly into the corner of the sofa, with a little frightened gesture, as though she had been told that a snake lay curled up beside her.

'Suddenly the blood spurted out from Harold's throat. There was a great red gash right across it.'

'Millicent,' cried Kathleen, springing up and almost leaping towards her, 'what in God's name do you mean?'

Mrs. Skinner stood staring at her with wide startled eyes, her mouth open.

'The parang wasn't on the wall any more. It was on the bed. Then Harold opened his eyes. They were just like Joan's.'

'I don't understand,' said Mr. Skinner. 'How could he have committed suicide if he was in the state you describe?'

Kathleen took her sister's arm and shook her angrily.

'Millicent, for God's sake explain.'

Millicent released herself.

'The parang was on the wall, I told you. I don't know what happened. There was all the blood, and Harold opened his eyes. He died almost at once. He never spoke, but he gave a sort of gasp.'

At last Mr. Skinner found his voice.

'But, you wretched woman, it was murder.'

Millicent, her face mottled with red, gave him such a look of scornful hatred that he shrank back. Mrs. Skinner cried out.

'Millicent, you didn't do it, did you?'

Then Millicent did something that made them all feel as though their blood were turned to ice in their veins. She chuckled.

'I don't know who else did,' she said.

'My God,' muttered Mr. Skinner.

Kathleen had been standing bolt upright, with her hands to her heart, as though its beating were intolerable.

'And what happened then?' she said.

'I screamed. I went to the window and flung it open. I called for the ayah. She came across the compound with Joan. "Not Joan," I cried. "Don't let her come." She called the cook and told him to take the child. I cried to her to hurry. And when she came I showed her Harold. "The Tuan's killed himself!" I cried. She gave a scream and ran out of the house.

'No one would come near. They were all frightened out of their wits. I wrote a letter to Mr. Francis, telling him what had happened and asking him to come at once.'

'How do you mean you told him what had happened?'

'I said, on my return from the mouth of the river, I'd found Harold with his throat cut. You know, in the tropics you have to bury people quickly. I got a Chinese coffin, and the soldiers dug a grave behind the Fort. When Mr. Francis came, Harold had been buried for nearly two days. He was only a boy. I could do anything I wanted with him. I told him I'd found the parang in Harold's hand and there was no doubt he'd killed himself in an attack of *delirium tremens*. I showed him the empty bottle. The servants said he'd been drinking hard ever since I left to go to the sea. I told the same story at Kuala Solor. Everyone was very kind to me, and the Government granted me a pension.'

For a little while nobody spoke. At last Mr. Skinner gathered himself together.

'I am a member of the legal profession. I'm a solicitor. I have certain duties. We've always had a most respectable practice. You've put me in a monstrous position.'

He fumbled, searching for the phrases that played at hide and seek in his scattered wits. Millicent looked at him with scorn.

'What are you going to do about it?'

'It was murder, that's what it was; do you think I can possibly connive at it?'

'Don't talk nonsense, father,' said Kathleen sharply. 'You can't give up your own daughter.'

'You've put me in a monstrous position,' he repeated.

Millicent shrugged her shoulders again.

'You made me tell you. And I've borne it long enough by myself. It was time that all of you bore it too.'

At that moment the door was opened by the maid.

'Davis has brought the car round, sir,' she said.

Kathleen had the presence of mind to say something, and the maid withdrew.

'We'd better be starting,' said Millicent.

'I can't go to the party now,' cried Mrs. Skinner, with horror. 'I'm far too upset. How can we face the Heywoods? And the Bishop will want to be introduced to you.'

Millicent made a gesture of indifference. Her eyes held their ironical expression.

'We must go, mother,' said Kathleen. 'It would look so funny if we stayed away.' She turned on Millicent furiously. 'Oh, I think the whole thing is such frightfully bad form.'

Mrs. Skinner looked helplessly at her husband. He went to her and gave her his hand to help her up from the sofa.

'I'm afraid we must go, mother,' he said.

'And me with the ospreys in my toque that Harold gave me with his own hands,' she moaned.

He led her out of the room, Kathleen followed close on their heels, and a step or two behind came Millicent.

'You'll get used to it, you know,' she said quietly. 'At first I thought of it all the time, but now I forget it for two or three days together. It's not as if there was any danger.'

They did not answer. They walked through the hall and out of the front door. The three ladies got into the back of the car and Mr. Skinner seated himself beside the driver. They had no self-starter; it was an old car, and Davis went to the bonnet to crank it up. Mr. Skinner turned round and looked petulantly at Millicent.

'I ought never to have been told,' he said. 'I think it was most selfish of you.'

Davis took his seat and they drove off to the Canon's garden-party.

Mr. Know-all

I was prepared to dislike Max Kelada even before I knew him. The war had just finished and the passenger traffic in the ocean-going liners was heavy. Accommodation was very hard to get and you had to put up with whatever the agents chose to offer you. You could not hope for a cabin to yourself and I was thankful to be given one in which there were only two berths. But when I was told the name of my companion my heart sank. It suggested closed port-holes and the night air rigidly excluded. It was bad enough to share a cabin for fourteen days with anyone (I was going from San Francisco to Yokohama), but I should have looked upon it with less dismay if my fellow-passenger's name had been Smith or Brown.

When I went on board I found Mr. Kelada's luggage already below. I did not like the look of it; there were too many labels on the suitcases, and the wardrobe trunk was too big. He had unpacked his toilet things, and I observed that he was a patron of the excellent Monsieur Coty; for I saw on the washing-stand his scent, his hair-wash and his brilliantine. Mr. Kelada's brushes, ebony with his monogram in gold, would have been all the better for a scrub. I did not at all like Mr. Kelada. I made my way into the smoking-room. I called for a pack of cards and began to play patience. I had scarcely started before a man came up to me and asked me if he was right in thinking my name was so-and-so.

'I am Mr. Kelada,' he added, with a smile that showed a row of flashing teeth, and sat down.

'Oh, yes, we're sharing a cabin, I think.'

'Bit of luck, I call it. You never know who you're going to be put in with. I was jolly glad when I heard you were English. I'm all for us English sticking together when we're abroad, if you understand what I mean.'

I blinked.

'Are you English?' I asked, perhaps tactlessly.

'Rather. You don't think I look like an American, do you? British to the backbone, that's what I am.'

To prove it, Mr. Kelada took out of his pocket a passport and airily waved it under my nose.

King George has many strange subjects. Mr. Kelada was short and of a sturdy build, clean-shaven and dark-skinned, with a fleshy, hooked nose and very large, lustrous and liquid eyes. His long black hair was sleek and curly. He spoke with a fluency in which there was nothing English and his gestures were exuberant. I felt pretty sure that a closer inspection of that British passport would have betrayed the fact that Mr. Kelada was born under a bluer sky than is generally seen in England.

'What will you have?' he asked me.

I looked at him doubtfully. Prohibition was in force and to all appearances the ship was bone-dry. When I am not thirsty I do not know which I dislike more, ginger-ale or lemon-squash. But Mr. Kelada flashed an oriental smile at me.

'Whisky and soda or a dry Martini, you have only to say the word.'

From each of his hip-pockets he fished a flask and laid them on the table before me. I chose the Martini, and calling the steward he ordered a tumbler of ice and a couple of glasses.

'A very good cocktail,' I said.

'Well, there are plenty more where that came from, and if you've got any friends on board, you tell them you've got a pal who's got all the liquor in the world.'

Mr. Kelada was chatty. He talked of New York and of San Francisco. He discussed plays, pictures, and politics. He was patriotic. The Union Jack is an impressive piece of drapery, but when it is flourished by a gentleman from Alexandria or Beirut, I cannot but feel that it loses somewhat in dignity. Mr. Kelada was familiar. I do not wish to put on airs, but I cannot help feeling that it is seemly in a total stranger to put mister before my name when he addresses me. Mr. Kelada, doubtless to set me at my ease, used no such formality. I did not like Mr. Kelada. I had put aside the cards when he sat down, but now thinking that for this first occasion our conversation had lasted long enough, I went on with my game.

'The three on the four,' said Mr. Kelada.

There is nothing more exasperating when you are playing patience than to be told where to put the card you have turned up before you have had a chance to look for yourself.

'It's coming out, it's coming out,' he cried. 'The ten on the knave.'

With rage and hatred in my heart I finished. Then he seized the pack.

'Do you like card tricks?'

'No, I hate card tricks,' I answered.

'Well, I'll just show you this one.'

He showed me three. Then I said I would go down to the dining-room and get my seat at table.

'Oh, that's all right,' he said. 'I've already taken a seat for you. I thought that as we were in the same state-room we might just as well sit at the same table.'

I did not like Mr. Kelada.

I not only shared a cabin with him and ate three meals a day at the same table, but I could not walk round the deck without his joining me. It was impossible to snub him. It never occurred to him that he was not wanted. He was certain that you were as glad to see him as he was to see you. In your own house you might have kicked him downstairs and slammed the door in his face without the suspicion dawning on him that he was not a welcome visitor. He was a good mixer, and in three days knew everyone on board. He ran everything. He managed the sweeps, conducted the auctions, collected money for prizes at the sports, got up quoit and golf matches, organized the concert and arranged the fancy dress ball. He was everywhere and always. He was certainly the best-hated man in the ship. We called him Mr. Know-All, even to his face. He took it as a compliment. But it was at meal times that he was most intolerable. For the better part of an hour then he had us at his mercy. He was hearty, jovial, loquacious and argumentative. He knew everything better than anybody else, and it was an affront to his overweening vanity that you should disagree with him. He would not drop a subject, however unimportant, till he had brought you round to his way of thinking. The possibility that he could be mistaken never occurred to him. He was the chap who knew. We sat at the doctor's table. Mr. Kelada would certainly have had it all his own way, for the doctor was lazy and I was frigidly indifferent, except for a man called Ramsay who sat there also. He was as dogmatic as Mr. Kelada and resented bitterly the Levantine's cocksureness. The discussions they had were acrimonious and interminable.

Ramsay was in the American Consular Service, and was stationed at Kobe. He was a great heavy fellow from the Middle West, with loose fat under a tight skin, and he bulged out of his ready-made clothes. He was on his way back to resume his post, having been on a flying visit to New York to fetch his wife who had been spending a year at home. Mrs. Ramsay was a very pretty little thing, with pleasant manners and a sense of humour. The Consular Service is ill paid, and she was dressed always very simply; but she knew how to wear her clothes.

She achieved an effect of quiet distinction. I should not have paid any particular attention to her but that she possessed a quality that may be common enough in women, but nowadays is not obvious in their demeanour. You could not look at her without being struck by her modesty. It shone in her like a flower on a coat.

One evening at dinner the conversation by chance drifted to the subject of pearls. There had been in the papers a good deal of talk about the culture pearls which the cunning Japanese were making, and the doctor remarked that they must inevitably diminish the value of real ones. They were very good already; they would soon be perfect. Mr. Kelada, as was his habit, rushed into the new topic. He told us all that was to be known about pearls. I do not believe Ramsay knew anything about them at all, but he could not resist the opportunity to have a fling at the Levantine, and in five minutes we were in the middle of a heated argument. I had seen Mr. Kelada vehement and voluble before, but never so voluble and vehement as now. At last something that Ramsay said stung him, for he thumped the table and shouted:

'Well, I ought to know what I am talking about. I'm going to Japan just to look into this Japanese pearl business. I'm in the trade and there's not a man in it who won't tell you that what I say about pearls goes. I know all the best pearls in the world, and what I don't know about pearls isn't worth knowing.'

Here was news for us, for Mr. Kelada, with all his loquacity, had never told anyone what his business was. We only knew vaguely that he was going to Japan on some commercial errand. He looked round the table triumphantly.

'They'll never be able to get a culture pearl that an expert like me can't tell with half an eye.' He pointed to a chain that Mrs. Ramsay wore. 'You take my word for it, Mrs. Ramsay, that chain you're wearing will never be worth a cent less than it is now.'

Mrs. Ramsay in her modest way flushed a little and slipped the chain inside her dress. Ramsay leaned forward. He gave us all a look and a smile flickered in his eyes.

'That's a pretty chain of Mrs. Ramsay's, isn't it?'

'I noticed it at once,' answered Mr. Kelada. 'Gee, I said to myself, those are pearls all right.'

'I didn't buy it myself, of course. I'd be interested to know how much you think it cost.'

'Oh, in the trade somewhere round fifteen thousand dollars. But if it was bought on Fifth Avenue I shouldn't be surprised to hear that anything up to thirty thousand was paid for it.'

Ramsay smiled grimly.

'You'll be surprised to hear that Mrs. Ramsay bought that string at a department store the day before we left New York, for eighteen dollars.'

Mr. Kelada flushed.

'Rot. It's not only real, but it's as fine a string for its size as I've ever seen.'

'Will you bet on it? I'll bet you a hundred dollars it's imitation.'

'Done.'

'Oh, Elmer, you can't bet on a certainty,' said Mrs. Ramsay.

She had a little smile on her lips and her tone was gently deprecating.

'Can't I? If I get a chance of easy money like that I should be all sorts of a fool not to take it.'

'But how can it be proved?' she continued. 'It's only my word against Mr. Kelada's.'

'Let me look at the chain, and if it's imitation I'll tell you quickly enough. I can afford to lose a hundred dollars,' said Mr. Kelada.

'Take it off, dear. Let the gentleman look at it as much as he wants.'

Mrs. Ramsay hesitated a moment. She put her hands to the clasp.

'I can't undo it,' she said. 'Mr. Kelada will just have to take my word for it.'

I had a sudden suspicion that something unfortunate was about to occur, but I could think of nothing to say.

Ramsay jumped up.

'I'll undo it.'

He handed the chain to Mr. Kelada. The Levantine took a magnifying glass from his pocket and closely examined it. A smile of triumph spread over his smooth and swarthy face. He handed back the chain. He was about to speak. Suddenly he caught sight of Mrs. Ramsay's face. It was so white that she looked as though she were about to faint. She was staring at him with wide and terrified eyes. They held a desperate appeal; it was so clear that I wondered why her husband did not see it.

Mr. Kelada stopped with his mouth open. He flushed deeply. You could almost *see* the effort he was making over himself.

'I was mistaken,' he said. 'It's a very good imitation, but of course as soon as I looked through my glass I saw that it wasn't real. I think eighteen dollars is just about as much as the damned thing's worth.'

He took out his pocket-book and from it a hundred-dollar bill. He handed it to Ramsay without a word.

'Perhaps that'll teach you not to be so cocksure another time, my young friend,' said Ramsay as he took the note.

I noticed that Mr. Kelada's hands were trembling.

The story spread over the ship as stories do, and he had to put up with a good deal of chaff that evening. It was a fine joke that Mr. Know-All had been caught out. But Mrs. Ramsay retired to her state-room with a headache.

Next morning I got up and began to shave. Mr. Kelada lay on his bed smoking a cigarette. Suddenly there was a small scraping sound and I saw a letter pushed under the door. I opened the door and looked out. There was nobody there. I picked up the letter and saw that it was addressed to Max Kelada. The name was written in block letters. I handed it to him.

'Who's this from?' He opened it. 'Oh!'

He took out of the envelope, not a letter, but a hundred-dollar bill. He looked at me and again he reddened. He tore the envelope into little bits and gave them to me.

'Do you mind just throwing them out of the port-hole?'

I did as he asked, and then I looked at him with a smile.

'No one likes being made to look a perfect damned fool,' he said.

'Were the pearls real?'

'If I had a pretty little wife I shouldn't let her spend a year in New York while I stayed at Kobe,' said he.

At that moment I did not entirely dislike Mr. Kelada. He reached out for his pocket-book and carefully put in it the hundred-dollar note.

Neil MacAdam

Captain Bredon was good-natured. When Angus Munro, the Curator of the museum at Kuala Solor, told him that he had advised Neil MacAdam, his new assistant, on his arrival at Singapore to put up at the Van Dyke Hotel, and asked him to see that the lad got into no mischief during the few days he must spend there, he said he would do his best. Captain Bredon commanded the 'Sultan Ahmed', and when he was at Singapore always stayed at the Van Dyke. He had a Japanese wife and kept a room there. It was his home. When he got back after his fortnight's trip along the coast of Borneo the Dutch manager told him that Neil had been there for two days. The boy was sitting in the little dusty garden of the hotel reading old numbers of 'The Straits Times'. Captain Bredon took a look at him first and then went up.

'You're MacAdam, aren't you?'

Neil rose to his feet, flushed to the roots of his hair and answered shyly: 'I am.'

'My name's Bredon. I'm skipper of the "Sultan Ahmed". You're sailing with me next Tuesday. Munro asked me to look after you. What about a stengah? I suppose you've learned what that means by now.'

'Thank you very much, but I don't drink.'

He spoke with a broad Scots accent.

'I don't blame you. Drink's been the ruin of many a good man in this country.'

He called the Chinese boy and ordered himself a double whisky and a small soda.

'What have you been doing with yourself since you got in?'

'Walking about.'

'There's nothing much to see in Singapore.'

'I've found plenty.'

Of course the first thing he had done was to go to the museum. There was little that he had not seen at home, but the fact that those beasts and birds, those reptiles, moths, butterflies and insects, were native to the country excited him. There was one section devoted to that part of Borneo of which Kuala Solor was the capital, and since these were the creatures that for the next three years would chiefly concern him, he examined them with attention. But it was outside, in the streets, that it was most thrilling, and except that he was a grave and sober young man he would have laughed aloud with joy. Everything was new to him. He walked till he was footsore. He stood at the corner of a busy street and wondered at the long line of rickshaws and the little men between the shafts running with dogged steps. He stood on a bridge over a canal and looked at the sampans wedged up against one another like sardines in a tin. He peered into the Chinese shops in Victoria Road where so many strange things were sold. Bombay merchants, fat and exuberant, stood at their shop doors and sought to sell him silks and tinsel jewellery. He watched the Tamils, pensive and forlorn, who walked with a sinister grace, and the bearded Arabs, in white skull-caps, who bore themselves with scornful dignity. The sun shone upon the varied scene with a hard, acrid brilliance. He was confused. He thought it would take him years to find his bearings in this multi-coloured and excessive world.

After dinner that night Captain Bredon asked him if he would like to go round the town.

'You ought to see a bit of life while you're here,' he said.

They stepped into rickshaws and drove to the Chinese quarter. The Captain, who never drank at sea, had been making up for his abstinence during the day. He was feeling good. The rickshaws stopped at a house in a side street and they knocked at the door. It was opened and they passed through a narrow passage into a large room with benches all round it covered with red plush. A number of women were sitting about – French, Italian and American. A mechanical piano was grinding out harsh music and a few couples were dancing. Captain Bredon ordered drinks. Two or three women, waiting for an invitation, gave them inciting glances.

'Well, young feller, is there anyone you fancy here?' the Captain asked facetiously.

'To sleep with, d'you mean? No.'

'No white girls where you're going, you know.'

'Oh, well.'

'Like to go an' see some natives?'

'I don't mind.'

The Captain paid for the drinks and they strolled on. They went to another house. Here the girls were Chinese, small and dainty, with tiny feet and hands like flowers, and they wore suits of flowered silk. But their painted faces were like masks. They looked at the strangers with black derisive eyes. They were strangely inhuman.

'I brought you here because I thought you ought to see the place,' said Captain Bredon, with the air of a man doing his bounden duty, 'but just look see is all. They don't like us for some reason. In some of these Chinese joints they won't even let a white man in. Fact is, they say we stink. Funny, ain't it? They say we smell of corpses.'

'We?'

'Give me Japs,' said the Captain. 'They're fine. My wife's a Jap, you know. You come along with me and I'll take you to a place where they have Japanese girls, and if you don't see something you like there I'm a Dutchman.'

Their rickshaws were waiting and they stepped into them. Captain Bredon gave a direction and the boys started off. They were let into the house by a stout middle-aged Japanese woman, who bowed low as they entered. She took them into a neat, clean room furnished only with mats on the floor; they sat down and presently a little girl came in with a tray on which were two bowls of pale tea. With a shy bow she handed one to each of them. The Captain spoke to the middle-aged woman and she looked at Neil and giggled. She said something to the child, who went out, and presently four girls tripped in. They were sweet in their kimonos, with their shining black hair artfully dressed; they were small and plump, with round faces and laughing eyes. They bowed low as they came in and with good manners murmured polite greetings. Their speech sounded like the twittering of birds. Then they knelt, one on each side of the two men, and charmingly flirted with them. Captain Bredon soon had his arms round two slim waists. They all talked nineteen to the dozen. They were very gay. It seemed to Neil that the Captain's girls were mocking him, for their gleaming eyes were mischievously turned towards him, and he blushed. But the other two cuddled up to him, smiling, and spoke in Japanese as though he understood every word they said. They seemed so happy and guileless that he laughed. They were very attentive. They handed him the bowl so that he should drink his tea, and then took it from him so that he should not have the trouble of holding it. They lit his cigarette for him and one put out a small, delicate hand to take the ash so that it should not fall on his clothes. They stroked his smooth face and looked with curiosity at his large young hands. They were as playful as kittens.

'Well, which is it to be?' said the Captain after a while. 'Made your choice yet?'

'What d'you mean?'

'I'll just wait and see you settled and then I'll fix myself up.'

'Oh, I don't want either of them. I'm going home to bed.'

'Why, what's the matter? You're not scared, are you?'

'No, I just don't fancy it. But don't let me stand in your way. I'll get back to the hotel all right.'

'Oh, if you're not going to do anything I won't either. I only wanted to be matey.'

He spoke to the middle-aged woman and what he said caused the girls to look at Neil with sudden surprise. She answered and the Captain shrugged his shoulders. Then one of the girls made a remark that set them all laughing.

'What does she say?' asked Neil.

'She's pulling your leg,' replied the Captain, smiling.

But he gave Neil a curious look. The girl, having made them laugh once, now said something directly to Neil. He could not understand, but the mockery of her eyes made him blush and frown. He did not like to be made fun of. Then she laughed outright and throwing her arm round his neck lightly kissed him.

'Come on, let's be going,' said the Captain.

When they dismissed their rickshaws and walked into the hotel Neil asked him:

'What was it that girl said that made them all laugh?'

'She said you were a virgin.'

'I don't see anything to laugh at in that,' said Neil, with his slow Scots accent.

'Is it true?'

'I suppose it is.'

'How old are you?'

'Twenty-two.'

'What are you waiting for?'

'Till I marry.'

The Captain was silent. At the top of the stairs he held out his hand. There was a twinkle in his eyes when he bade the lad good-night, but Neil met it with a level, candid and untroubled gaze.

Three days later they sailed. Neil was the only white passenger. When the Captain was busy he read. He was reading again Wallace's 'Malay Archipelago'. He had read it as a boy, but now it had a new and absorbing interest for him. When the Captain was at leisure they played cribbage or sat in long chairs on the deck, smoking, and talked. Neil was the son of a country doctor, and he could not remember when he had not been interested in natural history. When he had done with school he went to the University of Edinburgh and there took a B.Sc. with Honours. He was looking out for a job as demonstrator in biology when he chanced to see in 'Nature' an advertisement for an assistant curator of the museum at Kuala Solor. The Curator, Angus Munro, had been at Edinburgh with his uncle, a Glasgow merchant, and his uncle wrote to ask him if he would give the boy a trial. Though Neil was especially interested in entomology he was a trained taxidermist, which the advertisement said was essential; he enclosed certificates from Neil's old teachers; he added that Neil had played football for his university. In a few weeks a cable arrived engaging him and a fortnight later he sailed.

'What's Mr. Munro like?' asked Neil.

'Good fellow. Everybody likes him.'

'I looked out his papers in the scientific journals. He had one in the last number of "The Ibis" on the Gymnathidæ.'

'I don't know anything about that. I know he's got a Russian wife. They don't like her much.'

'I got a letter from him at Singapore saying they'd put

me up for a bit till I could look round and see what I
wanted to do.'

Now they were steaming up the river. At the mouth
was a straggling fishermen's village standing on piles in
the water; on the bank grew thickly nipah palm and the
tortured mangrove; beyond stretched the dense green
of the virgin forest. In the distance, darkly silhouetted
against the blue sky, was the rugged outline of a mountain. Neil, his heart beating with the excitement that
possessed him, devoured the scene with eager eyes. He
was surprised. He knew his Conrad almost by heart and
he was expecting a land of brooding mystery. He was not
prepared for the blue milky sky. Little white clouds on
the horizon, like sailing boats becalmed, shone in the
sun. The green trees of the forest glittered in the brilliant
light. Here and there, on the banks, were Malay houses
with thatched roofs, and they nestled cosily among fruit
trees. Natives in dug-outs rowed, standing, up the river.
Neil had no feeling of being shut in, nor in that radiant
morning, of gloom, but of space and freedom. The
country offered him a gracious welcome. He knew he
was going to be happy in it. Captain Bredon from the
bridge threw a friendly glance at the lad standing below
him. He had taken quite a fancy to him during the four
days the journey had lasted. It was true he did not drink,
and when you made a joke he was as likely as not to take
you seriously, but there was something very taking in his
seriousness; everything was interesting and important to
him – that, of course, was why he did not find your jokes
amusing; but even though he didn't see them he laughed,
because he felt you expected it. He laughed because life
was grand. He was grateful for every little thing you told
him. He was very polite. He never asked you to pass
him anything without saying 'please' and always said
'thank you' when you gave it. And he was a good-looking
fellow, no one could deny that. Neil was standing with

his hands on the rail, bare-headed, looking at the passing bank. He was tall, six foot two, with long, loose limbs, broad shoulders and narrow hips; there was something charmingly coltish about him, so that you expected him at any moment to break into a caper. He had brown curly hair with a peculiar shine in it; sometimes when the light caught it, it glittered like gold. His eyes, large and very blue, shone with good humour. They reflected his happy disposition. His nose was short and blunt and his mouth big, his chin determined; his face was rather broad. But his most striking feature was his skin; it was very white and smooth, with a lovely patch of red on either cheek. It would have been a beautiful skin even for a woman. Captain Bredon made the same joke to him every morning.

'Well, my lad, have you shaved to-day?'

Neil passed his hand over his chin.

'No, d'you think I need it?'

The Captain always laughed at this.

'Need it? Why, you've got a face like a baby's bottom.'

And invariably Neil reddened to the roots of his hair.

'I shave once a week,' he retorted.

But it wasn't only his looks that made you like him. It was his ingenuousness, his candour and the freshness with which he confronted the world. For all his intentness and the solemn way in which he took everything, and his inclination to argue upon every point that came up, there was something strangely simple in him that gave you quite an odd feeling. The Captain couldn't make it out.

'I wonder if it's because he's never had a woman,' he said to himself. 'Funny. I should have thought the girls never left him alone. With a complexion like that.'

But the 'Sultan Ahmed' was nearing the bend after rounding which Kuala Solor would be in sight and the

Captain's reflections were interrupted by the necessities of his work. He rang down to the engine room. The ship slackened to half speed. Kuala Solor straggled along the left bank of the river, a white neat and trim little town, and on the right on a hill were the fort and the Sultan's Palace. There was a breeze and the Sultan's flag, at the top of a tall staff, waved bravely against the sky. They anchored in midstream. The doctor and a police officer came on board in the government launch. They were accompanied by a tall thin man in white ducks. The Captain stood at the head of the gangway and shook hands with them. Then he turned to the last comer.

'Well, I've brought you your young hopeful safe and sound.' And with a glance at Neil: 'This is Munro.'

The tall thin man held out his hand and gave Neil an appraising look. Neil flushed a little and smiled. He had beautiful teeth.

'How do you do, sir?'

Munro did not smile with his lips, but faintly with his grey eyes. His cheeks were hollow and he had a thin aquiline nose and pale lips. He was deeply sunburned. His face looked tired, but his expression was very gentle, and Neil immediately felt confidence in him. The Captain introduced him to the doctor and the policeman and suggested that they should have a drink. When they sat down and the boy brought bottles of beer Munro took off his topi. Neil saw that he had close-cropped brown hair turning grey. He was a man of forty, quiet, self-possessed in manner, with an intellectual air that distinguished him from the brisk little doctor and the heavy swaggering police officer.

'MacAdam doesn't drink,' said the Captain when the boy poured out four glasses of beer.

'All the better,' said Munro. 'I hope you haven't been trying to lure him into evil ways.'

'I tried to in Singapore,' returned the Captain, with a twinkle in his eyes, 'but there was nothing doing.'

When he had finished his beer Munro turned to Neil.

'Well, we'll be getting ashore, shall we?'

Neil's baggage was put in charge of Munro's boy and the two men got into a sampan. They landed.

'Do you want to go straight up to the bungalow or would you like to have a look round first? We've got a couple of hours before tiffin.'

'Couldn't we go to the museum?' said Neil.

Munro's eyes smiled gently. He was pleased. Neil was shy and Munro not by nature talkative, so they walked in silence. By the river were the native huts and here, living their immemorial lives, dwelt the Malays. They were busy, but without haste, and you were conscious of a happy, normal activity. There was a sense of the rhythm of life of which the pattern was birth and death, love and the affairs common to mankind. They came to the bazaars, narrow streets with arcades, where the teeming Chinese, working and eating, noisily talking, as is their way, indefatigably strove with eternity.

'It's not much after Singapore,' said Munro, 'but I always think it's rather picturesque.'

He spoke with an accent less broad than Neil's, but the Scots burr was there and it put Neil at his ease. He could never quite get it out of his head that the English of English people was affected.

The museum was a handsome stone building and as they entered its portals Munro instinctively straightened himself. The attendant at the door saluted and Munro spoke to him in Malay, evidently explaining who Neil was, for the attendant gave him a smile and saluted again. It was cool in there in comparison with the heat without and the light was pleasant after the glare of the street.

'I'm afraid you'll be disappointed,' said Munro. 'We haven't got half the things we ought to have, but up to now we've been handicapped by lack of money. We've had to do the best we could. So you must make allowances.'

Neil stepped in like a swimmer diving confidently into a summer sea. The specimens were admirably arranged. Munro had sought to please as well as to instruct, and birds and beasts and reptiles were presented, as far as possible in their natural surroundings, in such a way as to give a vivid impression of life. Neil lost his shyness and began with boyish enthusiasm to talk of this and that. He asked an infinity of questions. He was excited. Neither of them was conscious of the passage of time, and when Munro glanced at his watch he was surprised to see what the hour was. They got into rickshaws and drove to the bungalow.

Munro led the young man into a drawing-room. A woman was lying on a sofa reading a book and as they came in she slowly rose.

'This is my wife. I'm afraid we're dreadfully late, Darya.'

'What does it matter?' she smiled. 'What is more unimportant than time?'

She held out her hand, a rather large hand, to Neil and gave him a long, reflective, but friendly look.

'I suppose you've been showing him the museum.'

She was a woman of five-and-thirty, of medium height, with a pale brown face of a uniform colour and pale blue eyes. Her hair, parted in the middle and wound into a knot on the nape of her neck, was untidy; it had a moth-like quality and was of a curious pale brown. Her face was broad, with high cheek-bones, and she had a rather fleshy nose. She was not a pretty woman, but there was in her slow movements a sensual grace and in her manner as it were a physical casualness that only very dull people could have failed to find interesting. She wore a frock of green cotton. She spoke English perfectly, but with a slight accent.

They sat down to tiffin. Neil was overcome once more with shyness, but Darya did not seem to notice it. She talked freely and easily. She asked him about his journey and what he had thought of Singapore. She told him about the people he would have to meet. That afternoon Munro was to take him to call on the Resident, the Sultan being away, and later they would go to the club. There he would see everybody.

'You will be popular,' she said, her pale blue eyes resting on him with attention. A man less ingenuous than Neil might have noticed that she took stock of his size and youthful virility, his shiny, curling hair and his lovely skin. 'They don't think much of us.'

'Oh, nonsense, Darya. You're too sensitive. They're English, that's all.'

'They think it's rather funny of Angus to be a scientist and they think it's rather vulgar of me to be a Russian. I don't care. They're fools. They're the most commonplace, the most narrow-minded, the most conventional people it has ever been my misfortune to live amongst.'

'Don't put MacAdam off the moment he arrives. He'll find them kind and hospitable.'

'What is your first name?' she asked the boy.

'Neil.'

'I shall call you by it. And you must call me Darya. I hate being called Mrs. Munro. It makes me feel like a minister's wife.'

Neil blushed. He was embarrassed that she should ask him so soon to be so familiar. She went on.

'Some of the men are not bad.'

'They do their jobs competently and that's what they're here for,' said Munro.

'They shoot. They play football and tennis and cricket. I get on with them quite well. The women are intolerable.

They are jealous and spiteful and lazy. They can talk of nothing. If you introduce an intellectual subject they look down their noses as though you were indecent. What can they talk about? They're interested in nothing. If you speak of the body they think you improper, and if you speak of the soul they think you priggish.'

'You mustn't take what my wife says too literally,' smiled Munro, in his gentle, tolerant way. 'The community here is just like any other in the East, neither very clever, nor very stupid, but amiable and kindly. And that's a good deal.'

'I don't want people to be amiable and kindly. I want them to be vital and passionate. I want them to be interested in mankind. I want them to attach more importance to the things of the spirit than to a gin pahit or a curry tiffin. I want art to matter to them and literature.' She addressed herself abruptly to Neil: 'Have you got a soul?'

'Oh, I don't know. I don't know exactly what you mean.'

'Why do you blush when I ask you? Why should you be ashamed of your soul? It is what is important in you. Tell me about it. I am interested in you and I want to know.'

It seemed very awkward to Neil to be tackled in this way by a perfect stranger. He had never met anyone like this. But he was a serious young man and when he was asked a question straight out he did his best to answer it. It was Munro's presence that embarrassed him.

'I don't know what you mean by the soul. If you mean an immaterial or spiritual entity, separately produced by the creator, in temporary conjunction with the material body, then my answer is in the negative. It seems to me that such a radically dualistic view of human personality cannot be defended by anyone who is able to take a calm view of the evidence. If, on the other hand, you mean by soul the aggregate of psychic elements which form what we know as the personality of the individual, then, of course, I have.'

'You're very sweet and you're wonderfully handsome,' she said, smiling. 'No, I mean the heart with its longings and the body with its desires and the infinite in us. Tell me, what did you read on the journey, or did you only play deck tennis?'

Neil was taken aback at the inconsequence of her reply. He would have been a little affronted except for the good humour in her eyes and the naturalness in her manner. Munro smiled quietly at the young man's bewilderment. When he smiled the lines that ran from the wings of his nostrils to the corners of his mouth became deep furrows.

'I read a lot of Conrad.'

'For pleasure or to improve your mind?'

'Both. I admire him awfully.'

Darya threw up her arms in an extravagant gesture of protest.

'That Pole,' she cried. 'How can you English ever have let yourselves be taken in by that wordy mountebank? He has all the superficiality of his countrymen. That stream of words, those involved sentences, the showy rhetoric, that affectation of profundity: when you get through all that to the thought at the bottom, what do you find but a trivial commonplace? He was like a second-rate actor who puts on a romantic dress and declaims a play by Victor Hugo. For five minutes you say this is heroic, and then your whole soul revolts and you cry, no, this is false, false, false.'

She spoke with a passion that Neil had never known anyone show when speaking of art or literature. Her cheeks, usually colourless, flushed and her pale eyes glowed.

'There's no one who got atmosphere like Conrad,'

said Neil. 'I can smell and see and feel the East when I read him.'

'Nonsense. What do you know about the East? Everyone will tell you that he made the grossest blunders. Ask Angus.'

'Of course he was not always accurate,' said Munro, in his measured, reflective way. 'The Borneo he described is not the Borneo we know. He saw it from the deck of a merchant vessel and he was not an acute observer even of what he saw. But does it matter? I don't know why fiction should be hampered by fact. I don't think it's a mean achievement to have created a country, a dark, sinister, romantic and heroic country of the soul.'

'You're a sentimentalist, my poor Angus.' And then again to Neil: 'You must read Turgeniev, you must read Tolstoi, you must read Dostoevsky.'

Neil did not in the least know what to make of Darya Munro. She skipped over the first stages of acquaintance and treated him at once like someone she had known intimately all her life. It puzzled him. It seemed so reckless. When he met anyone his own instinct was to go cautiously. He was amiable, but he did not like to step too far before he saw his way before him. He did not want to give anyone his confidence before he thought himself justified. But with Darya you could not help yourself; she forced your confidence. She poured out the feelings and thoughts that most people keep to themselves like a prodigal flinging gold pieces to a scrambling crowd. She did not talk, she did not act like anyone he had ever known. She did not mind what she said. She would speak of the natural functions of the human animal in a way that brought the blushes coursing to his cheeks. They excited her ridicule.

'Oh, what a prig you are! What is there indecent in it? When I'm going to take a purge, why shouldn't I say so and when I think you want one, why shouldn't I tell you?'

'Theoretically I daresay you're right,' said Neil, always judicious and reasonable.

She made him tell her of his father and mother, his brothers, his life at school and at the university. She told him about herself. Her father was a general killed in the war and her mother a Princess Lutchkov. They were in Eastern Russia when the Bolsheviks seized power, and fled to Yokohama. Here they had subsisted miserably on the sale of their jewels and such objects of art as they had been able to save, and here she married a fellow exile. She was unhappy with him and in two years divorced him. Her mother died and, penniless, she was driven to earn her living as best she could. She was employed by an American relief organisation. She taught in a mission school. She worked in a hospital. She made Neil's blood boil, and at the same time embarrassed him very much, when she spoke of the men who tried to take advantage of her defencelessness and her poverty. She spared him no details.

'Brutes,' he said.

'Oh, all men are like that,' she replied, with a shrug of her shoulders.

She told him how once she protected her virtue at the point of her revolver.

'I swore I'd kill him if he took another step, and if he had I'd have shot him like a dog.'

'Gosh!' said Neil.

It was at Yokohama that she met Angus. He was spending his leave in Japan. She was captivated by his straightforwardness, the decency which was so obvious in him, his tenderness and his consideration. He was not a business man; he was a scientist, and science is milk-brother to art. He offered her peace. He offered her security. And she was tired of Japan. Borneo was a land of mystery. They had been married for five years.

She gave Neil the Russian novelists to read. She gave him 'Fathers and Sons,' 'Anna Karenina' and 'The Brothers Karamazoff'.

'Those are the three peaks of our literature. Read them. They are the greatest novels the world has ever seen.'

Like many of her countrymen she talked as though no other literature counted, and as though a few novels and stories, some indifferent poetry and half a dozen good plays had made whatever else the world has produced negligible. Neil was fascinated and overwhelmed.

'You're rather like Alyosha yourself, Neil,' she said, looking at him with eyes that were now so soft and tender, 'an Alyosha with a Scotch dourness, suspicious and prudent, that will not let the soul in you, the spiritual beauty, come out.'

'I'm not a bit like Alyosha,' he answered self-consciously.

'You don't know what you're like. You don't know anything about yourself. Why are you a naturalist? Is it for money? You could have made much more money by going into your uncle's office in Glasgow. I feel in you something strange and unearthly. I could bow down at your feet as Father Zossima did to Dimitri.'

'Please don't,' he said, smiling, but flushing a little too.

But the novels he read made her seem a little less strange to him. They gave her an environment and he recognised in her traits which, however unusual in the women he knew in Scotland, his mother and the daughters of his uncle in Glasgow, were common to many of the characters in Russian fiction. He no longer wondered that she should like to sit up so late, drinking innumerable cups of tea, and lie on the sofa nearly all day long reading and incessantly smoking cigarettes. She could do nothing at all for days on end without being bored. She had a curious mixture of languor and zest. She often said, with a shrug of her shoulders, that she was an Oriental and a European only by chance. She had a feline grace that indeed suggested the Oriental. She was immensely untidy and it did not seem to affect her that cigarette ends, old papers and empty tins should lie about their living-room. But he thought she had something of Anna Karenina in her, and he transferred to her the sympathy he felt for that pathetic creature. He understood her arrogance. It was not unnatural that she despised the women of the community, whose acquaintance little by little he made; they *were* commonplace; her mind was quicker than theirs, she had a wider culture, and she had above all a sort of tremulous sensitiveness that made *them* extraordinarily colourless. She certainly took no pains to conciliate them. Though at home she slopped about in a sarong and baju, when she and Angus went out to dinner she dressed with a splendour that was somewhat out of place. She liked to display her ample bosom and her shapely back. She painted her cheeks and made up her eyes like an actress for the footlights. Though it made Neil angry to see the amused or outraged glances that her appearance provoked, he could not in his heart but think it a pity that she should make such an object of herself. She looked grand, of course, but if you hadn't known who she was you would have thought she wasn't respectable. There were things about her that he could never get over. She had an enormous appetite and it fashed him that she ate more than he and Angus together. He could never quite get used to the bluntness with which she discussed sexual matters. She took it for granted that at home and in Edinburgh he had had affairs with a host of women. She pressed him for details of his adventures. His Scotch pawkiness helped him to parry her thrusts and he evaded her questions with native caution. She laughed at his reticence.

Sometimes she shocked him. He grew accustomed to the frankness with which she admired his looks, and when she told him that he was as beautiful as a young Norse god he did not turn a hair. Flattery fell off him like water from a duck's back. But he did not like it when she ran her hand, though large, very soft, with caressing fingers, through his curly hair or, a smile on her lips, stroked his smooth face. He couldn't bear being mussed about. One day she wanted a drink of tonic water and began pouring some out in a glass that stood on the table.

'That's my glass,' he said quickly. 'I've just been drinking out of it.'

'Well, what of it? You haven't got syphilis, have you?'

'I hate drinking out of other people's glasses myself.'

She was funny about cigarettes too. Once, when he hadn't been there very long, he had just lit one, when she passed and said:

'I want that.'

She took it out of his mouth and began to smoke it. After two or three puffs, she said she did not want any more and handed it back to him. The end she had had in her mouth was red from the rouge on her lips, and he didn't want to go on smoking it at all. But he was afraid she would think it rude if he threw it away. It somewhat disgusted him. Often she would ask him for a cigarette and when he handed it to her, say:

'Oh, light it for me, will you?'

When he did so, and held it out to her, she opened her mouth so that he should put it in. He hadn't been able to help wetting the end a little. He wondered she could bear to put it in her mouth after it had been in his. The whole thing seemed to him awfully familiar. He was sure Munro wouldn't like it. She had even done this once or twice at the club. Neil had felt himself go purple. He wished she hadn't got these rather unpleasant habits, but he supposed they were Russian, and one couldn't deny that she was wonderfully good company. Her conversation was very stimulating. It was like champagne (which Neil had tasted once and thought wretched stuff), 'metaphorically speaking'. There was nothing she couldn't talk about. She didn't talk like a man; with a man you generally knew what he would say next, but with her you never did; her intuition was quite remarkable. She gave you ideas. She enlarged your mind and excited your imagination. Neil felt alive as he had never felt alive before. He seemed to walk on mountain peaks and the horizons of the spirit were unbounded. Neil felt a certain complacency when he stopped to reflect on what an exalted plane his mind communed with hers. Such conversations made very small beer of the vaunted pleasure of sense. She was in many ways (he was of a cautious nature and seldom made a statement even to himself that he did not qualify) the most intelligent woman he had ever met. And besides, she was Angus Munro's wife.

For, whatever Neil's reservations were about Darya, he had none about Munro, and she would have had to be a much less remarkable woman not to profit by the enormous admiration he conceived for her husband. With him Neil let himself go. He felt for him what he had never felt for anyone before. He was so sane, so balanced, so tolerant. This was the sort of man he would himself like to be when he was older. He talked little, but when he did, with good sense. He was wise. He had a dry humour that Neil understood. It made the hearty English fun of the men at the club seem inane. He was kind and patient. He had a dignity that made it impossible to conceive of anyone taking a liberty with him, but he was neither pompous nor solemn. He was honest and absolutely truthful. But Neil admired him no less as a scientist than as a man. He had imagination. He was careful and painstaking. Though his interest was in research he did the routine work of the museum conscientiously. He was just then much interested in stick-insects and intended to write a paper on their powers of parthenogenetic reproduction. An incident occurred in connection with the experiments he was making that made a great impression on Neil. One day, a little captive gibbon escaped from its chain and ate up all the larvæ and so destroyed the whole of Munro's evidence. Neil nearly cried. Angus Munro took the gibbon in his arms and, smiling, stroked it.

'Diamond, Diamond,' he said, quoting Sir Isaac Newton, 'you little know the damage you have done.'

He was also studying mimicry and instilled into Neil his absorbed interest in this controversial subject. They had interminable talks about it. Neil was astonished at the Curator's wonderful knowledge. It was encyclopædic, and he was abashed at his own ignorance. But it was when Munro spoke of the trips into the country to collect specimens that his enthusiasm was most contagious. That was the perfect life, a life of hardship, difficulty, often of privation and sometimes of danger, but rewarded by the thrill of finding a rare, or even a new species, by the beauty of the scenery and the intimate observation of nature, and above all by the sense of freedom from every tie. It was for this part of the work that Neil had been chiefly engaged. Munro was occupied in research work that made it difficult for him to be away from home for several weeks at a time, and Darya had always refused to accompany him. She had an unreasoning fear of the jungle. She was terrified of wild beasts, snakes and venomous insects. Though Munro had told her over and over again that no animal hurt you unless you molested or frightened it, she could not get over her instinctive horror. He did not like leaving her. She cared little for the local society and with him away he realised that life for her must be intolerably dull. But the Sultan was keenly interested in natural history and was anxious that the museum should be completely representative of the country's fauna. One expedition Munro and Neil were to make together, so that Neil should learn how to go to work, and the plans for this were discussed by them for months. Neil looked forward to it as he had never looked forward to anything in his life.

Meanwhile he learned Malay and acquired a smattering of the dialects that would be useful to him on future journeys. He played tennis and football. He soon knew everyone in the community. On the football field he threw off his absorption in science and his interest in Russian fiction and gave himself up to the pleasure of the game. He was strong, quick and active. After it was all over it was grand to have a sluice down and a long tonic with a slice of lemon and go over it all with the other fellows. It had never been intended that Neil should live permanently with the Munros. There was a roomy Rest House at Kuala Solor, but the rule was that no one should stay in it for more than a fortnight and such of the bachelors as had no official quarters clubbed together and took a house between them. When Neil arrived it so happened that there was no vacancy in any of these messes. One evening, however, when he had been about four months in the colony, two men, Waring and Jonson, when they were sitting together after a game of tennis, told him that one member of their mess was going home and if he would like to join them they would be glad to have him. They were young fellows of his own age, in the football team, and Neil liked them both. Waring was in the customs and Jonson in the police. He jumped at the suggestion. They told him how much it would cost and fixed a day, a fortnight later, when it would be convenient for him to move in.

At dinner he told the Munros.

'It's been awfully good of you to let me stay so long. It's made me very uncomfortable planting myself on you like this, I've been quite ashamed, but now there's no excuse for me.'

'But we like having you here,' said Darya. 'You don't need an excuse.'

'I can hardly go on staying here indefinitely?'

'Why not? Your salary's miserable, what's the use of wasting it on board and lodging? You'd be bored stiff with Jonson and Waring. Stupids. They haven't an idea in their heads outside playing the gramophone and knocking balls about.'

It was true that it had been very convenient to live free of cost. He had saved the greater part of his salary. He had a thrifty soul and had never been used to spending money when it wasn't necessary, but he was proud. He could not go on living at other people's expense. Darya looked at him with her quiet, observant eyes.

'Angus and I have got used to you now. I think we'd miss you. If you like, you can pay us for your board. You don't cost anything, but if it'll make you easier I'll find out exactly what difference you make in cookie's book and you can pay that.'

'It must be an awful nuisance having a stranger in the house,' he answered uncertainly.

'It'll be miserable for you there. Good heavens, the filth they eat.'

It was true also that at the Munros' you ate better than anywhere else at Kuala Solor. He had dined out now and then, and even at the Resident's you didn't get a very good dinner. Darya liked her food and kept the cook up to the mark. He made Russian dishes which were a fair treat. That cabbage soup of Darya's was worth walking five miles for. But Munro hadn't said anything.

'I'd be glad if you'd stay here,' he said now. 'It's very

convenient to have you on the spot. If anything comes up we can talk it over there and then. Waring and Jonson are very good fellows, but I daresay you'd find them rather limited after a bit.'

'Oh, well, then I'll be very pleased. Heaven knows, I couldn't want anything better than this. I was only afraid I was in the way.'

Next day it was raining cats and dogs and it was impossible to play tennis or football, but towards six Neil put on a mackintosh and went to the club. It was empty but for the Resident, who was sitting in an armchair reading 'The Fortnightly'. His name was Trevelyan, and he claimed to be related to the friend of Byron. He was a tall fat man, with close-cropped white hair and the large red face of a comic actor. He was fond of amateur theatricals and specialised in cynical dukes and facetious butlers. He was a bachelor, but generally supposed to be fond of the girls, and he liked his gin pahit before dinner. He owed his position to the Sultan's friendship. He was a slack, complacent man, a great talker, not very fond of work, who wanted everything to go smoothly and no one to give trouble. Though not considered especially competent he was popular in the community because he was easy-going and hospitable, and he certainly made life more comfortable than if he had been energetic and efficient. He nodded to Neil.

'Well, young fellow, how are bugs to-day?'

'Feeling the weather, sir,' said Neil gravely.

'Hi-hi.'

In a few minutes Waring, Jonson and another man, called Bishop, came in. He was in the Civil Service. Neil did not play bridge, so Bishop went up to the Resident.

'Would you care to make a fourth, sir?' he asked him. 'There's nobody much in the club to-day.'

The Resident gave the others a glance.

'All right. I'll just finish this article and join you. Cut for me and deal. I shall only be five minutes.'

Neil went up to the three men.

'Oh, I say, Waring, thanks awfully, but I can't move over to you after all. The Munros have asked me to stay on with them for good.'

A broad smile broke on Waring's face.

'Fancy that.'

'It's awfully nice of them, isn't it? They made rather a point of it. I couldn't very well refuse.'

'What did I tell you?' said Bishop.

'I don't blame the boy,' said Waring.

There was something in their manner that Neil did not like. They seemed to be amused. He flushed.

'What the hell are you talking about?' he cried.

'Oh, come off it,' said Bishop. 'We know our Darya. You're not the first good-looking young fellow she's had a romp with, and you won't be the last.'

The words were hardly out of his mouth before Neil's clenched fist shot out like a flash. He hit Bishop on the face and he fell heavily to the floor. Jonson sprang at Neil and seized him round the middle, for he was beside himself.

'Let me go,' he shouted. 'If he doesn't withdraw that I'll kill him.'

The Resident, startled by the commotion, looked up and rose to his feet. He walked heavily towards them.

'What's this? What's this? What the hell are you boys playing at?'

They were taken aback. They had forgotten him. He was their master. Jonson let go of Neil and Bishop picked himself up. The Resident, a frown on his face, spoke to Neil sharply.

'What's the meaning of this? Did you hit Bishop?'

'Yes, sir.'

'Why?'

'He made a foul suggestion reflecting on a woman's honour,' said Neil, very haughtily, and still white with rage.

The Resident's eyes twinkled, but he kept a grave face.

'What woman?'

'I refuse to answer,' said Neil, throwing back his head and drawing himself up to his full imposing height.

It would have been more effective if the Resident hadn't been a good two inches taller, and very much stouter.

'Don't be a damned young fool.'

'Darya Munro,' said Jonson.

'What did you say, Bishop?'

'I forget the exact words I used. I said she'd hopped into bed with a good many young chaps here, and I supposed she hadn't missed the chance of doing the same with MacAdam.'

'It was a most offensive suggestion. Will you be so good as to apologise and shake hands. Both of you.'

'I've had a hell of a biff, sir. My eye's going to look like the devil. I'm damned if I apologise for telling the truth.'

'You're old enough to know that the fact that your statement is true only makes it more offensive, and as far as your eye is concerned I'm told that a raw beef-steak is very efficacious in these circumstances. Though I put my desire that you should apologise in the form of a request out of politeness, it is in point of fact an order.'

There was a moment's silence. The Resident looked bland.

'I apologise for what I said, sir,' Bishop said sulkily.

'Now then, MacAdam.'

'I'm sorry I hit him, sir. I apologise, too.'

'Shake hands.'

The two young men solemnly did so.

'I shouldn't like this to go any further. It wouldn't be very nice for Munro, whom I think we all like. Can I count on you all holding your tongues?'

They nodded.

'Now be off with you. You stay, MacAdam, I want to have a few words with you.'

When the two of them were left alone, the Resident sat down and lit himself a cheroot. He offered one to Neil, but he only smoked cigarettes.

'You're a very violent young man,' said the Resident, with a smile. 'I don't like my officers to make scenes in a public place like this.'

'Mrs. Munro is a great friend of mine. She's been kindness itself to me. I won't hear a word said against her.'

'Then I'm afraid you'll have your job cut out for you if you stay here much longer.'

Neil was silent for a moment. He stood, tall and slim, before the Resident, and his grave young face was guileless. He flung back his head defiantly. His emotion made him speak in broader Scots even than usual.

'I've lived with the Munros for four months, and I give you my word of honour that so far as I am concerned there is not an iota of truth in what that beast said. Mrs. Munro has never treated me with anything that you could call undue familiarity. She's never by word or deed given me the smallest hint that she had an improper idea in her head. She's been like a mother to me or an elder sister.'

The Resident watched him with ironical eyes.

'I'm very glad to hear it. That's the best thing I've heard about her for a long time.'

'You believe me, sir, don't you?'

'Of course. Perhaps you've reformed her.' He called out. 'Boy. Bring me a gin pahit.' And then to Neil. 'That'll do. You can go now if you want to. But no more fighting, mind you, or you'll get the order of the boot.'

When Neil walked back to the Munros' bungalow the rain had stopped and the velvet sky was bright with stars. In the garden the fire-flies were flitting here and there. From the earth rose a scented warmth and you felt that if you stopped you would hear the growth of that luxuriant vegetation. A white flower of the night gave forth an overwhelming perfume. In the verandah Munro was typing some notes and Darya, lying at full length on a long chair, was reading. The lamp behind her lit her smoky hair so that it shone like an aureole. She looked up at Neil and putting down her book, smiled. Her smile was very friendly.

'Where have you been, Neil?'

'At the club.'

'Anybody there?'

The scene was so cosy and domestic, Darya's manner so peaceful and quietly assured, that it was impossible not to be touched. The two of them there, each occupied with his own concerns, seemed so united, their intimacy so natural, that no one could have conceived that they were not perfectly happy in one another. Neil did not believe a single word of what Bishop had said and the Resident had hinted. It was incredible. After all, he knew that what they had suspected of *him* was untrue, so what reason was there to think that the rest was any truer? They had dirty minds, all those people; because they were a lot of swine they thought everyone else as bad as they were. His knuckle hurt him a little. He was glad he had hit Bishop. He wished he knew who had started that filthy story. He'd wring his neck.

But now Munro fixed a date for the expedition that they had so much discussed, and in his careful way began to make preparations so that at the last moment nothing should be forgotten. The plan was to go as far up the river as possible and then make their way through the jungle and hunt for specimens on the little-known

Mount Hitam. They expected to be away two months. As the day on which they were to start grew nearer Munro's spirits rose, and though he did not say very much, though he remained quiet and self-controlled, you could tell by the light in his eyes and the jauntiness of his step how much he looked forward to it. One morning, at the museum, he was almost sprightly.

'I've got some good news for you,' he said suddenly to Neil, after they had been looking at some experiments they were making, 'Darya's coming with us.'

'Is she? That's grand.'

Neil was delighted. That made it perfect.

'It's the first time I've ever been able to induce her to accompany me. I told her she'd enjoy it, but she would never listen to me. Queer cattle, women. I'd given it up and never thought of asking her to come this time, and suddenly, last night, out of a blue sky she said she'd like to.'

'I'm awfully glad,' said Neil.

'I didn't much like the idea of leaving her by herself so long; now we can stay just as long as we want to.'

They started early one morning in four prahus, manned by Malays, and besides themselves the party consisted of their servants and four Dyak hunters. The three of them lay on cushions side by side, under an awning; in the other boats were the Chinese servants and the Dyaks. They carried bags of rice for the whole party, provisions for themselves, clothes, books and all that was necessary for their work. It was heavenly to leave civilisation behind them and they were all excited. They talked. They smoked. They read. The motion of the river was exquisitely soothing. They lunched on a grassy bank. Dusk fell and they moored for the night. They slept at a long house and their Dyak hosts celebrated their visit with arak, eloquence and a fantastic dance. Next day the river, narrowing, gave them more definitely the feeling that they were adventuring into the unknown, and the exotic vegetation that crowded the banks to the water's edge, like an excited mob pushed from behind by a multitude, caused Neil a breathless ravishment. O wonder and delight! On the third day, because the water was shallower and the stream more rapid, they changed into lighter boats, and soon it grew so strong that the boatmen could paddle no longer, and they poled against the current with powerful and magnificent gestures. Now and then they came to rapids and had to disembark, unload and haul the boats through a rock-strewn passage. After five days they reached a point beyond which they could go no further. There was a government bungalow there, and they settled in for a couple of nights while Munro made arrangements for their excursion into the interior. He wanted bearers for their baggage, and men to build a house for them when they reached Mount Hitam. It was necessary for Munro to see the headman of a village in the vicinity and thinking it would save time if he went himself rather than let the headman come to him, the day after they arrived he set out at dawn with a guide and a couple of Dyaks. He expected to be back in a few hours. When he had seen him off Neil thought he would have a bathe. There was a pool a little way from the bungalow, and the water was so clear that you saw every grain of the sandy bottom. The river was so narrow there that the trees over-arched it. It was a lovely spot. It reminded Neil of the pools in Scotch streams he had bathed in as a boy, and yet it was strangely different. It had an air of romance, a feeling of virgin nature, that filled him with sensations that he found hard to analyse. He tried, of course, but older heads than his have found it difficult to anatomize happiness. A kingfisher was sitting on an overhanging branch and its vivid blue was reflected as bluely in the crystal stream. It flew away with a flashing glitter of jewelled wings when Neil, slipping off his sarong and baju, scrambled down into the water. It was fresh without being cold. He splashed and tumbled about. He enjoyed the movement of his strong limbs. He floated and looked at the blue sky peeping through the leaves and the sun that here and there gilded the water. Suddenly he heard a voice.

'How white your body is, Neil.'

With a gasp he let himself sink and turning round saw Darya standing on the bank.

'I say, I haven't got any clothes on.'

'So I saw. It's much nicer bathing without. Wait a minute, I'll come in, it looks lovely.'

She also was wearing a sarong and a baju. He turned away his head quickly, for he saw that she was taking them off. He heard her splash into the water. He gave two or three strokes in order that she should have room to swim about at a good distance from him, but she swam up to him.

'Isn't the feel of the water on one's body lovely?' she said.

She laughed and opening her hand splashed water in his face. He was so embarrassed he did not know which way to look. In that limpid water it was impossible not to see that she was stark naked. It was not so bad now, but he could not help thinking how difficult it would be to get out. She seemed to be having a grand time.

'I don't care if I do get my hair wet,' she said.

She turned over on her back and with strong strokes swam round the pool. When she wanted to get out, he thought, the best thing would be if he turned his back, and when she was dressed she could go and he would get out later. She seemed quite unconscious of the awkwardness of the situation. He was vexed with her. It really was rather tactless to behave like that. She kept on talking to him just as if they were on dry land and properly dressed. She even called his attention to herself.

'Does my hair look awful? It's so fine it gets like rat tails when it's wet. Hold me under the shoulders a moment while I try to screw it up.'

'Oh, it's all right,' he said. 'You'd better leave it now.'

'I'm getting frightfully hungry,' she said presently. 'What about breakfast?'

'If you'll get out first and put on your things, I'll follow you in a minute.'

'All right.'

She swam the two strokes needed to bring her to the side, and he modestly looked away so that he should not see her get out nude from the water.

'I can't get up,' she cried. 'You'll have to help me.'

It had been easy enough to get in, but the bank overhung the water and one had to lift oneself up by the branch of a tree.

'I can't. I haven't got a stitch of clothing on.'

'I know that. Don't be so Scotch. Get up on the bank and give me a hand.'

There was no help for it. Neil swung himself up and pulled her after him. She had left her sarong beside his. She took it up unconcernedly and began to dry herself with it. There was nothing for him but to do the same, but for decency's sake he turned his back on her.

'You really have a most lovely skin,' she said. 'It's as smooth and white as a woman's. It's funny on such a manly virile figure. And you haven't got a hair on your chest.'

Neil wrapped the sarong round him and slipped his arms into the baju.

'Are you ready?'

She had porridge for breakfast, and eggs and bacon, cold meat and marmalade. Neil was a trifle sulky. She was really almost too Russian. It was stupid of her to behave like that; of course there was no harm in it, but it was just that sort of thing that made people think the things they did about her. The worst of it was that you couldn't give her a hint. She'd only laugh at you. But the fact was that if any of those men at Kuala Solor had seen them bathing like that together, stark naked, nothing would have persuaded them that something improper hadn't happened. In his judicious way Neil admitted to himself that you could hardly blame them. It was too bad of her. She had no right to put a fellow in such a position. He had felt such a fool. And say what you liked it was indecent.

Next morning, having seen their carriers on the way, a long procession in single file, each man carrying his load in a creel on his back, with their servants, guides and hunters, they started to walk. The path ran over the foothills of the mountain, through scrub and tall grass, and now and then they came to narrow streams which they crossed by rickety bridges of bamboo. The sun beat on them fiercely. In the afternoon they reached the shade of a bamboo forest, grateful after the glare, and the bamboos in their slender elegance rose to incredible heights, and the green light was like the light under the sea. At last they reached the primeval forest, huge trees swathed in luxuriant creepers, an inextricable tangle, and awe descended upon them. They cut their way through the undergrowth. They walked in twilight and only now and then caught through the dense foliage above them a glimpse of sunshine. They saw neither man nor beast, for the denizens of the jungle are shy and at the first sound of footsteps vanish from sight. They heard birds up high in the tall trees, but saw none save the twittering sunbirds that flew in the underwoods and delicately coquetted with the wild flowers. They halted for the night. The carriers made a floor of branches and on this spread water-proof sheets. The Chinese cook made them their dinner and then they turned in.

It was the first night Neil had ever spent in the jungle

and he could not sleep. The darkness was profound. The noise was deafening of innumerable insects, but like the roar of traffic in a great city it was so constant that in a little while it was like an impenetrable silence, and when on a sudden he heard the shriek of a monkey seized by a snake or the scream of a night-bird he nearly jumped out of his skin. He had a mysterious sensation that all around creatures were watching them. Over there, beyond the camp fires, savage warfare was waged and they three on their bed of branches were defenceless and alone in face of the horror of nature. By his side Munro was breathing quietly in his deep sleep.

'Are you awake, Neil?' Darya whispered.

'Yes. Is anything the matter?'

'I'm terrified.'

'It's all right. There's nothing to be afraid of.'

'The silence is so awful. I wish I hadn't come.'

She lit a cigarette.

Neil, having at last dozed off, was awakened by the hammering of a woodpecker, and its complacent laugh as it flew from one tree to another seemed to mock the sluggards. A hurried breakfast and the caravan started. The gibbons swung from branch to branch, gathering in the dawn dew from the leaves, and their strange cry was like the call of a bird. The light had driven away Darya's fears, and notwithstanding a sleepless night she was alert and gay. They continued to climb. In the afternoon they reached the spot that the guides had told them would be a good camping place, and here Munro decided to build a house. The men set to work. With their long knives they cut palm leaves and saplings and soon had erected a two-roomed hut raised on piles from the ground. It was neat and fresh and green. It smelt good.

The Munros, he from old habit, she because she had for years wandered about the world and had a catlike knack of making herself comfortable wherever she went, were at home anywhere. In a day they had arranged everything and settled down. Their routine was invariable. Every morning early Neil and Munro started out separately, collecting. The afternoon was devoted to pinning insects in boxes, placing butterflies between sheets of paper and skinning birds. When dusk came they caught moths. Darya busied herself with the hut and the servants, sewed and read and smoked innumerable cigarettes. The days passed very pleasantly, monotonous but eventful. Neil was enraptured. He explored the mountain in all directions. One day, to his pride, he found a new species of stick-insect. Munro named it Cuniculina MacAdami. This was fame. Neil (at twenty-two) realised that he had not lived in vain. But another day he only just escaped being bitten by a viper. Owing to its green colour he had not seen it and was only saved from lurching against it by the Dyak hunter who was with him. They killed it and brought it back to camp. Darya shuddered at the sight of it. She had a terror of the wild creatures of the jungle that was almost hysterical. She would never go more than a few yards from the camp for fear of being lost.

'Has Angus ever told you how he was lost?' she asked Neil one evening when they were sitting quietly together after dinner.

'It wasn't a very pleasant experience,' he smiled.

'Tell him, Angus.'

He hesitated a little. It was not a thing he liked to recall.

'It was some years ago, I'd gone out with my butterfly net and I'd been very lucky, I'd got several rare specimens that I'd been looking for a long time. After a while I thought I was getting hungry so I turned back. I walked for some time and it struck me I'd come a good deal farther than I knew. Suddenly I caught sight of an empty match-box. I swore. I knew at once what had happened. I'd thrown it away when I started to come back, I'd been walking in a circle and was exactly where I was an hour before. I was not pleased. But I had a look round and set off again. It was fearfully hot and I was simply dripping with sweat. I knew more or less the direction the camp was in and I looked about for traces of my passage to see if I had come that way. I thought I found one or two and went on hopefully. I was frightfully thirsty. I walked on and on, picking my way over snags and trailing plants, and suddenly I knew I was lost. I couldn't have gone so far in the right direction without hitting the camp. I can tell you I was startled. I knew I must keep my head, so I sat down and thought the situation over. I was tortured by thirst. It was long past midday and in three or four hours it would be dark. I didn't like the idea of spending a night in the jungle at all. The only thing I could think of was to try and find a stream; if I followed its course, it would eventually bring me to a larger stream and sooner or later to the river. But of course it might take a couple of days. I cursed myself for being such a fool, but there was nothing better to do and I began walking. At all events if I found a stream I should be able to get a drink. I couldn't find a trickle of water anywhere, not the smallest brook that might lead to something like a stream. I began to be alarmed. I saw myself wandering on till at last I fell exhausted. I knew there was a lot of game in the forest and if I came upon a rhino I was done for. The maddening thing was I knew I couldn't be more than ten miles from my camp. I forced myself to keep my head. The day was waning and in the depths of the jungle it was growing dark already. If I'd brought a gun I could have fired it. In the camp they must have realised I was lost and would be looking for me. The undergrowth was so thick that I couldn't see six feet into it and presently, I don't know if it was nerves or not, I had the sensation that some animal was walking stealthily beside me. I stopped and it stopped too. I went on and it went on. I couldn't see it. I could see no movement in the undergrowth. I didn't even hear the breaking of a twig or the brushing of a body through leaves, but I knew how silently those beasts could move, and I was positive something was stalking me. My heart beat so violently against my ribs that I thought it would break. I was scared out of my wits. It was only by the exercise of all the self-control I had that I prevented myself from breaking into a run. I knew if I did that I was lost. I should be tripped up before I had gone twenty yards by a tangled root and when I was down it would spring on me. And if I started to run God knew where I should get to. And I had to husband my strength. I felt very like crying. And that intolerable thirst. I've never been so frightened in my life. Believe me, if I'd had a revolver I think I'd have blown my brains out. It was so awful I just wanted to finish with it. I was so exhausted I could hardly stagger. If I had an enemy who'd done me a deadly injury I wouldn't wish him the agony I endured then. Suddenly I heard two shots. My heart stood still. They were looking for me. Then I did lose my head. I ran in the direction of the sound, screaming at the top of my voice, I fell, I picked myself up again, I ran on, I shouted till I thought my lungs would burst, there was another shot, nearer, I shouted again, I heard answering shouts; there was a scramble of men in the undergrowth. In a minute I was surrounded by Dyak hunters. They wrung and kissed my hands. They laughed and cried. I very nearly cried too. I was down and out, but they gave me a drink. We were only three miles from the camp. It was pitch dark when we got back. By God, it was a near thing.'

A convulsive shudder passed through Darya.

'Believe me, I don't want to be lost in the jungle again.'

'What would have happened if you hadn't been found?'

'I can tell you. I should have gone mad. If I hadn't been

stung by a snake or attacked by a rhino I should have gone on blindly till I fell exhausted. I should have starved to death. I should have died of thirst. Wild beasts would have eaten my body and ants cleaned my bones.'

Silence fell upon them.

Then it happened, when they had spent nearly a month on Mount Hitam, that Neil, notwithstanding the quinine Munro had made him take regularly, was stricken with fever. It was not a bad attack, but he felt very sorry for himself and was obliged to stay in bed. Darya nursed him. He was ashamed to give her so much trouble, but she would not listen to his protests. She was certainly very capable. He resigned himself to letting her do things for him that one of the Chinese boys could have done just as well. He was touched. She waited on him hand and foot. But when the fever was at its height and she sponged him all over with cold water, though the comfort was indescribable, he was excessively embarrassed. She insisted on washing him night and morning.

'I wasn't in the British hospital at Yokohama for six months without learning at least the routine of nursing,' she said, smiling.

She kissed him on the lips each time after she had finished. It was friendly and sweet of her. He rather liked it, but attached no importance to it; he even went so far, a rare thing for him, as to be facetious on the subject.

'Did you always kiss your patients at the hospital?' he asked her.

'Don't you like me to kiss you?' she smiled.

'It doesn't do me any harm.'

'It may even hasten your recovery,' she mocked.

One night he dreamt of her. He awoke with a start. He was sweating profusely. The relief was wonderful, and he knew that his temperature had fallen; he was well. He did not care. For what he had dreamt filled him with shame. He was horrified. That he should have such thoughts, even in his sleep, made him feel awful. He must be a monster of depravity. Day was breaking, and he heard Munro getting up in the room next door that he occupied with Darya. She slept late, and he took care not to disturb her. When he passed through Neil's room, Neil in a low voice called him.

'Hullo, are you awake?'

'Yes, I've had the crisis. I'm all right now.'

'Good. You'd better stay in bed to-day. Tomorrow you'll be as fit as a fiddle.'

'Send Ah Tan to me when you've had your breakfast, will you?'

'Right-ho.'

He heard Munro start out. The Chinese boy came and asked him what he wanted. An hour later Darya awoke. She came in to bid him good morning. He could hardly look at her.

'I'll just have my breakfast and then I'll come in and wash you,' she said.

'I'm washed. I got Ah Tan to do it.'

'Why?'

'I wanted to spare you the trouble.'

'It isn't a trouble. I like doing it.'

She came over to the bed and bent down to kiss him, but he turned away his head.

'Oh, don't,' he said.

'Why not?'

'It's silly.'

She looked at him for a moment, surprised, and then with a slight shrug of the shoulders left him. A little later she came back to see if there was anything he wanted. He pretended to be asleep. She very gently stroked his cheek.

'For God's sake don't do that,' he cried.

'I thought you were sleeping. What's the matter with you to-day?'

'Nothing.'

'Why are you being horrid to me? Have I done anything to offend you?'

'No.'

'Tell me what it is.'

She sat down on the bed and took his hand. He turned his face to the wall. He was so ashamed he could hardly speak.

'You seem to forget I'm a man. You treat me as if I was a boy of twelve.'

'Oh?'

He was blushing furiously. He was angry with himself and vexed with her. She really should be more tactful. He plucked nervously at the sheet.

'I know it means nothing to you and it ought not to mean anything to me. It doesn't when I'm well and up and about. One can't help one's dreams, but they are an indication of what is going on in the subconscious.'

'Have you been dreaming about me? Well, I don't think there's any harm in that.'

He turned his head and looked at her. Her eyes were gleaming, but his were sombre with remorse.

'You don't know men,' he said.

She gave a little burble of laughter. She bent down and threw her arms round his neck. She had nothing on but her sarong and baju.

'You darling,' she cried. 'Tell me, what did you dream?'

He was startled out of his wits. He pushed her violently aside.

'What are you doing? You're crazy.'

He jumped half out of bed.

'Don't you know that I'm madly in love with you?' she said.

'What *are* you talking about?'

He sat down on the side of the bed. He was frankly bewildered. She chuckled.

'Why do you suppose I came up to this horrible place? To be with you, ducky. Don't you know I'm scared stiff of the jungle? Even in here I'm frightened there'll be snakes or scorpions or something. I adore you.'

'You have no right to speak to me like that,' he said sternly.

'Oh, don't be so prim,' she smiled.

'Let's get out of here.'

He walked out on to the verandah and she followed him. He threw himself into a chair. She knelt by his side and tried to take his hands, but he withdrew them.

'I think you must be mad. I hope to God you don't mean what you say.'

'I do. Every word of it,' she smiled.

It exasperated him that she seemed unconscious of the frightfulness of her confession.

'Have you forgotten your husband?'

'Oh, what does he matter?'

'Darya.'

'I can't be bothered about Angus now.'

'I'm afraid you're a very wicked woman,' he said slowly, a frown darkening his smooth brow.

She giggled.

'Because I've fallen in love with you? Darling, you shouldn't be so absurdly good-looking.'

'For God's sake don't laugh.'

'I can't help it; you're comic – but still adorable. I love your white skin and your shining curly hair. I love you because you're so prim and Scotch and humourless. I love your strength. I love your youth.'

Her eyes glowed and her breath came quickly. She stooped and kissed his naked feet. He drew them away quickly, with a cry of protest, and in the agitation of his gesture nearly overthrew the rickety chair.

'Woman, you're insane. Have you no shame?'

'No.'

'What do you want of me?' he asked fiercely.

'Love.'

'What sort of a man do you take me for?'

'A man like any other,' she replied calmly.

'Do you think after all that Angus Munro has done for me I could be such a damned beast as to play about with his wife? I admire him more than any man I've ever known. He's grand. He's worth a dozen of me and you put together. I'd sooner kill myself than betray him. I don't know how you can think me capable of such a dastardly act.'

'Oh, my dear, don't talk such bilge. What harm is it going to do him? You mustn't take that sort of thing so tragically. After all, life is very short; we're fools if we don't take what pleasure we can out of it.'

'You can't make wrong right by talking about it.'

'I don't know about that. I think that's a very controvertible statement.'

He looked at her with amazement. She was sitting at his feet, cool to all appearance and collected, and she seemed to be enjoying the situation. She seemed quite unconscious of its seriousness.

'Do you know that I knocked a fellow down at the club because he made an insulting remark about you?'

'Who?'

'Bishop.'

'Dirty dog. What did he say?'

'He said you'd had affairs with men.'

'I don't know why people won't mind their own business. Anyhow, who cares what they say? I love you. I've never loved anyone like you. I'm absolutely sick with love for you.'

'Be quiet. Be quiet.'

'Listen, to-night when Angus is asleep, I'll slip into your room. He sleeps like a rock. There's no risk.'

'You mustn't do that.'

'Why not?'

'No, no, no.'

He was frightened out of his wits. Suddenly she sprang to her feet and went into the house.

Munro came back at noon, and in the afternoon they busied themselves as usual. Darya, as she sometimes did, worked with them. She was in high spirits. She was so gay that Munro suggested that she was beginning to enjoy the life.

'It's not so bad,' she admitted. 'I'm feeling happy to-day.'

She teased Neil. She seemed not to notice that he was silent and kept his eyes averted from her.

'Neil's very quiet,' said Munro. 'I suppose you're feeling a bit weak still.'

'No, I just don't feel very talkative.'

He was harassed. He was convinced that Darya was capable of anything. He remembered the hysterical frenzy of Nastasya Filipovna in 'The Idiot', and felt that she too could behave with that unfortunate lack of balance. He had seen her more than once fly into a temper with one of the Chinese servants and he knew how completely she could lose her self-control. Resistance only exasperated her. If she did not immediately get what she wanted she would go almost insane with rage. Fortunately she lost interest in a thing with the same suddenness with which she hankered for it, and if you could distract her attention for a minute she forgot all about it. It was in such situations that Neil had most admired Munro's tact. He had often been slyly amused to see with what a pawky and yet tender cunning he appeased her feminine tantrums. It was on Munro's account that Neil's indignation was so great. Munro was a saint, and from what a state of humiliation and penury and random shifts had he not taken her to make her his wife! She owed everything to him. His name protected her. She had respectability. The commonest gratitude should have made it impossible for her to harbour such thoughts as she had that morning expressed. It was all very well for men to make advances, that was what men did, but for women to do so was disgusting. His modesty was outraged. The passion he had seen in her face, and the indelicacy of her gestures, scandalised him.

He wondered whether she would really carry out her threat to come to his room. He didn't think she would dare. But when night came and they all went to bed, he was so terrified that he could not sleep. He lay there listening anxiously. The silence was broken only by the repeated and monotonous cry of an owl. Through the thin wall of woven palm leaves he heard Munro's steady breathing. Suddenly he was conscious that someone was stealthily creeping into his room. He had already made up his mind what to do.

'Is that you, Mr. Munro?' he called in a loud voice.

Darya stopped suddenly. Munro awoke.

'There's someone in my room. I thought it was you.'

'It's all right,' said Darya. 'It's only me. I couldn't sleep, so I thought I'd go and smoke a cigarette on the verandah.'

'Oh, is that all?' said Munro. 'Don't catch cold.'

She walked through Neil's room and out. He saw her light a cigarette. Presently she went back and he heard her get into bed.

He did not see her next morning, for he started out collecting before she was up, and he took care not to get in till he was pretty sure Munro also would be back. He avoided being alone with her till it was dark and Munro went down for a few minutes to arrange the moth-traps.

'Why did you wake Angus last night?' she said in a low angry whisper.

He shrugged his shoulders and going on with his work did not answer.

227

'Were you frightened?'

'I have a certain sense of decency.'

'Oh, don't be such a prig.'

'I'd rather be a prig than a dirty swine.'

'I hate you.'

'Then leave me alone.'

She did not answer, but with her open hand smartly slapped his face. He flushed, but did not speak. Munro returned and they pretended to be intent on whatever they were doing.

For the next few days Darya, except at meal-times and in the evenings, never spoke to Neil. Without pre-arrangement they exerted themselves to conceal from Munro that their relations were strained. But the effort with which Darya roused herself from a brooding silence would have been obvious to anyone more suspicious than Angus, and sometimes she could not help herself from being a trifle sharp with Neil. She chaffed him, but in her chaff was a sting. She knew how to wound and caught him on the raw, but he took care not to let her see it. He had an inkling that the good humour he affected infuriated her.

Then, one day when Neil came back from collecting, though he had delayed till the last possible minute before tiffin, he was surprised to find that Munro had not yet returned. Darya was lying on a mattress on the verandah, sipping a gin pahit and smoking. She did not speak to him when he passed through to wash. In a minute the Chinese boy came into his room and told him that tiffin was ready. He walked out.

'Where's Mr. Munro?' he asked.

'He's not coming,' said Darya. 'He sent a message to say that the place he's at is so good he won't come down till night.'

Munro had set out that morning for the summit of the mountain. The lower levels had yielded poor results in the way of mammals, and Munro's idea was, if he could find a good place higher up, with a supply of water, to transfer the camp. Neil and Darya ate their meal in silence. After they had finished he went into the house and came out again with his topi and his collecting gear. It was unusual for him to go out in the afternoon.

'Where are you going?' she asked abruptly.

'Out.'

'Why?'

'I don't feel tired. I've got nothing much else to do this afternoon.'

Suddenly she burst into tears.

'How can you be so unkind to me?' she sobbed. 'Oh, it is cruel to treat me like this.'

He looked down at her from his great height, his handsome, somewhat stolid face bearing a harassed look.

'What have *I* done?'

'You've been beastly to me. Bad as I am I haven't deserved to suffer like this. I've done everything in the world for you. Tell me one single little thing I could do that I haven't done gladly. I'm so terribly unhappy.'

He moved on his feet uneasily. It was horrible to hear her say that. He loathed and feared her, but he had still the respect for her that he had always felt, not only because she was a woman, but because she was Angus Munro's wife. She wept uncontrollably. Fortunately the Dyak hunters had gone that morning with Munro. There was no one about the camp but the three Chinese servants and they, after tiffin, were asleep in their own quarters fifty yards away. They were alone.

'I don't want to make you unhappy. It's all so silly. It's absurd of a woman like you to fall in love with a fellow like me. It makes me look such a fool. Haven't you got any self-control?'

'Oh, God. Self-control!'

'I mean, if you really cared for me you couldn't want

229

me to be such a cad. Doesn't it mean anything to you that your husband trusts us implicitly? The mere fact of his leaving us alone like this puts us on our honour. He's a man who would never hurt a fly. I should never respect myself again if I betrayed his confidence.'

She looked up suddenly.

'What makes you think he would never hurt a fly? Why, all those bottles and cases are full of the harmless animals he's killed.'

'In the interests of science. That's quite another thing.'

'Oh, you fool, you fool.'

'Well, if I am a fool I can't help it. Why do you bother about me?'

'Do you think I wanted to fall in love with you?'

'You ought to be ashamed of yourself.'

'Ashamed? How stupid! My God, what have I done that I should eat my heart out for such a pretentious ass?'

'You talk about what you've done for me. What has Munro done for you?'

'Munro bores me to death. I'm sick of him. Sick to death of him.'

'Then I'm not the first?'

Ever since her amazing avowal he had been tortured by the suspicion that what those men at Kuala Solor had said of her was true. He had refused to believe a word of it, and even now he could not bring himself to think that she could be such a monster of depravity. It was frightful to think that Angus Munro, so trusting and tender, should have lived in a fool's paradise. She could not be as bad as that. But she misunderstood him. She smiled through her tears.

'Of course not. How can you be so silly? Oh, darling, don't be so desperately serious. I love you.'

Then it was true. He had sought to persuade himself that what she felt for him was exceptional, a madness that together they could contend with and vanquish. But she was simply promiscuous.

'Aren't you afraid Munro will find out?'

She was not crying any more. She adored talking about herself, and she had a feeling that she was inveigling Neil into a new interest in her.

'I sometimes wonder if he doesn't know, if not with his mind, then with his heart. He's got the intuition of a woman and a woman's sensitiveness. Sometimes I've been certain he suspected and in his anguish I've sensed a strange, spiritual exaltation. I've wondered if in his pain he didn't find an infinitely subtle pleasure. There are souls, you know, that feel a voluptuous joy in laceration.'

'How horrible!' Neil had no patience with these conceits. 'The only excuse for you is that you're insane.'

She was now much more sure of herself. She gave him a bold look.

'Don't you think I'm attractive? A good many men have. You must have had dozens of women in Scotland who weren't so well made as I am.'

She looked down at her shapely, sensual figure with calm pride.

'I've never had a woman,' he said gravely.

'Why not?'

She was so surprised that she sprang to her feet. He shrugged his shoulders. He could not bring himself to tell her how disgusting the idea of such a thing was to him, and how vile he had thought the haphazard amours of his fellow-students at Edinburgh. He took a mystical joy in his purity. Love was sacred. The sexual act horrified him. Its excuse was the procreation of children and its sanctification marriage. But Darya, her whole body rigid, stared at him, panting; and suddenly, with a sobbing cry in which there was exultation and at the same time wild desire, she flung herself on her knees and seizing his hand passionately kissed it.

'Alyosha,' she gasped. 'Alyosha.'

And then, crying and laughing, she crumpled up in a heap at his feet. Strange, hardly human sounds issued from her throat and convulsive tremors passed through her body so that you would have thought she was receiving one electric shock after another. Neil did not know if it was an attack of hysteria or an epileptic fit.

'Stop it,' he cried. 'Stop it.'

He took her up in his strong arms and laid her in the chair. But when he tried to leave her she would not let him. She flung her arms round his neck and held him. She covered his face with kisses. He struggled. He turned his face away. He put his hand between her face and his to protect himself. Suddenly she dug her teeth into it. The pain was so great that, without thinking, he gave her a great swinging blow.

'You devil,' he cried.

His violent gesture had forced her to release him. He held his hand and looked at it. She had caught him by the fleshy part on the side and it was bleeding. Her eyes blazed. She was feeling alert and active.

'I've had enough of this. I'm going out,' he said.

She sprang to her feet.

'I'll come with you.'

He put on his topi and, snatching up his collecting gear, without a word turned on his heel. With one stride he leaped down the three steps that led from the floor of the house to the ground. She followed him.

'I'm going into the jungle,' he said.

'I don't care.'

In the ravening desire that possessed her she forgot her morbid fear of the jungle. She recked nothing of snakes and wild beasts. She did not mind the branches that hit her face or the creepers that entangled her feet. For a month Neil had explored all that part of the forest and he knew every yard of it. He told himself grimly that he'd teach her to come with him. He forced his way through the undergrowth with rapid strides; she followed him, stumbling but determined; he crashed on, blind with rage, and she crashed after him. She talked; he did not listen to what she said. She besought him to have pity on her. She bemoaned her fate. She made herself humble. She wept and wrung her hands. She tried to cajole him. The words poured from her lips in an unceasing stream. She was like a mad woman. At last in a little clearing he stopped suddenly and turning round faced her.

'This is impossible,' he cried. 'I'm fed up. When Angus comes back I must tell him I've got to go. I shall go back to Kuala Solor to-morrow morning and go home.'

'He won't let you go, he wants you. He finds you invaluable.'

'I don't care. I'll fake up something.'

'What?'

He mistook her.

'Oh, you needn't be frightened, I shan't tell him the truth. You can break his heart if you want to; I'm not going to.'

'You worship him, don't you? That dull, phlegmatic man.'

'He's worth a hundred of you.'

'It would be rather funny if I told him you'd gone because I wouldn't yield to your advances.'

He gave a slight start and looked at her to see if she was serious.

'Don't be such a fool. You don't think he'd believe that, do you? He knows it would never occur to me.'

'Don't be too sure.'

She had spoken carelessly, with no particular intention other than to continue the argument, but she saw that

233

he was frightened and some instinct of cruelty made her press the advantage.

'Do you expect mercy from me? You've humiliated me beyond endurance. You've treated me like dirt. I swear that if you make any suggestion of going I shall go straight to Angus and say that you took advantage of his absence to try and assault me.'

'I can deny it. After all it's only your word against mine.'

'Yes, but my word'll count. I can prove what I say.'

'What do you mean?'

'I bruise easily. I can show him the bruise where you struck me. And look at your hand.' He turned and gave it a sudden glance. 'How did those teeth marks get there?'

He stared at her stupidly. He had gone quite pale. How could he explain that bruise and that scar? If he was forced to in self-defence he could tell the truth, but was it likely that Angus would believe it? He worshipped Darya. He would take her word against anyone's. What monstrous ingratitude it would seem for all Munro's kindness and what treachery in return for so much confidence! He would think him a filthy skunk and from his standpoint with justice. That was what shattered him, the thought that Munro, for whom he would willingly have laid down his life, should think ill of him. He was so unhappy that tears, unmanly tears that he hated, came to his eyes. Darya saw that he was broken. She exulted. She was paying him back for the misery he had made her suffer. She held him now. He was in her power. She savoured her triumph and in the midst of her anguish laughed in her heart because he was such a fool. At that moment she did not know whether she loved or despised him.

'Now will you be good?' she said.

He gave a sob and blindly, with a sudden instinct of

escape from that abominable woman, took to his heels and ran as hard as he could. He plunged through the jungle, like a wounded animal, not looking where he was going, till he was out of breath. Then, panting, he stopped. He took out his handkerchief and wiped away the sweat that was pouring into his eyes and blinding him. He was exhausted and he sat down to rest.

'I must take care I don't get lost,' he said to himself.

That was the least of his troubles, but all the same he was glad that he had a pocket compass, and he knew in which direction he must go. He heaved a deep sigh and rose wearily to his feet. He started walking. He watched his way and with another part of his mind miserably asked himself what he should do. He was convinced that Darya would do what she had threatened. They were to be another three weeks in that accursed place. He dared not go; he dared not stay. His mind was in a whirl. The only thing was to get back to camp and think it out quietly. In about a quarter of an hour he came to a spot that he recognised. In an hour he was back. He flung himself miserably into a chair. And it was Angus who filled his thoughts. His heart bled for him. Neil saw now all sorts of things that before had been dark to him. They were revealed to him in a flash of bitter insight. He knew why the women at Kuala Solor were so hostile to Darya and why they looked at Angus so strangely. They treated him with a sort of affectionate levity. Neil thought it was because Angus was a man of science and so in their foolish eyes somewhat absurd. He knew now it was because they were sorry for him and at the same time found him ridiculous. Darya had made him the laughing-stock of the community. If ever there was a man who hadn't deserved ill usage at a woman's hands it was he. Suddenly Neil gasped and began to tremble all over. It had suddenly occurred to him that Darya did not know her way through the jungle; in his anguish he had hardly been conscious of where they went. Supposing she could not find her way home? She would be terrified. He remembered the ghastly story Angus had told them of being lost in the forest. His first instinct was to go back and find her, and he sprang to his feet. Then a fierce anger seized him. No, let her shift for herself. She had gone of her own free will. Let her find her own way back. She was an abominable woman and deserved all that might come to her. Neil threw back his head defiantly, a frown of indignation on his smooth young brow, and clenched his hands. Courage. He made up his mind. It would be better for Angus if she never returned. He sat down and began trying to make a skin of a Mountain Trogon. But the Trogon has a skin like wet tissue-paper and his hands trembled. He tried to apply his mind to the work he was doing, but his thoughts fluttered desperately, like moths in a trap, and he could not control them. What was happening over there in the jungle? What had she done when he suddenly bolted? Every now and then, against his will, he looked up. At any moment she might appear in the clearing and walk calmly up to the house. He was not to blame. It was the hand of God. He shuddered. Storm clouds were gathering in the sky and night fell quickly.

Just after dusk Munro arrived.

'Just in time,' he said. 'There's going to be a hell of a storm.'

He was in great spirits. He had come upon a fine plateau, with lots of water, from which there was a magnificent view to the sea. He had found two or three rare butterflies and a flying squirrel. He was full of plans to move the camp to this new place. All about it he had seen abundant evidence of animal life. Presently he went into the house to take off his heavy walking boots. He came out at once.

'Where's Darya?'

Neil stiffened himself to behave with naturalness.

'Isn't she in her room?'

'No. Perhaps she's gone down to the servants' quarters for something.'

He walked down the steps and strolled a few yards.

'Darya,' he called. 'Darya.' There was no answer. 'Boy.'

A Chinese servant came running up and Angus asked him where his mistress was. He did not know. He had not seen her since tiffin.

'Where can she be?' asked Munro, coming back, puzzled.

He went to the back of the house and shouted.

'She can't have gone out. There's nowhere to go. When did you see her last, Neil?'

'I went out collecting after tiffin. I'd had a rather unsatisfactory morning and I thought I'd try my luck again.'

'Strange.'

They hunted everywhere round the camp. Munro thought she might have made herself comfortable somewhere and gone to sleep.

'It's too bad of her to frighten one like this.'

The whole party joined in the search. Munro began to grow alarmed.

'It's not possible that she should have gone for a stroll in the jungle and lost her way. She's never moved more than a hundred yards from the house to the best of my knowledge since we've been here.'

Neil saw the fear in Munro's eyes and looked down.

'We'd better get everyone along and start hunting. There's one thing, she can't be far. She knows that if you get lost the best thing is to stay where you are and wait for people to come and find you. She'll be scared out of her wits, poor thing.'

He called out the Dyak hunters and told the Chinese

servants to bring lanterns. He fired his gun as a signal. They separated into two parties, one under Munro, the other under Neil, and went down the two rough paths that in the course of the month they had made in their comings and goings. It was arranged that whoever found Darya should fire three shots in quick succession. Neil walked with his face stern and set. His conscience was clear. He seemed to bear in his hands the decree of imminent justice. He knew that Darya would never be found. The two parties met. It was not necessary to look at Munro's face. He was distracted. Neil felt like a surgeon who is forced to perform a dangerous operation without assistance or appliances to save the life of someone he loves. It behoved him to be firm.

'She could never have got so far as this,' said Munro. 'We must go back and beat the jungle within the radius of a mile from the house inch by inch. The only explanation is that she was frightened by something or fainted or was stung by a snake.'

Neil did not answer. They started out again and, making lines, combed the undergrowth. They shouted. Every now and then they fired a gun and listened for a faint call in answer. Birds of the night flew with a whirring of wings, frightened, as they advanced with their lanterns; and now and then they half saw, half guessed at an animal, deer, boar or rhino, that fled at their approach. The storm broke suddenly. A great wind blew and then the lightning rent the darkness, like the scream of a woman in pain, and the tortured flashes, quick, quick, one on the heels of the other, like demon dancers in a frantic reel, wriggled down the night. The horror of the forest was revealed in an unearthly day. The thunder crashed down the sky in huge rollers, peal upon peal, like vast, primeval waves dashing against the shores of eternity. That fearful din hurtled through space as though sound had size and weight. The rain pelted in fierce torrents. Rocks and gigantic trees came tumbling down the mountain. The tumult was awful. The Dyak hunters cowered, gibbering in terror of the angry spirits who spoke in the storm, but Munro urged them on. The rain fell all night, with lightning and thunder, and did not cease till dawn. Wet through and shivering they returned to the camp. They were exhausted. When they had eaten Munro meant to resume the desperate search. But he knew that it was hopeless. They would never see her alive again. He flung himself down wearily. His face was tired and white and anguished.

'Poor child. Poor child.'

The End of the Flight

I shook hands with the skipper and he wished me luck. Then I went down to the lower deck crowded with passengers, Malays, Chinese and Dyaks, and made my way to the ladder. Looking over the ship's side I saw that my luggage was already in the boat. It was a large, clumsy-looking craft, with a great square sail of bamboo matting, and it was crammed full of gesticulating natives. I scrambled in and a place was made for me. We were about three miles from the shore and a stiff breeze was blowing. As we drew near I saw that the coconut trees in a green abundance grew to the water's edge, and among them I saw the brown roofs of the village. A Chinese who spoke English pointed out to me a white bungalow as the residence of the district officer. Though he did not know it, it was with him that I was going to stay. I had a letter of introduction to him in my pocket.

I felt somewhat forlorn when I landed and my bags were set down beside me on the glistening beach. This was a remote spot to find myself in, this little town on the north coast of Borneo, and I felt a trifle shy at the thought of presenting myself to a total stranger with the announcement that I was going to sleep under his roof, eat his food and drink his whisky, till another boat came in to take me to the port for which I was bound.

But I might have spared myself these misgivings, for the moment I reached the bungalow and sent in my letter he came out, a sturdy, ruddy, jovial man, of thirty-five perhaps, and greeted me with heartiness. While he held my hand he shouted to a boy to bring drinks and to another to look after my luggage. He cut short my apologies.

'Good God, man, you have no idea how glad I am to see you. Don't think I'm doing anything for you in putting you up. The boot's on the other leg. And stay as long as you damned well like. Stay a year.'

I laughed. He put away his day's work, assuring me that he had nothing to do that could not wait till the morrow, and threw himself into a long chair. We talked and drank and talked. When the heat of the day wore off we went for a long tramp in the jungle and came back wet to the skin. A bath and a change were very grateful, and then we dined. I was tired out and though my host was plainly willing to go on talking straight through the night I was obliged to beg him to allow me to go to bed.

'All right, I'll just come along to your room and see everything's all right.'

It was a large room with verandahs on two sides of it, sparsely furnished, but with a huge bed protected by mosquito netting.

'The bed is rather hard. Do you mind?'

'Not a bit. I shall sleep without rocking to-night.'

My host looked at the bed reflectively.

'It was a Dutchman who slept in it last. Do you want to hear a funny story?'

I wanted chiefly to go to bed, but he *was* my host, and being at times somewhat of a humorist myself I know that it is hard to have an amusing story to tell and find no listener.

'He came on the boat that brought you, on its last journey along the coast, he came into my office and asked where the dak bungalow was. I told him there wasn't one, but if he hadn't anywhere to go I didn't mind putting him up. He jumped at the invitation. I told him to have his kit sent along.

'"This is all I've got," he said.

'He held out a little shiny black grip. It seemed a bit scanty, but it was no business of mine, so I told him to go along to the bungalow and I'd come as soon as I was through with my work. While I was speaking the door of my office was opened and my clerk came in. The Dutchman had his back to the door and it may be that my clerk opened it a bit suddenly. Anyhow, the Dutchman gave a shout, he jumped about two feet into the air and whipped out a revolver.

'"What the hell are you doing?" I said.

'When he saw it was the clerk he collapsed. He leaned against the desk, panting, and upon my word he was shaking as though he'd got fever.

'"I beg your pardon," he said. "It's my nerves. My nerves are terrible."

'"It looks like it," I said.

'I was rather short with him. To tell you the truth I wished I hadn't asked him to stop with me. He didn't look as though he'd been drinking a lot and I wondered if he was some fellow the police were after. If he were, I said to myself, he could hardly be such a fool as to walk right into the lion's den.

'"You'd better go and lie down," I said.

'He took himself off, and when I got back to my bungalow I found him sitting quite quietly, but bolt upright, on the verandah. He'd had a bath and shaved and put on clean things and he looked fairly presentable.

'"Why are you sitting in the middle of the place like that?" I asked him. "You'll be much more comfortable in one of the long chairs."

'"I prefer to sit up," he said.

'Queer, I thought. But if a man in this heat would rather sit up than lie down it's his own lookout. He wasn't much to look at, tallish and heavily built, with a square head and close-cropped bristly hair. I should think he was about forty. The thing that chiefly struck me about him was his expression. There was a look in his eyes, blue eyes they were and rather small, that beat me altogether; and his face sagged as it were; it gave you the feeling he was going to cry. He had a way of looking quickly over his left shoulder as though he thought he heard something. By God, he was nervous. But we had a couple of drinks and he began to talk. He spoke English very well; except for a slight accent you'd never have known that he was a foreigner, and I'm bound to admit he was a good talker. He'd been everywhere and he'd read any amount. It was a treat to listen to him.

'We had three or four whiskies in the afternoon and a lot of gin pahits later on, so that when dinner came along we were by way of being rather hilarious and I'd come to the conclusion that he was a damned good fellow. Of course we had a lot of whisky at dinner and I happened to have a bottle of Benedictine, so we had some liqueurs afterwards. I can't help thinking we both got very tight.

'And at last he told me why he'd come. It was a rum story.'

My host stopped and looked at me with his mouth slightly open as though, remembering it now, he was struck again with its rumness.

'He came from Sumatra, the Dutchman, and he'd done something to an Achinese and the Achinese had sworn to kill him. At first he made light of it, but the fellow tried two or three times and it began to be rather a nuisance, so he thought he'd better go away for a bit. He went over to Batavia and made up his mind to have a good time. But when he'd been there a week he saw the fellow slinking along a wall. By God, he'd followed him. It looked as though he meant business. The Dutchman began to think it was getting beyond a joke and he thought the best thing he could do would be to skip off to Soerabaya. Well, he was strolling about there one day, you know how crowded the streets are, when he happened to turn round and saw the Achinese walking quite quietly just behind him. It gave him a turn. It would give anyone a turn.

'The Dutchman went straight back to his hotel, packed his things, and took the next boat to Singapore. Of course he put up at the Van Wyck, all the Dutch stay there, and one day when he was having a drink in the courtyard in front of the hotel, the Achinese walked in as bold as brass, looked at him for a minute, and walked out again. The Dutchman told me he was just paralysed. The fellow could have stuck his kriss into him there and then and he wouldn't have been able to move a hand to defend himself. The Dutchman knew he was just biding his time, that damned native was going to kill him, he saw it in his eyes; and he went all to pieces.'

'But why didn't he go to the police?' I asked.

'I don't know. I expect it wasn't a thing he wanted the police to be mixed up in.'

'But what had he done to the man?'

'I don't know that either. He wouldn't tell me. But by the look he gave when I asked him, I expect it was something pretty rotten. I have an idea he knew he deserved whatever the Achinese could do.'

My host lit a cigarette.

'Go on,' I said.

'The skipper of the boat that runs between Singapore and Kuching lives at the Van Wyck between trips and the boat was starting at dawn. The Dutchman thought it a grand chance to give the fellow the slip; he left his luggage at the hotel and walked down to the ship with the skipper, as if he were just going to see him off, and stayed on her when she sailed. His nerves were all anyhow by then. He didn't care about anything but getting rid of the Achinese. He felt pretty safe at Kuching. He got a room at the rest-house and bought himself a couple of suits and some shirts in the Chinese shops. But he told me he couldn't sleep. He dreamt of that man and half a dozen times he awakened just as he thought a kriss was being drawn across his throat. By God, I felt quite sorry for him. He just shook as he talked to me and his voice was hoarse with terror. That was the meaning of the look I had noticed. You remember, I told you he had a funny look on his face and I couldn't tell what it meant. Well, it was fear.

'And one day when he was in the club at Kuching he looked out of the window and saw the Achinese sitting there. Their eyes met. The Dutchman just crumpled up and fainted. When he came to, his first idea was to get out. Well, you know, there's not a hell of a lot of traffic at Kuching and this boat that brought you was the only one that gave him a chance to get away quickly. He got on her. He was positive the man was not on board.'

'But what made him come here?'

'Well, the old tramp stops at a dozen places on the coast and the Achinese couldn't possibly guess he'd chosen this one because he only made up his mind to get off when he saw there was only one boat to take the passengers ashore, and there weren't more than a dozen people in it.

'"I'm safe here for a bit at all events," he said, "and if I can only be quiet for a while I shall get my nerve back."

'"Stay as long as you like," I said. "You're all right here, at all events till the boat comes along next month, and if you like we'll watch the people who come off."

'He was all over me. I could see what a relief it was to him.

'It was pretty late and I suggested to him that we should turn in. I took him to his room to see that it was all right. He locked the door of the bathhouse and bolted the shutters, though I told him there was no risk, and when I left him I heard him lock the door I had just gone out of.

245

'Next morning when the boy brought me my tea I asked him if he'd called the Dutchman. He said he was just going to. I heard him knock and knock again. Funny, I thought. The boy hammered on the door, but there was no answer. I felt a little nervous, so I got up. I knocked too. We made enough noise to rouse the dead, but the Dutchman slept on. Then I broke down the door. The mosquito curtains were neatly tucked in round the bed. I pulled them apart. He was lying there on his back with his eyes wide open. He was as dead as mutton. A kriss lay across his throat, and say I'm a liar if you like, but I swear to God it's true, there wasn't a wound about him anywhere. The room was empty.

'Funny, wasn't it?'

'Well, that all depends on your idea of humour,' I replied.

My host looked at me quickly.

'You don't mind sleeping in that bed, do you?'

'N-no. But I'd just as soon you'd told me the story to-morrow morning.'

The Force of Circumstance

She was sitting on the verandah waiting for her husband to come in for luncheon. The Malay boy had drawn the blinds when the morning lost its freshness, but she had partly raised one of them so that she could look at the river. Under the breathless sun of midday it had the white pallor of death. A native was paddling along in a dug-out so small that it hardly showed above the surface of the water. The colours of the day were ashy and wan. They were but the various tones of the heat. (It was like an Eastern melody, in the minor key, which exacerbates the nerves by its ambiguous monotony; and the ear awaits impatiently a resolution, but waits in vain.) The cicadas sang their grating song with a frenzied energy; it was as continual and monotonous as the rustling of a brook over the stones; but on a sudden it was drowned by the loud singing of a bird, mellifluous and rich; and for an instant, with a catch at her heart, she thought of the English blackbird.

Then she heard her husband's step on the gravel path behind the bungalow, the path that led to the court-house in which he had been working, and she rose from her chair to greet him. He ran up the short flight of steps, for the bungalow was built on piles, and at the door the boy was waiting to take his topee. He came into the room which served them as a dining-room and parlour, and his eyes lit up with pleasure as he saw her.

'Hulloa, Doris. Hungry?'

'Ravenous.'

'It'll only take me a minute to have a bath and then I'm ready.'

'Be quick,' she smiled.

He disappeared into his dressing-room and she heard him whistling cheerily while, with the carelessness with which she was always remonstrating, he tore off his clothes and flung them on the floor. He was twenty-nine, but he was still a school-boy; he would never grow up. That was why she had fallen in love with him, perhaps, for no amount of affection could persuade her that he was good-looking. He was a little round man, with a red face like the full moon, and blue eyes. He was rather pimply. She had examined him carefully and had been forced to confess to him that he had not a single feature which she could praise. She had told him often that he wasn't her type at all.

'I never said I was a beauty,' he laughed.

'I can't think what it is I see in you.'

But of course she knew perfectly well. He was a gay, jolly little man, who took nothing very solemnly, and he was constantly laughing. He made her laugh too. He found life an amusing rather than a serious business, and he had a charming smile. When she was with him she felt happy and good-tempered. And the deep affection which she saw in those merry blue eyes of his touched her. It was very satisfactory to be loved like that. Once, sitting on his knees, during their honeymoon she had taken his face in her hands and said to him:

'You're an ugly, little fat man, Guy, but you've got charm. I can't help loving you.'

A wave of emotion swept over her and her eyes filled with tears. She saw his face contorted for a moment with the extremity of his feeling and his voice was a little shaky when he answered.

'It's a terrible thing for me to have married a woman who's mentally deficient,' he said.

She chuckled. It was the characteristic answer which she would have liked him to make.

It was hard to realise that nine months ago she had never even heard of him. She had met him at a small place by the seaside where she was spending a month's holiday with her mother. Doris was secretary to a member of parliament. Guy was home on leave. They were staying at the same hotel, and he quickly told her all about himself. He was born in Sembulu, where his father had served for thirty years under the second Sultan, and on leaving school he had entered the same service. He was devoted to the country.

'After all England's a foreign land to me,' he told her. 'My home's Sembulu.'

And now it was her home too. He asked her to marry him at the end of the month's holiday. She had known he was going to, and had decided to refuse him. She was her widowed mother's only child and she could not go so far away from her, but when the moment came she did not quite know what happened to her, she was carried off her feet by an unexpected emotion, and she accepted him. They had been settled now for four months in the little outstation of which he was in charge. She was very happy.

She told him once that she had quite made up her mind to refuse him.

'Are you sorry you didn't?' he asked, with a merry smile in his twinkling blue eyes.

'I should have been a perfect fool if I had. What a bit of luck that fate or chance or whatever it was stepped in and took the matter entirely out of my hands!'

Now she heard Guy clatter down the steps to the bath-house. He was a noisy fellow and even with bare feet he could not be quiet. But he uttered an exclamation. He said two or three words in the local dialect and she could not understand. Then she heard someone speaking to him, not aloud, but in a sibilant whisper. Really it was too bad of people to waylay him when he was going to have his bath. He spoke again and though his voice was low she could hear that he was vexed. The other voice was raised now; it was a woman's. Doris supposed it was someone who had a complaint to make. It was like a Malay woman to come in that surreptitious way. But she was evidently getting very little from Guy, for she heard him say: get out. That at all events she understood, and then she heard him bolt the door. There was a sound of the water he was throwing over himself (the bathing arrangements still amused her, the bath-houses were under the bedrooms, on the ground; you had a large tub of water and you sluiced yourself with a little tin pail) and in a couple of minutes he was back again in the dining-room. His hair was still wet. They sat down to luncheon.

'It's lucky I'm not a suspicious or a jealous person,' she laughed. 'I don't know that I should altogether approve of your having animated conversations with ladies while you're having your bath.'

His face, usually so cheerful, had borne a sullen look when he came in, but now it brightened.

'I wasn't exactly pleased to see her.'

'So I judged by the tone of your voice. In fact, I thought you were rather short with the young person.'

'Damned cheek, waylaying me like that!'

'What did she want?'

'Oh, I don't know. It's a woman from the kampong. She's had a row with her husband or something.'

'I wonder if it's the same one who was hanging about this morning.'

He frowned a little.

'Was there someone hanging about?'

'Yes, I went into your dressing-room to see that everything was nice and tidy, and then I went down to the

250

bath-house. I saw someone slink out of the door as I went down the steps and when I looked out I saw a woman standing there.'

'Did you speak to her?'

'I asked her what she wanted and she said something, but I couldn't understand.'

'I'm not going to have all sorts of stray people prowling about here,' he said. 'They've got no right to come.'

He smiled, but Doris, with the quick perception of a woman in love, noticed that he smiled only with his lips, not as usual with his eyes also, and wondered what it was that troubled him.

'What have you been doing this morning?' he asked.

'Oh, nothing much. I went for a little walk.'

'Through the kampong?'

'Yes. I saw a man send a chained monkey up a tree to pick coconuts, which rather thrilled me.'

'It's rather a lark, isn't it?'

'Oh, Guy, there were two little boys watching him who were much whiter than the others. I wondered if they were half-castes. I spoke to them, but they didn't know a word of English.'

'There are two or three half-caste children in the kampong,' he answered.

'Who do they belong to?'

'Their mother is one of the village girls.'

'Who is their father?'

'Oh, my dear, that's the sort of question we think it a little dangerous to ask out here.' He paused. 'A lot of fellows have native wives, and then when they go home or marry they pension them off and send them back to their village.'

Doris was silent. The indifference with which he spoke seemed a little callous to her. There was almost a frown on her frank, open, pretty English face when she replied.

'But what about the children?'

'I have no doubt they're properly provided for. Within his means, a man generally sees that there's enough money to have them decently educated. They get jobs as clerks in a Government office, you know; they're all right.'

She gave him a slightly rueful smile.

'You can't expect me to think it's a very good system.'

'You mustn't be too hard,' he smiled back.

'I'm not hard. But I'm thankful you never had a Malay wife. I should have hated it. Just think if those two little brats were yours.'

The boy changed their plates. There was never much variety in their menu. They started luncheon with river fish, dull and insipid, so that a good deal of tomato ketchup was needed to make it palatable, and then went on to some kind of stew. Guy poured Worcester Sauce over it.

'The old Sultan didn't think it was a white woman's country,' he said presently. 'He rather encouraged people to – keep house with native girls. Of course things have changed now. The country's perfectly quiet and I suppose we know better how to cope with the climate.'

'But Guy, the eldest of those boys wasn't more than seven or eight and the other was about five.'

'It's awfully lonely on an out-station. Why, often one doesn't see another white man for six months on end. A fellow comes out here when he's only a boy.' He gave her that charming smile of his which transfigured his round, plain, face. 'There are excuses, you know.'

She always found that smile irresistible. It was his best argument. Her eyes grew once more soft and tender.

'I'm sure there are.' She stretched her hand across the little table and put it on his. 'I'm very lucky to have caught you so young. Honestly, it would upset me dreadfully if I were told that you had lived like that.'

He took her hand and pressed it.

'Are you happy here, darling?'

'Desperately.'

She looked very cool and fresh in her linen frock. The heat did not distress her. She had no more than the prettiness of youth, though her brown eyes were fine; but she had a pleasing frankness of expression, and her dark, short hair was neat and glossy. She gave you the impression of a girl of spirit and you felt sure that the member of parliament for whom she worked had in her a very competent secretary.

'I loved the country at once,' she said. 'Although I'm alone so much I don't think I've ever once felt lonely.'

Of course she had read novels about the Malay Archipelago and she had formed an impression of a sombre land with great ominous rivers and a silent, impenetrable jungle. When the little coasting steamer set them down at the mouth of the river, where a large boat, manned by a dozen Dyaks, was waiting to take them to the station, her breath was taken away by the beauty, friendly rather than awe-inspiring, of the scene. It had a gaiety, like the joyful singing of birds in the trees, which she had never expected. On each bank of the river were mangroves and nipah palms, and behind them the dense green of the forest. In the distance stretched blue mountains, range upon range, as far as the eye could see. She had no sense of confinement nor of gloom, but rather of openness and wide spaces where the exultant fancy could wander with delight. The green glittered in the sunshine and the sky was blithe and cheerful. The gracious land seemed to offer her a smiling welcome.

They rowed on, hugging a bank, and high overhead flew a pair of doves. A flash of colour, like a living jewel, dashed across their path. It was a kingfisher. Two monkeys, with their dangling tails, sat side by side on a branch. On the horizon, over there on the other side of the broad and turbid river, beyond the jungle, was a row of little white clouds, the only clouds in the sky, and they looked like a row of ballet-girls, dressed in white, waiting at the back of the stage, alert and merry, for the curtain to go up. Her heart was filled with joy; and now, remembering it all, her eyes rested on her husband with a grateful assured affection.

And what fun it had been to arrange their living-room! It was very big. On the floor, when she arrived, was a torn and dirty matting; on the walls of unpainted wood hung (much too high up) photogravures of Academy pictures, Dyak shields and parangs. The tables were covered with Dyak cloth in sombre colours, and on them stood pieces of Brunei brass-ware, much in need of cleaning, empty cigarette tins and bits of Malay silver. There was a rough wooden shelf with cheap editions of novels and a number of old travel books in battered leather; and another shelf was crowded with empty bottles. It was a bachelor's room, untidy but stiff; and though it amused her she found it intolerably pathetic. It was a dreary, comfortless life that Guy had led there, and she threw her arms round his neck and kissed him.

'You poor darling,' she laughed.

She had deft hands and she soon made the room habitable. She arranged this and that, and what she could not do with she turned out. Her wedding-presents helped. Now the room was friendly and comfortable. In glass vases were lovely orchids and in great bowls huge masses of flowering shrubs. She felt an inordinate pride because it was her house (she had never in her life lived in anything but a poky flat) and she had made it charming for him.

'Are you pleased with me?' she asked when she had finished.

'Quite,' he smiled.

The deliberate understatement was much to her mind. How jolly it was that they should understand each other so well! They were both of them shy of displaying emotion, and it was only at rare moments that they used with one another anything but ironic banter.

They finished luncheon and he threw himself into a long chair to have a sleep. She went towards her room. She was a little surprised that he drew her to him as she passed and, making her bend down, kissed her lips. They were not in the habit of exchanging embraces at odd hours of the day.

'A full tummy is making you sentimental, my poor lamb,' she chaffed him.

'Get out and don't let me see you again for at least two hours.'

'Don't snore.'

She left him. They had risen at dawn and in five minutes were fast asleep.

Doris was awakened by the sound of her husband's splashing in the bath-house. The walls of the bungalow were like a sounding-board and not a thing that one of them did escaped the other. She felt too lazy to move, but she heard the boy bring the tea things in, so she jumped up and ran down into her own bath-house. The water, not cold but cool, was deliciously refreshing. When she came into the sitting-room Guy was taking the rackets out of the press, for they played tennis in the short cool of the evening. The night fell at six.

The tennis-court was two or three hundred yards from the bungalow and after tea, anxious not to lose time, they strolled down to it.

'Oh, look,' said Doris, 'there's that girl that I saw this morning.'

Guy turned quickly. His eyes rested for a moment on a native woman, but he did not speak.

'What a pretty sarong she's got,' said Doris. 'I wonder where it comes from.'

They passed her. She was slight and small, with the large, dark, starry eyes of her race and a mass of raven hair. She did not stir as they went by, but stared at them strangely. Doris saw then that she was not quite so young as she had at first thought. Her features were a trifle heavy and her skin was dark, but she was very pretty. She held a small child in her arms. Doris smiled a little as she saw it, but no answering smile moved the woman's lips. Her face remained impassive. She did not look at Guy, she looked only at Doris, and he walked on as though he did not see her. Doris turned to him.

'Isn't that baby a duck?'

'I didn't notice.'

She was puzzled by the look on his face. It was deathly white, and the pimples which not a little distressed her were more than commonly red.

'Did you notice her hands and feet? She might be a duchess.'

'All natives have good hands and feet,' he answered, but not jovially as was his wont; it was as though he forced himself to speak.

But Doris was not intrigued.

'Who is she, d'you know?'

'She's one of the girls in the kampong.'

They had reached the court now. When Guy went up to the net to see that it was taut he looked back. The girl was still standing where they had passed her. Their eyes met.

'Shall I serve?' said Doris.

'Yes, you've got the balls on your side.'

He played very badly. Generally he gave her fifteen and beat her, but today she won easily. And he played silently. Generally he was a noisy player, shouting all the time, cursing his foolishness when he missed a ball and chaffing her when he placed one out of her reach.

'You're off your game, young man,' she cried.

'Not a bit,' he said.

He began to slam the balls, trying to beat her, and sent one after the other into the net. She had never seen him with that set face. Was it possible that he was a little out of temper because he was not playing well? The light fell, and they ceased to play. The woman whom they had passed stood in exactly the same position as when they came and once more, with expressionless face, she watched them go.

The blinds on the verandah were raised now and on the table between their two long chairs were bottles of soda-water. This was the hour at which they had the first drink of the day and Guy mixed a couple of gin slings. The river stretched widely before them and on the further bank the jungle was wrapped in the mystery of the approaching night. A native was silently rowing up stream, standing at the bow of the boat, with two oars.

'I played like a fool,' said Guy, breaking a silence. 'I'm feeling a bit under the weather.'

'I'm sorry. You're not going to have fever, are you?'

'Oh, no. I shall be all right tomorrow.'

Darkness closed in upon them. The frogs croaked loudly and now and then they heard a few short notes from some singing bird of the night. Fireflies flitted across the verandah and they made the trees that surrounded it look like Christmas trees lit with tiny candles. They sparkled softly. Doris thought she heard a little sigh. It vaguely disturbed her. Guy was always so full of gaiety.

'What is it, old man?' she said gently. 'Tell mother.'

'Nothing. Time for another drink,' he answered breezily.

Next day he was as cheerful as ever and the mail came. The coasting steamer passed the mouth of the river twice a month, once on its way to the coalfields and once on its way back. On the outward journey it brought mail, which Guy sent a boat down to fetch. Its arrival was the excitement of their uneventful lives. For the first day or two they skimmed rapidly all that had come, letters, English papers and papers from Singapore, magazines and books, leaving for the ensuing weeks a more exact perusal. They snatched the illustrated papers from one another. If Doris had not been so absorbed she might have noticed that there was a change in Guy. She would have found it hard to describe and harder still to explain. There was in his eyes a sort of watchfulness and in his mouth a slight droop of anxiety.

Then, perhaps a week later, one morning when she was sitting in the shaded room studying a Malay grammar (for she was industriously learning the language) she heard a commotion in the compound. She heard the house-boy's voice, he was speaking angrily, the voice of another man, perhaps it was the water-carrier's, and then a woman's, shrill and vituperative. There was a scuffle. She went to the window and opened the shutters. The water-carrier had hold of a woman's arm and was dragging her along, while the houseboy was pushing her from behind with both hands. Doris recognised her at once as the woman she had seen one morning loitering in the compound and later in the day outside the tennis-court. She was holding a baby against her breast. All three were shouting angrily.

'Stop,' cried Doris. 'What are you doing?'

At the sound of her voice the water-carrier let go suddenly and the woman, still pushed from behind, fell to the ground. There was a sudden silence and the house-boy looked sullenly into space. The water-carrier hesitated a moment and then slunk away. The woman raised herself slowly to her feet, arranged the baby on her arm, and stood impassive, staring at Doris. The boy said something to her which Doris could not have heard even if she had understood; the woman by no change of face showed that his words meant anything to her; but she slowly strolled away. The boy followed her to the gate of the compound. Doris called to him as he walked back, but he pretended not to hear. She was growing angry now and she called more sharply.

'Come here at once,' she cried.

Suddenly, avoiding her wrathful glance, he came towards the bungalow. He came in and stood at the door. He looked at her sulkily.

'What were you doing with that woman?' she asked abruptly.

'Tuan say she no come here.'

'You mustn't treat a woman like that. I won't have it. I shall tell the Tuan exactly what I saw.'

The boy did not answer. He looked away, but she felt that he was watching her through his long eyelashes. She dismissed him.

'That'll do.'

Without a word he turned and went back to the servants' quarters. She was exasperated and she found it impossible to give her attention once more to the Malay exercises. In a little while the boy came in to lay the cloth for luncheon. On a sudden he went to the door.

'What is it?' she asked.

'Tuan just coming.'

He went out to take Guy's hat from him. His quick ears had caught the footsteps before they were audible to her. Guy did not as usual come up the steps immediately; he paused, and Doris at once surmised that the boy had gone down to meet him in order to tell him of the morning's incident. She shrugged her shoulders. The boy evidently wanted to get his story in first. But she was astonished when Guy came in. His face was ashy.

'Guy, what on earth's the matter?'

259

He flushed a sudden hot red.

'Nothing. Why?'

She was so taken aback that she let him pass into his room without a word of what she had meant to speak of at once. It took him longer than usual to have his bath and change his clothes and luncheon was served when he came in.

'Guy,' she said, as they sat down,' that woman we saw the other day was here again this morning.'

'So I've heard,' he answered.

'The boys were treating her brutally. I had to stop them. You must really speak to them about it.'

Though the Malay understood every word she said, he made no sign that he heard. He handed her the toast.

'She's been told not to come here. I gave instructions that if she showed herself again she was to be turned out.'

'Were they obliged to be so rough?'

'She refused to go. I don't think they were any rougher than they could help.'

'It was horrible to see a woman treated like that. She had a baby in her arms.'

'Hardly a baby. It's three years old.'

'How d'you know?'

'I know all about her. She hasn't the least right to come here pestering everybody.'

'What does she want?'

'She wants to do exactly what she did. She wants to make a disturbance.'

For a little while Doris did not speak. She was surprised at her husband's tone. He spoke tersely. He spoke as though all this were no concern of hers. She thought him a little unkind. He was nervous and irritable.

'I doubt if we shall be able to play tennis this afternoon,' he said. 'It looks to me as though we were going to have a storm.'

The rain was falling when she awoke and it was impossible to go out. During tea Guy was silent and abstracted. She got her sewing and began to work. Guy sat down and read such of the English papers as he had not yet gone through from cover to cover; but he was restless; he walked up and down the large room and then went out on the verandah. He looked at the steady rain. What was he thinking of? Doris was vaguely uneasy.

It was not till after dinner that he spoke. During the simple meal he had exerted himself to be his usual gay self, but the exertion was apparent. The rain had ceased and the night was starry. They sat on the verandah. In order not to attract insects they had put out the lamp in the sitting-room. At their feet, with a mighty, formidable sluggishness, silent, mysterious and fatal, flowed the river. It had the terrible deliberation and the relentlessness of destiny.

'Doris, I've got something to say to you,' he said suddenly.

His voice was very strange. Was it her fancy that he had difficulty in keeping it quite steady? She felt a little pang in her heart because he was in distress, and she put her hand gently into his. He drew it away.

'It's rather a long story. I'm afraid it's not a very nice one and I find it rather difficult to tell. I'm going to ask you not to interrupt me, or to say anything, till I've finished.'

In the darkness she could not see his face, but she felt that it was haggard. She did not answer. He spoke in a voice so low that it hardly broke the silence of the night.

'I was only eighteen when I came out here. I came straight from school. I spent three months in Kuala Solor, and then I was sent to a station up the Sembulu River. Of course there was a Resident there and his wife. I lived in the court-house, but I used to have my meals with them and spend the evening with them. I had an awfully good time. Then the fellow who was here fell ill and had to go home. We were short of men on account of the war and I was put in charge of this place. Of course I was very young, but I spoke the language like a native, and they remembered my father. I was as pleased as punch to be on my own.'

He was silent while he knocked the ashes out of his pipe and refilled it. When he lit a match Doris, without looking at him, noticed that his hand was unsteady.

'I'd never been alone before. Of course at home there'd been father and mother and generally an assistant. And then at school naturally there were always fellows about. On the way out, on the boat, there were people all the time, and at K.S., and the same at my first post. The people there were almost like my own people. I seemed always to live in a crowd. I like people. I'm a noisy blighter. I like to have a good time. All sorts of things make me laugh and you must have somebody to laugh with. But it was different here. Of course it was all right in the day time; I had my work and I could talk to the Dyaks. Although they were head-hunters in those days and now and then I had a bit of trouble with them, they were an awfully decent lot of fellows. I got on very well with them. Of course I should have liked a white man to gas to, but they were better than nothing, and it was easier for me because they didn't look upon me quite as a stranger. I liked the work too. It was rather lonely in the evening to sit on the verandah and drink a gin and bitters by myself, but I could read. And the boys were about. My own boy was called Abdul. He'd known my father. When I got tired of reading I could give him a shout and have a bit of a jaw with him.

'It was the nights that did for me. After dinner the boys shut up and went away to sleep in the kampong. I was all alone. There wasn't a sound in the bungalow except now and then the croak of the chik-chak. It used to come out of the silence, suddenly, so that it made me jump. Over in the kampong I heard the sound of a gong or fire-crackers. They were having a good time, they weren't so far away, but I had to stay where I was. I was tired of reading. I couldn't have been more of a prisoner if I'd been in jail. Night after night it was the same. I tried drinking three or four whiskies, but it's poor fun drinking alone, and it didn't cheer me up; it only made me feel rather rotten next day. I tried going to bed immediately after dinner, but I couldn't sleep. I used to lie in bed, getting hotter and hotter, and more wide awake, till I didn't know what to do with myself. By George, those nights were long. D'you know, I got so low, I was so sorry for myself that sometimes – it makes me laugh now when I think of it, but I was only nineteen and a half – sometimes I used to cry.

'Then, one evening, after dinner, Abdul had cleared away and was just going off, when he gave a little cough. He said, wasn't I lonely in the house all night by myself? "Oh, no, that's all right," I said. I didn't want him to know what a damned fool I was, but I expect he knew all right. He stood there without speaking, and I knew he wanted to say something to me. "What is it?" I said. "Spit it out." Then he said that if I'd like to have a girl to come and live with me he knew one who was willing. She was a very good girl and he could recommend her. She'd be no trouble and it would be someone to have about the bungalow. She'd mend my things for me . . . I felt awfully low. It had been raining all day and I hadn't been able to get any exercise. I knew I shouldn't sleep for hours. It wouldn't cost me very much money, he said, her people were poor and they'd be quite satisfied with a small present. Two hundred Straits dollars. "You look," he said. "If you don't like her you send her away." I asked him where she was. "She's here," he said. "I call her."

263

He went to the door. She'd been waiting on the steps with her mother. They came in and sat down on the floor. I gave them some sweets. She was shy, of course, but cool enough, and when I said something to her she gave me a smile. She was very young, hardly more than a child, they said she was fifteen. She was awfully pretty, and she had her best clothes on. We began to talk. She didn't say much, but she laughed a lot when I chaffed her. Abdul said I'd find she had plenty to say for herself when she got to know me. He told her to come and sit by me. She giggled and refused, but her mother told her to come, and I made room for her on the chair. She blushed and laughed, but she came, and then she snuggled up to me. The boy laughed too. "You see, she's taken to you already," he said. "Do you want her to stay?" he asked. "Do you want to?" I said to her. She hid her face, laughing, on my shoulder. She was very soft and small. "Very well," I said, "let her stay." '

Guy leaned forward and helped himself to a whisky and soda.

'May I speak now?' asked Doris.

'Wait a minute, I haven't finished yet. I wasn't in love with her, not even at the beginning. I only took her so as to have somebody about the bungalow. I think I should have gone mad if I hadn't, or else taken to drink. I was at the end of my tether. I was too young to be quite alone. I was never in love with anyone but you.' He hesitated a moment. 'She lived here till I went home last year on leave. It's the woman you've seen hanging about.'

'Yes, I guessed that. She had a baby in her arms. Is that your child?'

'Yes. It's a little girl.'

'Is it the only one?'

'You saw the two small boys the other day in the kampong. You mentioned them.'

'She has three children then?'

'Yes.'

'It's quite a family you've got.'

She felt the sudden gesture which her remark forced from him, but he did not speak.

'Didn't she know that you were married till you suddenly turned up here with a wife?' asked Doris.

'She knew I was going to be married.'

'When?'

'I sent her back to the village before I left here. I told her it was all over. I gave her what I'd promised. She always knew it was only a temporary arrangement. I was fed up with it. I told her I was going to marry a white woman.'

'But you hadn't even seen me then.'

'No, I know. But I'd made up my mind to marry when I was home.' He chuckled in his old manner. 'I don't mind telling you that I was getting rather despondent about it when I met you. I fell in love with you at first sight and then I knew it was either you or nobody.'

'Why didn't you tell me? Don't you think it would have been only fair to give me a chance of judging for myself? It might have occurred to you that it would be rather a shock to a girl to find out that her husband had lived for ten years with another girl and had three children.'

'I couldn't expect you to understand. The circumstances out here are peculiar. It's the regular thing. Five men out of six do it. I thought perhaps it would shock you and I didn't want to lose you. You see, I was most awfully in love with you. I am now, darling. There was no reason that you should ever know. I didn't expect to come back here. One seldom goes back to the same station after home leave. When we came here I offered her money if she'd go to some other village. First she said she would and then she changed her mind.'

'Why have you told me now?'

'She's been making the most awful scenes. I don't

know how she found out that you knew nothing about it. As soon as she did she began to blackmail me. I've had to give her an awful lot of money. I gave orders that she wasn't to be allowed in the compound. This morning she made that scene just to attract your attention. She wanted to frighten me. It couldn't go on like that. I thought the only thing was to make a clean breast of it.'

There was a long silence as he finished. At last he put his hand on hers.

'You do understand, Doris, don't you? I know I've been to blame.'

She did not move her hand. He felt it cold beneath his.

'Is she jealous?'

'I daresay there were all sorts of perks when she was living here, and I don't suppose she much likes not getting them any longer. But she was never in love with me any more than I was in love with her. Native women never do really care for white men, you know.'

'And the children?'

'Oh, the children are all right. I've provided for them. As soon as the boys are old enough I shall send them to school at Singapore.'

'Do they mean nothing to you at all?'

He hesitated.

'I want to be quite frank with you. I should be sorry if anything happened to them. When the first one was expected I thought I'd be much fonder of it than I ever had been of its mother. I suppose I should have been if it had been white. Of course, when it was a baby it was rather funny and touching, but I had no particular feeling that it was mine. I think that's what it is; you see, I have no sense of their belonging to me. I've reproached myself sometimes, because it seemed rather unnatural, but the honest truth is that they're no more to me than if they were somebody else's children. Of course a lot of slush is talked about children by people who haven't got any.'

Now she had heard everything. He waited for her to speak, but she said nothing. She sat motionless.

'Is there anything more you want to ask me, Doris?' he said at last.

'No, I've got rather a headache. I think I shall go to bed.' Her voice was as steady as ever. 'I don't quite know what to say. Of course it's been all very unexpected. You must give me a little time to think.'

'Are you very angry with me?'

'No. Not at all. Only – only I must be left to myself for a while. Don't move. I'm going to bed.'

She rose from her long chair and put her hand on his shoulder.

'It's so very hot tonight. I wish you'd sleep in your dressing-room. Goodnight.'

She was gone. He heard her lock the door of her bedroom.

She was pale next day and he could see that she had not slept. There was no bitterness in her manner, she talked as usual, but without ease; she spoke of this and that as though she were making conversation with a stranger. They had never had a quarrel, but it seemed to Guy that so would she talk if they had had a disagreement and the subsequent reconciliation had left her still wounded. The look in her eyes puzzled him; he seemed to read in them a strange fear. Immediately after dinner she said:

'I'm not feeling very well tonight. I think I shall go straight to bed.'

'Oh, my poor darling, I'm so sorry,' he cried.

'It's nothing. I shall be all right in a day or two.'

'I shall come in and say goodnight to you later.'

'No, don't do that. I shall try and get straight off to sleep.'

'Well, then, kiss me before you go.'

He saw that she flushed. For an instant she seemed to hesitate; then, with averted eyes, she leaned towards him. He took her in his arms and sought her lips, but she turned her face away and he kissed her cheek. She left him quickly and again he heard the key turn softly in the lock of her door. He flung himself heavily on the chair. He tried to read, but his ear was attentive to the smallest sound in his wife's room. She had said she was going to bed, but he did not hear her move. The silence in there made him unaccountably nervous. Shading the lamp with his hand he saw that there was a glimmer under her door; she had not put out her light. What on earth was she doing? He put down his book. It would not have surprised him if she had been angry and had made him a scene, or if she had cried; he could have coped with that; but her calmness frightened him. And then what was that fear which he had seen so plainly in her eyes? He thought once more over all he had said to her on the previous night. He didn't know how else he could have put it. After all, the chief point was that he'd done the same as everybody else, and it was all over long before he met her. Of course as things turned out he had been a fool, but anyone could be wise after the event. He put his hand to his heart. Funny how it hurt him there.

'I suppose that's the sort of thing people mean when they say they're heartbroken,' he said to himself. 'I wonder how long it's going on like this?'

Should he knock at the door and tell her he must speak to her? It was better to have it out. He *must* make her understand. But the silence scared him. Not a sound! Perhaps it was better to leave her alone. Of course it had been a shock. He must give her as long as she wanted. After all, she knew how devotedly he loved her. Patience, that was the only thing; perhaps she was fighting it out with herself; he must give her time; he must have patience.

Next morning he asked her if she had slept better.

'Yes, much,' she said.

'Are you very angry with me?' he asked piteously.

She looked at him with candid, open eyes.

'Not a bit.'

'Oh, my dear, I'm so glad. I've been a brute and a beast. I know it's been hateful for you. But do forgive me. I've been so miserable.'

'I do forgive you. I don't even blame you.'

He gave her a little rueful smile, and there was in his eyes the look of a whipped dog.

'I haven't much liked sleeping by myself the last two nights.'

She glanced away. Her face grew a trifle paler.

'I've had the bed in my room taken away. It took up so much space. I've had a little camp bed put there instead.'

'My dear, what are you talking about?'

Now she looked at him steadily.

'I'm not going to live with you as your wife again.'

'Never?'

She shook her head. He looked at her in a puzzled way. He could hardly believe he had heard aright and his heart began to beat painfully.

'But that's awfully unfair to me, Doris.'

'Don't you think it was a little unfair to me to bring me out here in the circumstances?'

'But you just said you didn't blame me.'

'That quite true. But the other's different. I can't do it.'

'But how are we going to live together like that?'

She stared at the floor. She seemed to ponder deeply.

'When you wanted to kiss me on the lips last night I – it almost made me sick.'

'Doris.'

She looked at him suddenly and her eyes were cold and hostile.

'That bed I slept on, is that the bed in which she had her children?' She saw him flush deeply. 'Oh, it's horrible. How could you?' She wrung her hands, and her twisting, tortured fingers looked like little writhing snakes. But she made a great effort and controlled herself. 'My mind is quite made up. I don't want to be unkind to you, but there are some things that you can't ask me to do. I've thought it all over. I've been thinking of nothing else since you told me, night and day, till I'm exhausted. My first instinct was to get up and go. At once. The steamer will be here in two or three days.'

'Doesn't it mean anything to you that I love you?'

'Oh, I know you love me. I'm not going to do that. I want to give us both a chance. I have loved you so, Guy.' Her voice broke, but she did not cry. 'I don't want to be unreasonable. Heaven knows, I don't want to be unkind. Guy, will you give me time?'

'I don't know quite what you mean.'

'I just want you to leave me alone. I'm frightened by the feelings that I have.'

He had been right then; she was afraid.

'What feelings?'

'Please don't ask me. I don't want to say anything to wound you. Perhaps I shall get over them. Heaven knows, I want to. I'll try, I promise you. I'll try. Give me six months. I'll do everything in the world for you, but just that one thing.' She made a little gesture of appeal. 'There's no reason why we shouldn't be happy enough together. If you really love me you'll – you'll have patience.'

He sighed deeply.

'Very well,' he said. 'Naturally I don't want to force you to do anything you don't like. It shall be as you say.'

He sat heavily for a little, as though, on a sudden grown old, it was an effort to move; then he got up.

'I'll be getting along to the office.'

He took his topee and went out.

A month passed. Women conceal their feelings better than men and a stranger visiting them would never have guessed that Doris was in any way troubled. But in Guy the strain was obvious; his round, good-natured face was drawn, and in his eyes was a hungry, harassed look. He watched Doris. She was gay and she chaffed him as she had been used to do; they played tennis together; they chatted about one thing and another. But it was evident that she was merely playing a part, and at last, unable to contain himself, he tried to speak again of his connection with the Malay woman.

'Oh, Guy, there's no object in going back on all that,' she answered breezily. 'We've said all we had to say about it and I don't blame you for anything.'

'Why do you punish me then?'

'My poor boy, I don't want to punish you. It's not my fault if . . . ' she shrugged her shoulders. 'Human nature is very odd.'

'I don't understand.'

'Don't try.'

The words might have been harsh, but she softened them with a pleasant, friendly smile. Every night when she went to bed she leaned over Guy and lightly kissed his cheek. Her lips only touched it. It was as though a moth had just brushed his face in its flight.

A second month passed, then a third, and suddenly the six months which had seemed so interminable were over. Guy asked himself whether she remembered. He gave a strained attention now to everything she said, to every look on her face and to every gesture of her hands. She remained impenetrable. She had asked him to give her six months; well, he had.

The coasting steamer passed the mouth of the river, dropped their mail, and went on its way. Guy busily wrote the letters which it would pick up on the return journey. Two or three days passed by. It was a Tuesday and the prahu was to start at dawn on Thursday to await the steamer. Except at meal time when Doris exerted herself to make conversation they had not of late talked very much together; and after dinner as usual they took their books and began to read; but when the boy had finished clearing away and was gone for the night Doris put down hers.

'Guy, I have something I want to say to you,' she murmured.

His heart gave a sudden thud against his ribs and he felt himself change colour.

'Oh, my dear, don't look like that, it's not so very terrible,' she laughed.

But he thought her voice trembled a little.

'Well?'

'I want you to do something for me.'

'My darling, I'll do anything in the world for you.'

He put out his hand to take hers, but she drew it away.

'I want you to let me go home.'

'You?' he cried aghast. 'When? Why?'

'I've borne it as long as I can. I'm at the end of my tether.'

'How long do you want to go for? For always?'

'I don't know. I think so.' She gathered determination. 'Yes, for always.'

'Oh, my God!'

His voice broke and she thought he was going to cry.

'Oh, Guy, don't blame me. It really is not my fault. I can't help myself.'

'You asked me for six months. I accepted your terms. You can't say I've made a nuisance of myself.'

'No, no.'

'I've tried not to let you see what a rotten time I was having.'

'I know. I'm very grateful to you. You've been awfully kind to me. Listen, Guy, I want to tell you again that I don't blame you for a single thing you did. After all, you were only a boy, and you did no more than the others; I know what the loneliness is here. Oh, my dear, I'm so dreadfully sorry for you. I knew all that from the beginning. That's why I asked for six months. My common sense tells me that I'm making a mountain out of a molehill. I'm unreasonable; I'm being unfair to you. But, you see, common sense has nothing to do with it; my whole soul is in revolt. When I see the woman and her children in the village I just feel my legs shaking. Everything in this house; when I think of that bed I slept in it gives me goose-flesh . . . You don't know what I've endured.'

'I think I've persuaded her to go away. And I've applied for a transfer.'

'That wouldn't help. She'd be there always. You belong to them, you don't belong to me. I think perhaps I could have stood it if there'd only been one child, but three; and the boys are quite big boys. For ten years you lived with her.' And now she came out with what she had been working up to. She was desperate. 'It's a physical thing, I can't help it, it's stronger than I am. I think of those thin black arms of hers round you and it fills me with a physical nausea. I think of you holding those little black babies in your arms. Oh, its loathsome. The touch of you is odious to me. Each night, when I've kissed you, I've had to brace myself up to it, I've had to clench my hands and force myself to touch your cheek.' Now she was clasping and unclasping her fingers in a nervous agony, and her voice was out of control. 'I know it's I who am to blame now. I'm a silly, hysterical woman. I thought

273

I'd get over it. I can't, and now I never shall. I've brought it all on myself; I'm willing to take the consequences; if you say I must stay here, I'll stay, but if I stay I shall die. I beseech you to let me go.'

And now the tears which she had restrained so long overflowed and she wept broken-heartedly. He had never seen her cry before.

'Of course I don't want to keep you here against your will,' he said hoarsely.

Exhausted, she leaned back in her chair. Her features were all twisted and awry. It was horribly painful to see the abandonment of grief on that face which was habitually so placid.

'I'm so sorry, Guy. I've broken your life, but I've broken mine too. And we might have been so happy.'

'When do you want to go? On Thursday?'

'Yes.'

She looked at him piteously. He buried his face in his hands. At last he looked up.

'I'm tired out,' he muttered.

'May I go?'

'Yes.'

For two minutes perhaps they sat there without a word. She started when the chik-chak gave its piercing, hoarse and strangely human cry. Guy rose and went out on to the verandah. He leaned against the rail and looked at the softly flowing water. He heard Doris go into her room.

Next morning, up earlier than usual, he went to her door and knocked.

'Yes?'

'I have to go up river today. I shan't be back till late.'

'All right.'

She understood. He had arranged to be away all day in order not to be about while she was packing. It was heartbreaking work. When she had packed her clothes she looked round the sitting-room at the things that belonged to her. It seemed dreadful to take them. She left everything but the photograph of her mother. Guy did not come in till ten o'clock at night.

'I'm sorry I couldn't get back to dinner,' he said. 'The headman at the village I had to go to had a lot of things for me to attend to.'

She saw his eyes wander about the room and notice that her mother's photograph no longer stood in its place.

'Is everything quite ready?' he asked. 'I've ordered the boatman to be at the steps at dawn.

'I've told the boy to wake me at five.'

'I'd better give you some money.' He went to his desk and wrote out a cheque. He took some notes from a drawer. 'Here's some cash to take you as far as Singapore and at Singapore you'll be able to change the cheque.'

'Thank you.'

'Would you like me to come to the mouth of the river with you?'

'Oh, I think it would be better if we said goodbye here.'

'All right. I think I shall turn in. I've had a long day and I'm dead beat.'

He did not even touch her hand. He went into his room. In a few minutes she heard him throw himself on his bed. For a little while she sat looking for the last time round that room in which she had been so happy and so miserable. She sighed deeply. She got up and went into her own room. Everything was packed except the one or two things she needed for the night.

It was dark when the boy awakened them. They dressed hurriedly and when they were ready breakfast was waiting for them. Presently they heard the boat row up to the landing-stage below the bungalow, and then the servants carried down her luggage. It was a poor pretence they made of eating. The darkness thinned away

275

and the river was ghostly. It was not yet day, but it was
no longer night. In the silence the voices of the natives
at the landing-stage were very clear. Guy glanced at his
wife's untouched plate.

'If you're finished we might stroll down. I think you
ought to be starting.'

She did not answer. She rose from the table. She went
into her room to see that nothing had been forgotten
and then side by side with him walked down the steps.
A little winding path led them to the river. At the
landing-stage the native guards in their smart uniform
were lined up and they presented arms as Guy and
Doris passed. The head boatman gave her his hand as
she stepped into the boat. She turned and looked at Guy.
She wanted desperately to say one last word of comfort,
once more to ask for his forgiveness, but she seemed to
be struck dumb.

He stretched out his hand.

'Well, good-bye, I hope you'll have a jolly journey.'

They shook hands.

Guy nodded to the head boatman and the boat pushed
off. The dawn now was creeping along the river mistily,
but the night lurked still in the dark trees of the jungle.
He stood at the landing-stage till the boat was lost in the
shadows of the morning. With a sigh he turned away.
He nodded absent-mindedly when the guard once more
presented arms. But when he reached the bungalow he
called the boy. He went round the room picking out
everything that had belonged to Doris.

'Pack all these things up,' he said. 'It's no good leaving
them about.'

Then he sat on the verandah and watched the day
advance gradually like a bitter, an unmerited and an
overwhelming sorrow. At last he looked at his watch.
It was time for him to go to the office.

In the afternoon he could not sleep, his head ached

miserably, so he took his gun and went for a tramp in the jungle. He shot nothing, but he walked in order to tire himself out. Towards sunset he came back and had two or three drinks, and then it was time to dress for dinner. There wasn't much use in dressing now; he might just as well be comfortable; he put on a loose native jacket and a sarong. That was what he had been accustomed to wear before Doris came. He was bare-foot. He ate his dinner listlessly and the boy cleared away and went. He sat down to read 'The Tatler'. The bungalow was very silent. He could not read and let the paper fall on his knees. He was exhausted. He could not think and his mind was strangely vacant. The chik-chak was noisy that night and its hoarse and sudden cry seemed to mock him. You could hardly believe that this reverberating sound came from so small a throat. Presently he heard a discreet cough.

'Who's there?' he cried.

There was a pause. He looked at the door. The chik-chak laughed harshly. A small boy sidled in and stood on the threshold. It was a little half-caste boy in a tattered singlet and a sarong. It was the elder of his two sons.

'What do you want?' said Guy.

The boy came forward into the room and sat down, tucking his legs away under him.

'Who told you to come here?'

'My mother sent me. She says, do you want anything?'

Guy looked at the boy intently. The boy said nothing more. He sat and waited, his eyes cast down shyly. Then Guy in deep and bitter reflection buried his face in his hands. What was the use? It was finished. Finished! He surrendered. He sat back in his chair and sighed deeply.

'Tell your mother to pack up her things and yours. She can come back.'

'When?' asked the boy, impassively.

Hot tears trickled down Guy's funny, round, spotty face.

'Tonight.'

Also by W. Somerset Maugham
and available from Mandarin Paperbacks

Cakes and Ale

The book that roused a storm of controversy when it was first published, *Cakes and Ale* is a wickedly satirical novel about contemporary literary poseurs and a skilfully crafted study of freedom. It was also the book by which Maugham most wanted to be remembered – and it probably still is.

As he traces the fortunes of Edward Driffield and his extraordinary wife, Rosie, one of the most delightful heroines of twentieth century literature, Maugham's sardonic wit and lyrical warmth expertly combine in this accomplished and unforgettable novel.

'One of my favourite writers' *Gabriel Garcia Marquez*

Of Human Bondage

The first, and most autobiographical of Maugham's masterpieces, *Of Human Bondage* is the story of Philip Carey, a club-footed orphan eager for life, love and adventure.

A few months spent studying in Heidelberg followed by a brief spell in Paris as a would-be artist find Philip in London training as a doctor. And that is where he meets Mildred, the loud but irresistible waitress with whom he plunges into a formative, tortured and masochistic affair which very nearly ruins him.

It is in *Of Human Bondage* that the essential themes of autonomy and enslavement which predominate so much of Maugham's writing are most profoundly explored.

'A writer of great dedication'   *Graham Greene*

TITLES AVAILABLE IN MANDARIN

☐ The Good Companions	J. B. Priestley	£7.99
☐ Angel Pavement	J. B. Priestley	£6.99
☐ Lost Empires	J. B. Priestley	£5.99
☐ A Question of Upbringing	Anthony Powell	£3.99
☐ A Buyer's Market	Anthony Powell	£3.99
☐ What's Become of Waring?	Anthony Powell	£5.99
☐ The Moon and Sixpence	W. Somerset Maugham	£5.99
☐ Cakes and Ale	W. Somerset Maugham	£5.99
☐ Of Human Bondage	W. Somerset Maugham	£7.99
☐ To Kill a Mockingbird	Harper Lee	£4.99
☐ The Balkan Trilogy	Olivia Manning	£9.99
☐ School for Love	Olivia Manning	£4.50
☐ The Doves of Venus	Olivia Manning	£4.99
☐ A Romantic Hero	Olivia Manning	£4.99
☐ Of Mice and Men	John Steinbeck	£4.99
☐ The Grapes of Wrath	John Steinbeck	£6.99
☐ East of Eden	John Steinbeck	£6.99

ALL ARROW BOOKS ARE AVAILABLE THROUGH MAIL ORDER OR FROM YOUR LOCAL BOOKSHOP AND NEWSAGENT.

PLEASE SEND CHEQUE/EUROCHEQUE/POSTAL ORDER (STERLING ONLY) ACCESS, VISA, MASTERCARD, DINERS CARD, SWITCH OR AMEX.

EXPIRY DATE................ SIGNATURE..

PLEASE ALLOW 75 PENCE PER BOOK FOR POST AND PACKING U.K.

OVERSEAS CUSTOMERS PLEASE ALLOW £1.00 PER COPY FOR POST AND PACKING.

ALL ORDERS TO:

ARROW BOOKS, BOOKS BY POST, TBS LIMITED, THE BOOK SERVICE, COLCHESTER ROAD, FRATING GREEN, COLCHESTER, ESSEX CO7 7DW.

NAME ....

ADDRESS ....

....

Please allow 28 days for delivery. Please tick box if you do not wish to receive any additional information ☐

Prices and availability subject to change without notice.